Trial By Fire

by
Margarita Gakis

Print Edition, License Notes

Trial By Fire
Book 1 of Covencraft

Published by Castalian Springs Press

Cover by Steven Novak
Edited by Donna Serafinus

To my family and friends, here and hereafter, I write by myself but I never write alone.

CHAPTER ONE

As it turned out, becoming suddenly pyrokinetic wasn't as awesome as Jade would have thought.

In fact, it was pretty inconvenient.

She grabbed the fire extinguisher off the wall and liberally sprayed the ugly Formica countertop. She wasn't fast enough and the building's automatic sensors were already triggered, setting off a floor-wide alarm. Her coworkers crammed into the kitchen behind her - curious and already gossiping about the fire. They started pressing into the room like cattle, crowding into her personal space.

With an unspoken groan, she inched forward, preferring to be closer to the smoky, charred remains of the countertop rather than be jostled and bumped by gawkers. Questions, speculations, and a few hushed murmurs were directed at her. Jade just shrugged and said she came in and found the counter on fire.

What was she supposed to say? *I was thinking it was a hideous countertop and I'm pretty sure I set it on fire with my mind. Oops.*

It was her fourth fire this week.

Jade hadn't even been angry this time. She'd just been bored, distracted. Maybe a bit impatient with the coffee machine. She just glanced down at the counter top and thought, *that needs to burn - it's so ugly.*

And then it was on fire.

"Bet we have to shut down today due to smoke inhalation."

She tipped her head slightly backward, over her shoulder, toward the voice. Francis was part of Technical Services and sat two cubicles over from her. She pictured him stretching his meager height up on his tiptoes so he could whisper in her ear.

"You gonna round up of the rest of the brainiacs and go for laser tag?" she asked back, keeping her voice low. She didn't know why she bothered as the rest of their floor was too busy chatting to each other to listen to them.

"If I can round them up on such short notice. It's Tuesday. Half-price. Wanna come?"

She flicked her grey eyes back toward him and shrugged. "Maybe next time."

He popped back down onto his feet and gave her a dorky smirk. "One day you're going to say yes, Jade."

"You get that from the eightball on your desk?" Jade replied with a half-smile of her own.

"Statistical probability. I've run the numbers. You can't say no forever."

She laughed. "I'd like to see those numbers."

Building Security and Maintenance arrived and herded everyone out of the kitchen, sending Jade and Francis meandering back to their cubicles. Instead of sitting down, she prairie-dogged on the divider hanging over the half wall that separated her cube from Francis. They chatted about inconsequential stuff - the latest episode of the sci-fi show they both watched, how the coffee shop downstairs had switched coffee and neither one of them liked it now, the new software upgrade that had so many glitches it was a miracle they could get any work done. She was more than aware that the rest of the office found their friendship bizarre. The hunched over mousy tech was pretty much her opposite in every way. He was plump, she was lean. He had messy hair, hers was always secured in a sleek ponytail. His brown eyes darted around when he talked, and her steady gaze made people stutter when they didn't mean to. He was meek and she was about as subtle as a hungry bear in a campsite full of barbecue.

But she liked him. Francis was safe.

And he ended up being right; the day was shot. Not three minutes later, HR announced they were shutting the floor down until they could get Risk Management in to survey the damage and Building Maintenance to estimate the repairs.

Ah, bureaucracy. But if it got her out of work at noon, she'd take it.

Maybe I should set the kitchenette ablaze more often?

Which was very likely to happen if she didn't figure out what the hell was going on. The first couple of times, she explained it away. Flash flame of an already lit candle catching the plant she never watered – that could happen. Ten-year-old stereo shooting sparks and lighting the curtain on fire – old electronics can be faulty. Late for work, flicking on the bathroom lights to have all six bulbs burst in a hail of glass and sparks - freaky, but the light bulbs had been put in at the same time and, while it was unlikely they would all shatter at once, it wasn't impossible.

Then there was the kitchen fire in her apartment. She sighed.

Jade hadn't cooked since. Not that she was much of a cook in the first place. She had been trying to steam vegetables - vegetables she didn't even *like*- and the pot caught fire. She burned her hand, knocking the pot off the stove, shouting a string of curses that would make a pirate blush. Almost in response to her creative and impressive vulgarity, the dishes in the sink lit up.

They hadn't been near the stove.

The popping ceramic startled her and she'd shouted in surprise.

Her table then exploded into flames.

She'd just stood there, surrounded on three sides by fire wondering what the hell just happened.

The fire alarm went off as she'd stripped the kitchen curtains down, burning her palms as she stomped the flames out on the linoleum floor. She turned the water on and stuck both hands under it, trying to get the fiercely painful burning sensation to stop. The heel of her right palm was forming a blister, white and full of liquid. She wondered if she could manage to reach the first aid kit under the sink while keeping her hands in the cold water. The blister seemed to swell impossibly for a split second and then started to shrink, sucking itself back into the soft skin of her palm. She yanked her hands out from the water and ran her fingertips over the skin. Nothing. Perfectly unmarked, as before.

She met the fire department at the door and managed some lie about cooking and getting everything into the sink without hurting herself. She suffered through a rehearsed, well-used lecture on kitchen safety and some reminders about keeping an extinguisher close by. The fireman even plied a stern expression and disapproving voice.

That was two days ago and she still stopped every now and then to stare at her hand, trailing fingers over the soft, smooth skin.

It had been strictly takeout for dinner since.

With her floor shut down for the day, she stopped off at the nearby cafeteria and picked up enough food for lunch and dinner and headed home. She sat down in front of her computer and waggled her fingers a bit in nervous procrastination. Then she started doing what she should have done a few days ago.

She Googled.

Of course, she tried a few variations - pyrokinesis, pyrokinetic, suddenly setting things on fire... She skipped past anything that seemingly had to do with arson and serial criminals. The fires weren't intentional. They just sort of... happened.

The hits from her search scrolled down the screen, most of them dealing with witchcraft and covers or generic stuff that every school kid knew from their "Supernatural Awareness" class. She clicked on a few links, wondering if anything had changed since she'd taken the mandatory class in grade four.

Scrunching her nose, she realized it was still the standard stuff she remembered - broad details about supernaturals, witches included, and how they interacted with society with some brief details about unique abilities, pyrokenesis included.

But since witches were born only into a coven and she hadn't been, that info didn't really help her. There didn't seem to be anything about a regular person suddenly having the ability to set things on fire. She wasn't sure if she was disappointed or relieved.

She ended up completely sidetracked by an article on spontaneous human combustion as the hours melted away. After a few more halfhearted search terms, she clicked on some links but nothing jumped out at her from the screen.

She wondered if it was maybe all in her mind. A string of incredibly unlikely coincidences, but coincidences nonetheless. The light bulbs could have all blown at the same time. Her stove and pot could have caught fire, her dishes could have burst into flames all due to faulty manufacturing. The countertop at work could have wiring underneath it that she didn't know about.

Maybe it was all just random. Extraordinarily coincidental - nothing more. Maybe she was crazy to think that she could set things on fire with her mind.

It wouldn't be the first time she'd had some kind of nervous breakdown.

But she didn't like to think about that.

She opened up a few more browser tabs and busied herself with her usual evening activities - surfing the web, reading blogs and journals, streaming some shows online. The longer she sat there, the more she convinced herself that there couldn't possibly be anything supernatural or bizarre going on. She just needed to get more sleep or learn to relax or something.

People couldn't just become pyrokinetic. The universe didn't work that way.

#

Paris wouldn't have said he was sitting in his office waiting for Hannah to call even if that was exactly what he was doing.

He looked at the clock for the sixth time in ten minutes. The Council should have been adjourned by now; Hannah should be phoning in with her update, letting him know, letting the Coven know how they were to proceed.

He disliked having to wait on the word of the Council, especially when it came to Coven business, but unless he wanted all of the Fae, and likely most of the Vampires and Werewolves displeased and feeling hostile toward his Coven, he'd have to wait for their permission to act.

In many ways it was a formality. There was an unlisted, unknown witch somewhere practicing magic. Although it was rudimentary magic, it was unsanctioned and had to be dealt with. It was galling that someone had gone to the Council and informed the authority without coming to a coven - any coven - first.

Paris understood how politics worked but it didn't mean he had to like it. It had clearly been one of the other groups - the demi-Fae, the Shifters, another coven, or possibly even one of the Unaligned – that raised the alarm that there was unsanctioned magic about. Despite the fact that it was obviously happening in Paris' territory, the unknown informant hadn't come to him or another member of his Coven. Instead, he, she or it had gone directly to the Council and now Paris had to wait for permission to do what he'd been planning to do in the first place: find the unauthorized witch and figure out what was going on.

It had to be someone that had left or been ostracized from a coven, although he hadn't heard of anyone being exiled lately. He had enough on his plate running his own rather large coven and greasing his allies without keeping tabs on all of the smaller covens in and around the area.

The amount of magic being used was negligible but it was strangely disorganized and haphazard. If he didn't know better, he would think it was a child mucking about with their powers, but surely a missing witch-child would have made news across covens.

When his phone finally rang, he felt his shoulders loosen slightly at Hannah's name on the caller display.

"Yes?" he answered.

Hannah's calm, even tone came clearly over the phone. "You have the authority of the Council to pursue our rogue witch."

He ground his jaw slightly. "I would say you could extend my thanks to the Council but I presume you've already done that."

He heard a smile in Hannah's tone. "Don't get your British up," she teased, and even he could hear how his voice was more clipped when he was annoyed. "I imagine my thanks to them was a bit more gracious than yours might have been." She paused. "However-"

"Ah yes, the stipulations," he interrupted.

"We have only one month to find her and bring her into the coven-fold."

"Or?"

"Or the Council will take over the search and, once located, strip her of power."

He winced. Stripping a witch's power was painful, messy work and there weren't many witches strong enough to do it or at least do it well enough not to permanently damage the witch being stripped.

"That's rather... Harsh."

"The Council has been hypersensitive lately." Again Hannah paused and Paris could see her in his mind's eye, delicately poised as she tried to formulate what she wanted to say. He'd known her for years, since childhood, and had never known her to speak in anger or choose words without care. "There's more than magic afoot here. I'm not sure what it is but it's not just spell-casting gone awry," she said.

"Does the Council know that as well?"

"Some of them. Perhaps. The Fae most likely. The Vampires and Shifters? No, I don't think so. They aren't always as sensitive to the world as we are."

He made a noncommittal sound. "A month isn't a lot of time, Hannah."

"No. It isn't, but it's all we've got. When we find our truant witch, we'll have to do our best to convince her to join our Coven."

"I'm sure it will all make a very convincing argument. *Join my Coven or be stripped painfully of your powers by an amateur.*"

When Hannah didn't reply back he felt the skin on the back of his neck prickle. "Please tell me you didn't volunteer me to do it," he said tiredly.

"There are precious few witches who are sufficiently qualified to practice that kind of magic and you're one of them. Also, you're not cruel or malicious about it. People have died because it was done improperly and, though I know you hate it, I'd rather have you do it and hate it than see someone else do it poorly."

Paris sighed and leaned back in his chair. He knew she was right, just as he knew if it came to that - even if Hannah hadn't volunteered him - he would have likely stepped up to do it. He just didn't like having to dwell on it beforehand. Anyone who envied Paris' power was either foolish or idiotic. Or both.

"No, you're right. Of course you're right. If it becomes necessary, I'll do it. Better me than some hack."

"You know I would do it myself but my magic doesn't work that way."

"I know," he said crisply.

He'd known even as a child that there was something different about Hannah's magic. Though she was incredibly powerful, her magic was more like a strong undertow than the sharp, cresting wave needed to break a witch. She'd gotten stronger as she aged, her magic settling even deeper now that she had passed her centennial, but it still wasn't the whip-crack that witch-stripping required.

Not like Paris' magic, which, if left unchecked or unmanaged could be violent, relentless and raging. He preferred other means, but he would use his power if necessary.

"So," Hannah said briskly, interrupting his thoughts, "you've one month."

"I've already got Callie working on some locator spells to help us narrow down the area. I'm hopeful we can find whoever is doing this within the week and then have three weeks to convince them to join our Coven. Or another coven I suppose."

"No. It needs to be ours."

He was slightly taken aback by the surety in her tone. "May I ask why?"

"I had an uneasy feeling so I did a card reading last night. Before you say anything, I didn't do a card reading on you or for you - I did it on our unknown witch."

"All right," he said trying not to let his distaste of the Tarot cards color his voice. He had an extreme dislike of them and Hannah knew it far too well. For her to bring those up, it must be important.

"The cards were quite clear. The unknown witch belongs with us. In our Coven."

"Well, obviously I'll do my best, but if he or she doesn't want to join I can't force them."

"No, but you could try using some of that boyish charm I remember you having."

A ghost of a smile traced his lips. "That was a long time ago."

"Oh, did I miss the day you surpassed me in years, Paris?" she said sarcastically. "You sound like you're ancient when I know for a fact you're only in your thirties."

"There's more to age than years."

"Yes, there is," she agreed. "And once you've reached one hundred you can start lecturing me on age. But until then, you would do well to listen to your elders, young boy."

He wanted to laugh. Only Hannah could still call him a young boy and make it sound loving and chiding at the same time.

"Very well, Hannah."

"Go find us our lost witch, Paris. Bring her home."

CHAPTER TWO

Paris examined the locator spells researched by Callie and he pulled out the bits and pieces he liked, crafting them into a new spell of his own.

"Ugh, how do you do that?" Callie bemoaned, watching him as he jotted down the few lines he wanted from each spell.

His lips quirked, "Magic."

"Har-dee-har," she deadpanned, leaning over the table slightly, her long, fine blond hair slipping over her shoulder and swinging out in front of her. She tossed it back with an absent flick. "Seriously, I'd have to try each one, see how I could ply them, if they worked, and then spend the next four days trying to cobble something together that still wouldn't be half as effective."

"I think you're a very fine spell-crafter," he murmured, not looking up at her as he perused his notes. He absently made a move to stick the tip of his pen in his mouth but Callie deftly snatched it out of his hands.

"That's a gross habit and it's been gross since we were six."

He plucked his pen back from her hands. "It's *my* pen."

She appeared to consider something, perhaps a rude gesture, but she simply jerked her chin slightly at the spell he was tweaking. "How accurate do you think it will be?"

Paris looked over his words and ingredients and weighed them in his mind. He'd always had excellent instincts when it came to magic. He knew some people thought that his mother, as Coven Leader before him, had perhaps given him some extra books or knowledge that she had - things the rest of the coven didn't have access to.

He supposed in some way they were right. He'd had his mother to watch as she crafted spells. He couldn't think of anything else that would have taught him as well as watching her. She'd had a deft touch, a fine control. Looking through some of her spell-books and grimoires now, he was amazed at what she could do. There were spells in her books he didn't think any other witch on earth could understand, let alone cast, including himself.

He pushed those thoughts of his mother from his mind before he became too distracted. Knowing the spell-casting part of his kitchen nearly as well as hers, Callie helped him gather the ingredients he needed, setting them down on the counter next to his notes and then stepping back out of his space while he worked. She crossed over to his kitchen table and unfolded the oversized paper map she'd picked up from the travel agent, smoothing it down and weighting it with four paperweights Paris picked from his spell-chest. She placed one at each of the directional points then quietly took a place just outside the kitchen, off to the side, not wanting her energy to interfere with his.

He rolled up his shirt sleeves and only glanced once more at his notes before setting to work. He didn't so much measure the ingredients as intuit the amounts he wanted, allowing the scents to overlap as he breathed them in deep. The aroma of each spell was always unique but somehow still always smelled familiar and recognizable to him. When Paris was younger, he thought that it was his mother's perfume. As a child, he would sit on the floor next to her feet, or if he was very quiet, she'd pop him up on the counter while she worked. It wasn't until he started his spell-craft classes in middle school that he recognized his mother's "perfume" as the ingredients she often worked with - sage, vanilla, mint. She had, in fact, worn no perfume at all.

Paris felt his magic stir inside him, even before he called on it, almost like it was sitting up and paying attention as soon as he began mixing ingredients. He finished adding what he wanted to the mortar and then started grinding with the pestle - short, firm, counterclockwise movements until he got the fine powder he wanted. He thought about the unknown witch as he did, thought about how Hannah always referred to a 'she' or a 'her' and how Hannah was not very often wrong. He also considered the magic they could sense being used - distorted, disorganized, sharp and quick. Powerful but immature. Then, he thought about finding her, their lost unknown witch, and offering her a place in their Coven.

When he was satisfied with the powder, Paris stepped over to the map on the table, cradling the mortar in his hands. Looking down at the map, he scooped up the fine dust in his fist and then, putting his intent - his magic - behind it, blew it into the air above the map.

It hung, suspended in the air, a delicate cloud of dark grey each particle seemingly stopped for a moment in time.

Then, it began to move.

The cloud pulsed, undulated and swirled slowly like a long, powerful snake. It curled and coiled a meter above the map, becoming dense and then spreading out again. He could feel the magic in his head, feeding the motion - powering it, fueling it - a small, slight tug at the front of his brain. Then, like a string being plucked, it vibrated sharply and froze for another moment before collapsing in on itself, pulling together into a tight, dense knot and then funneling down to the map. He smelled a twinge of burning paper and a fine tendril of smoke lazily curled up from a corner of the map where a small, pinprick hole burned black.

"There you are," he breathed.

Callie returned to the kitchen behind him and he glanced over, his eyes meeting hers.

"I don't even know why I bother sitting around wondering if your magic is going to work. It always works."

He knocked on the table three times in automatic reflex. "You'll jinx it."

"You don't even believe in jinxes," she replied, bending over and holding her hair back so she could study the map.

Callie was right, Paris didn't believe in jinxes, but he'd had those reflexes drilled into him just the same, like people who toss salt over their shoulder after spilling it without knowing why.

"Hmm, not too far away. We could be there by tomorrow."

"We?" he asked, grabbing a dishcloth from the counter and wiping his hands.

She grinned. "I love the smell of a road trip."

CHAPTER THREE

Jade felt like she should have one of those signs they hang in construction sites or industrial plants.

Days Without Incident: 5.

A full five days without any exploding bulbs, leaping flames, scorched cabinets or singed countertops.

It was like sitting around waiting for your next hiccup. The body knows something's amiss and produces a strange, sick feeling in the gut, but it's still impossible to predict exactly when it might all go wrong. You just knew that it would.

Jade was too pragmatic to be optimistic. Despite the fact that yesterday night she had almost convinced herself she was having a nervous breakdown and not really suddenly setting things on fire with her mind, there was still a small voice inside her that whispered, *you know exactly what you're doing.*

Even if she didn't know how she was doing it.

But still, she had made it an entire five days without anything happening and that made her more nervous instead of less.

She decided to make a half pot of coffee to settle her nerves. It didn't matter that it was early evening. Contrary to most people, caffeine didn't rile Jade up and she instead found the ritual soothing. Toss old grounds, rinse permanent filter, dump old coffee, rinse pot. Fill with water, grind beans, pour into filter.

The first snap-hiss of the pot starting up always gave her a sense of trivial accomplishment. She eyeballed her half-full mug cupboard. It was time to do a complete search of the apartment and track down all her cups. She tended to drink coffee while she got ready in the morning, leaving her mug wherever she happened to be when she downed the last swallow. She would find one or two in the bathroom, maybe one on her dresser, one by her computer. Once she found one inside the freezer.

She grabbed a mug, saw that all her favorites were gone and made a note to go hunting for them.

As soon as she had a cup of coffee.

She pulled open the fridge and immediately scrunched her face when she picked up the half-and-half. She gave it a little shake.

Only enough for one cup.

Jade looked sideways at the cup on the counter and then back again at the nearly empty milk container. The math was already done. If she drank it now, there'd be none tomorrow morning. She'd already used up her emergency powdered creamer last week and had forgotten to restock.

But it was stupid not to drink it now as she'd already made the pot of coffee.

She'd have to go out and get more half-and-half if she wanted coffee tomorrow morning. Jade had tried to get into the habit of stopping somewhere on her way to work for coffee but that early in the morning she couldn't stand any conversation, let alone dialog with overly perky coffee baristas. Or worse, other customers. It was infinitely better to have her own coffee in her apartment while she got ready than trudge with the masses to the closest shop.

So, late evening trip to the grocery shop it would be.

Decision made, Jade poured the last bit of cream into her mug and then topped it off with coffee. The pot dribbled a bit onto the counter and she pushed around a tea towel that she kept close to the pot for just such occasions. Satisfied she made at least some kind of effort, she took her coffee and sat down on the sofa with the books she'd picked up over the week.

She'd grabbed a few on Wicca, some on actual witchcraft, two on various psychic phenomena and was slowly working her way through them. Even when the material didn't seem at all helpful, she still found it interesting. The one she liked the best so far was purely a neuroscience book. She enjoyed the crossover with mathematics and computer science but also the parts that delved into linguistics and philosophy.

It wasn't really helping her with her little 'setting things on fire' problem, but it was interesting reading. Jade kept her laptop open as she read and jotted a few things down here and there, making a note to pick up another one of the books in the reference section when something struck her fancy.

After making a decent dent in the books by the time she checked the clock, she had worked up the energy to go to the grocery store. She decided her current outfit of leggings and a t-shirt, while slightly threadbare, was passable to get groceries. She stuffed her feet into her runners and grabbed her wallet on the way out. After missing – no, make that skipping - her workout for the past three days, a swift, two-block walk made sense.

Dusk had arrived on the heels of the day with early fall not quite giving a nip to the air - enough that she was glad she was in a t-shirt and not a tank top, but not so much that she was wishing for a jacket or a sweater. Just outside her apartment building she paused, the hair on the back of her neck tingling. She stopped and absorbed her surroundings. Jade was suspicious by nature and she didn't care if people noticed her scrutinizing them or if she made others uncomfortable. She saw kids on skateboards, a couple out walking a dog, cars going by, and people waiting for the bus. Nothing out of the ordinary and yet her eyes were drawn upwards, to the building across the street and her gaze narrowed. She couldn't explain it. It was like there was an invisible string tugging on her forehead, pulling her face toward the building. She looked at the windows, the almost-set sun making the glass reflective and bright, giving nothing away.

Reluctantly, she turned away from the building and started heading toward the grocery store but the prickling on her neck remained, even as she put distance between her and the windows.

\#

From his vantage point in the building across the street, Paris watched Jade step out of her apartment building and then suddenly halt - taking a measured, shrewd look around. She threw her magic out, like a net and then pulled it back in toward her body. He felt her power brush up against his own and make the base of his skull tingle slightly. Unerringly, her eyes drifted up and settled on his building, at his window, right at his level. He stepped backwards even though intellectually he knew there was no way she could see him in the fading daylight, four floors below.

Jade stared intensely up at his location for a moment with an uncanny, eerie focus. Paris took another step back involuntarily. Then, as if some decision had been made, she reluctantly turned away from him and headed down the street. He let out the breath he didn't realize he had been holding.

The woman clearly had no idea what she was doing. The touch of her magic, though brief, was unfocused and confused, almost messy in its approach - thrown out quickly and dragged back just as fast - blunt and disorderly.

But not malicious. Merely... curious. Wary but interested. Like it was an extension of herself. He didn't think he'd ever felt magic with a personality before, but hers had been almost alive in its own right.

He'd wanted to watch her for a few days, see if he could get a sense of her first without approaching her. He knew her name and where she worked. She didn't socialize much, if at all. She spent her nights at home possibly watching TV, reading or on her computer. Without actually breaking into her apartment, there wasn't much he could do to figure out exactly how she spent her time.

Paris wasn't quite ready to commit breaking and entering, though he was sorely tempted.

Callie had accompanied him to search for and find out more about their missing witch. After one day in town, they'd managed to narrow down Jade's location quite easily and then, the next day, while trying to pick up the trail of magic in the air, Callie turned and stopped still where she stood.

Callie nearly pointed and squealed, but Paris grabbed her arm and hauled her into the nearest coffee shop just as Jade jogged by.

"Oh my god, that's her! Did you see her? That was her! It's so strange. A witch without a coven! I've got to look this up in some of the older grimoires. She doesn't even feel like another witch but she definitely felt like magic, didn't you think?" Callie babbled, her face almost pressed to the glass of the coffee shop like a kid in a toy store.

"And an amazing job you would have done introducing us by falling all over her," Paris said dryly.

Callie slapped him on the arm. She always did treat him more like a brother than her Coven Leader. "Shut up, I was caught off guard. I don't think she noticed us, do you think she noticed us?" Callie was heading back toward the door, pulling it open and leaning her head outside to look after where Jade had passed by.

"No, I don't think she did," agreed Paris, similarly drawn to gaze down the street, toward the direction Jade had gone.

Callie bounced a bit. "Ooh. So exciting! Okay. We're going to need some place close by..."

They'd been watching her for two days. Surveillance wasn't nearly as exciting as books and movies made it sound. Jade went to work at the same time each and every workday, came home at the same time each night, went jogging only the once. The lights in the apartment went out at the same time and came on again in the morning at the same time.

A creature of habit who, apparently, preferred the safety and solitude of her home.

So when Paris saw Jade heading out, he didn't think about it. He rushed to the door, calling over his shoulder to Callie as he did that Jade had gone out and he was going to follow her. He didn't wait for a response.

Paris rushed out the building but couldn't see Jade on the street. He closed his eyes for a moment and tried to feel her magic, feel where it went, follow its trail.

In his mind he could see it dimly, like a colored scarf trailing down the street, fading in her wake. Paris tracked her to the local grocery store, but stayed outside. He could easily see into the bank of front windows - the bright fluorescent lights illuminating the till area. He was close enough that, with the doors propped open for the end-of-summer breeze, he could even catch part of the conversations drifting out from the checkout area.

After about ten minutes Jade showed up at the nearest till, a small basket hooked over her arm but he couldn't see the contents from where he stood. She grabbed a tabloid as she stood in line, frowned at the cover and then put it back. She touched one of the chocolate bars and he could see the debate going on in her head, but she ultimately didn't pick it up, frowning again. Jade craned her neck slightly to see what was going on with the person in front of her and when she saw a man counting out pennies her large grey eyes widened and one of her eyebrows went up in annoyance.

The man in front of her fiddled with more change in his pocket, pulling out small coins and flipping through them with his fingertips. Paris was surprised when he saw Jade seemingly square her shoulders and lean forward.

"This is why people have credit cards," she snapped.

Paris' lip reading was fair, if underutilized, but Jade's voice was strong and even, carrying easily over the distance to his ears. Paris had to bite his lip to keep from laughing at the outraged look on the man's face. The man sputtered and coughed and Jade rolled her eyes at him before grabbing another tabloid magazine off the rack, flipping its pages without interest.

"I beg your pardon?" the man finally sputtered at Jade.

"With the amount of time you're taking, you totally should." She didn't even look up from her tabloid.

The man opened his mouth, closed it, and opened it again. Jade finally looked up at him.

"I think you want to pay and go," she said quietly.

Paris could almost see the magic flare out of her and push against the man. Curious, Paris let his own magic uncoil like a long, serpentine spring.

Although he had known she was using her power, he was still surprised when his power brushed up quietly against hers. Unlike the innocuous touch of her power earlier, this time her power lashed out at his sharply, slapping it away. It occurred to Paris that last time her power reached out to investigate, but this time it was reacting like his power was a trespasser - an enemy. It was fast, angry and Paris immediately snapped down on his automatic response to send his power flaring back. Regardless of what was going on magically, Jade didn't appear to notice his power, nor her own response. Instead she was focused on the man at the till as he turned, almost mindlessly and handed dollar bills to the cashier. The man grabbed his grocery bags and left, never once turning back to Jade; strangely and intensely focused on the door and the way out.

Doing exactly what he'd been told, Paris realized. *Paying and leaving.*

Jade placed the tabloid back on the rack and waited for her things to be rung through. Paris let his power drift closer to her again, slower this time, more carefully, circling her cautiously instead of approaching straight on. He closed his eyes as he tried to focus on her, to get a reading.

She was bleeding power from every part of her.

She watched her groceries as they were scanned, a bored look on her face. Then, she handed over her credit card, tapped her fingers against the pin pad of the cash machine and waited for her receipt - seemingly unaffected by the power she'd just flung out at the stranger in line before her and the power she was hemorrhaging as she stood there. As she picked up her bags, her power swirled up around her, almost like it was anxious to leave.

Paris waited for a moment and followed Jade out of the grocery store, staying far enough behind to not spook her. She started the walk back to her apartment, her grocery bags pulling down on her arms, laden with bananas, coffee cream and some other odds and ends he couldn't quite see. Even with the bags, she kept a brisk pace, not expending any extra motion other than her determined forward walk.

She halted suddenly and turned around. Paris spat out the quickest spell he could think of, an obfuscation spell, one he hadn't used since he was nine when he tried to sneak by his mother with a bag of cookies. The spell hadn't worked on his mother - his spells rarely did work on her - but it seemed to work on Jade. She stared intently at the space where he stood, but not directly at him. Most people would stop, look and then move on. But she was doggedly determined, staring at him for long enough that he thought she certainly must see him. Surprisingly, none of her magic appeared to slink out of her toward him. It darted all around her, like confused and abstract fireworks - jarring and unfocused - but nothing came close to him. It was chaotic, distracted. It reminded him of watching a hungry child find a buffet of treats - all excitable energy and frenzy but no intelligence about it.

Jade finally turned and started walking again, her first few steps slow and reluctant but then speeding up and returning to her normal pace. He breathed out slowly, waited a moment longer and followed. Jade's power jumped around as she walked, darting into corners, pulling ahead of her, reaching behind her. At one point, it came dangerously close to him, and he wondered if he would have to use another spell. He carefully pulled his own circle of energy back, folding it closer to himself than he usually kept it. Her power danced around, like it was looking for him, and then curled back toward her. He realized that was probably how she sensed him before. He hadn't felt it, but her power must have brushed up against his, and somehow she had known.

A car backfired, and although she gave no outward notice, she must have been startled. He saw her power jump out of her, a dark indigo flash, and the streetlight above her exploded. She stopped and glared up at the streetlight as glass and sparks showered down a few feet in front of her. Jade set her jaw tightly as she looked at the damage murderously. She shook her head sharply and continued walking. Like a distracted puppy, her power skipped along in front of her, unconcerned and oblivious.

#

Jade shouldered open her door and then dumped the grocery bags on the counter with a huff.

Days without incident: 0.

She knew, she *knew,* that light bulb exploding had been her doing. She'd almost felt it break in her hands - sharp, loud and crisp. On the way back from the grocery store, she'd felt on edge, like she was being watched. So much so that she had stopped and looked. She wasn't a shrinking violet. She knew the best way to defend herself was to be alert and assertive, so she had turned around to face whoever was behind her.

There'd been nothing there.

No. Not exactly nothing. There'd been no *one* there, but she still felt something. She just didn't know what it was.

So, yeah, she'd been uneasy - like a skittish cat in a loud room. If she'd had claws, they would have been out.

When a car backfired, Jade almost felt a part of her leap out and find the first thing it could easily break: a street lamp's bulb. As pieces showered down, she felt relieved, like something in her had been released. Then she felt angry and resentful because she knew she'd done it but she didn't know how.

Jade unpacked her groceries and put them away quickly, giving the fridge door a hip-check to shut it when she was done. She crossed her arms over her chest and glared at the books she had on witches, Wicca and brain function - she felt resentful of them suddenly, like they were somehow to blame for her predicament.

Oh no.

The pile of books gave a loud crack and then flames shot up from the covers. She cursed loudly and leapt toward her sink, turning the tap full on and grabbing a saucepan from the stove. It seemed to take forever to fill with water but, once done, she sprang over to her pile of books, aflame and charring her coffee table, and dumped water on the whole stack.

The fire snapped, hissed and as it seemed to die down a bit, she felt her shoulders start to relax...

There was a sharp knock at the door.

Startled, she jumped and the books broke out into flames again. *Jesus, who was at the door?* It had to be someone from the apartment complex or someone by mistake - she hadn't buzzed anyone in. Whoever it was, they could fucking wait.

Jade was back at the sink, filling another pot of water, eyeballing the burning books from where she stood, trying to decide if she should try to pick them up and dump them all in the shower and soak them there.

Another loud knock sounded against the door - this time firmer, harder.

"Go away!" Jade shouted, hauling her saucepan across the room to dump on her small - getting larger every moment - fire.

"I can help you."

She looked over at the closed door incredulously and then back down at the rapidly growing fire. *The hell you can*, she thought. Her entire coffee table was on fire and if she hadn't already deactivated the fire alarms in her apartment, they would have surely gone off. If Jade couldn't control this quickly, the smoke would set off the alarms in the hallway and she'd have a hell of a time explaining why there'd been two fires in two weeks in her apartment.

Panic wasn't something she typically gave in to. But in that moment, with a third knock coming from the door, with the coffee table wood crackling with flames, and her only holding an empty saucepan, she admitted it. She was panicking.

It took less than two strides for her to reach her door. Jade flung it open and found herself staring at a man with dark hair and impossibly blue eyes.

"You'd better not be lying," Jade shot out, her voice on edge and sharp. He took one look at her, his face calm, impassive, and then looked over her shoulder at the burning coffee table and books.

"I see," he said simply. He took a step inside her apartment and shut the door behind him with a soft click. She opened her mouth to say something, anything, possibly yell at him, when he raised a hand and then murmured a few quiet words.

It was like she could feel him pulling the fire from the table and books. She hunched over herself slightly, a look of distaste spreading over her face. It felt like someone had just curled a fist in her stomach - it wasn't painful but it was intrusive and she didn't like it. She wanted to push him away, punch him in the head or just - get him to stop what he was doing.

He looked sharply over at her. "Stop fighting me." His voice was low, commanding.

She shook her head and took a step away from him. She wasn't fighting him, she wasn't doing anything. She just... She was overwhelmed. It was like he was everywhere, all around her, crowding her.

"Please," he said, his voice softer, quieter. "Stop fighting me."

"I'm not!" Jade snapped.

He still had one hand raised facing the fire, and with the other, he reached out toward her and she flinched back. She felt the heat of the flames as they spiked, the entire room going hot and bright for a moment and all she could think was *away away away, get away.*

He dropped his hand quickly and this time, he took a step away from her, whispering other words that she couldn't make out or understand. His eyes flickered from Jade back to the fire and then he squared his shoulders sharply, narrowed his eyes and clenched the hand he was holding up hard, into a fist.

Jade felt squeezed, pinched and, not knowing why, she took a step toward him, wanting him to stop whatever he was doing, just stop.

He held out his other hand again, this time as if he was holding her off, and he squeezed his fist tighter. For a moment, Jade couldn't breathe and she wanted to push at him and then -

Everything released.

It was like being suddenly freed after being tied up. She gasped in a few deep breaths, looked over her shoulder where her scorched coffee table wasn't even smoking – it just sat there black and still. She turned back at the stranger in her apartment. He was taller than her by about three inches, but not overly muscled - slender like a runner or a swimmer. A faint sheen of sweat dotted his upper lip and brow even though it wasn't really hot in the apartment, despite the fire. He was dressed, neatly, in tailored slacks and a blue dress shirt, shoes perfectly shiny and crisp. But it was his eyes that made her stop. Those perfectly dark blue eyes that seemed genetically impossible.

Impossible for a human. She narrowed her own eyes at him and felt her whole body tensed up.

"What the fuck are you?"

"I'm a witch. And so are you, Jade," he said

She felt an icy trickle down her spine at the mention of her name. *Do not react, do not react*, she told herself and amazingly she could feel her face remain placid. She shook her head.

"Medication cart missed its rounds today?" Jade asked sarcastically.

He smiled. "You know what I'm talking about. Please don't insult me by pretending you don't. I only wish to talk to you."

They stood there, staring at each other, for a few heavy moments. He waited patiently, as though he had all the time in the world for her to make up her mind.

"So talk."

"May I sit?" he asked, gesturing to the sofa.

"No."

He nodded once and then seemed to gather his thoughts, looking briefly around her apartment. "If I make you nervous, I have a female partner. If you like, I can invite her to join us."

"You don't make me nervous," Jade said, not moving from where she stood. She wasn't sure if she was telling the truth or not. She wasn't scared, but she didn't exactly want to invite him in and offer him a cup of coffee either. "And even if you did, just because you have a woman with you, it wouldn't make you any safer."

"I suppose not." He paused for a moment and then inclined his head slightly. "My name is Paris."

She narrowed her brows. "Like France?"

He had a rueful expression. "Yes."

"You sound British," she accused, like he didn't already know what he sounded like.

He inclined his head once more. "My mother was from England, and perhaps had a sense of humor." He spoke to her like he already knew her, like he was telling her a confidence. She wanted to believe him but at the same time still felt wary and mistrustful. Paris waited a moment for Jade to say something else and when she didn't, he continued.

"I assume you know of the existence of witches? You likely had some sort of awareness class in school or perhaps a presentation?"

"Yeah. They said witches are born into a coven. I wasn't," she countered, keeping her voice cool.

Paris nodded slowly. "Yes, you're... Somewhat of an anomaly. We were unaware of your existence at all until a short while ago when you started bleeding magic."

Jade stiffened thinking of the spontaneous fires, the exploding street lamp. She didn't say anything but raised an eyebrow and gave him a look that she hoped conveyed 'continue.'

"We could sense your magic and realizing you weren't part of any coven, we came to find you. To ask you to join our Coven."

Jade knew what the word meant but still couldn't stop herself from saying, "The what?"

"The coven. My Coven. As a witch, you belong in one."

A disbelieving snort ripped from Jade's mouth before she had time to stifle it. "Right," she said. A nervous laugh escaped and she covered it up with a smirk. "Because I'm a witch."

"I'm quite serious, Jade," he said, unperturbed.

She snorted again. It felt so ridiculous. "You know, you're not the first person to tell me I'm a witch, but I usually get more of a chance to piss someone off first." She shook her head. "So what, you're here to suss me out and see if I want to join your little coven?"

"In a manner of speaking, yes. The amount of magic you've been expending is quite extraordinary for someone with no training or knowledge."

He took a small step toward her and she moved back immediately. She was listening but that didn't mean she was comfortable. He seemed to realize his mistake and returned to his original position. They remained like two boxers in their corners, each watching the other.

"So, how often does this happen?" she asked.

"Pardon?"

She waved a hand. "How often do you guys have to go out and 'collect,'" Jade made air quotes around the word, "witches who weren't born into a coven? I didn't read anything about it or find any references when I was looking this all up."

Paris hesitated and Jade's heart thumped in her chest madly.

"You're the first," he admitted. She could see his reluctance.

Jade huffed and tried to ignore the disappointment and uncertainty his words caused to creep up inside her chest. "I'm just a special snowflake then."

His lips curled slightly in a smile. "It would appear so."

"So, what do you want?"

Paris frowned slightly. "For you to join my Coven."

"Yeah, you said, but what does that mean? Is it like a membership or a subscription? Like joining a gym and then never going? Or are you gonna make me show up in a robe and chant freaky shit in a circle or what?"

He shook his head. "It's like neither of those things. A coven is your home, your family. We live in the same area, we work together, we practice magic with one another, sanction each other's spells, work as a unit."

She held her hands up and took a step backward. "That seems like a lot of togetherness and sharing."

"It's how witches are," Paris said with a shrug.

"I'm not a witch," she said immediately, instinctively.

"Yes," he said evenly. "You are," his eyes matched hers unblinking. "Come back to our Coven with us. My partner, Callie, and me. See what you think."

"I don't even know you," she snapped.

"You'll get to know us. We can give you a place to live. You can meet other witches, learn how to use your magic. I think you'll probably feel quite at home in a coven."

"I'm not much of a joiner," she said. "I don't want to sit in a circle and sing kumbaya with a bunch of people I don't know."

"Nothing like that," Paris soothed. "Just... Spend some time with us. Learn from us. It will be an opportunity for you to see what you can accomplish, how much magic you have."

"Or maybe for *you* to see how much magic I have?" she countered. Nothing was free in the world, supernatural or otherwise. If she did have magic, she wasn't stupid enough to think that other people with magic wouldn't be curious or envious of her.

He nodded a little reluctantly. "Yes. I admit, we're curious. As I said, you're the first witch we've known to exist outside a coven. You've sparked some curiosity."

Jade recoiled. "I won't be your freak show. I'm not going to go just so you can poke and prod me. Forget it."

"Nothing of the sort," Paris assured. "As I said, people are curious, but they will be respectful."

"How can you be sure?"

He gave her a small smile. "I'm Coven Leader. They will follow my example."

She wasn't sure if she was relieved or not. If the rest of his coven followed Paris' lead then it was logical to assume that the same would be expected of her if she joined. But still, she was tempted to go. To go somewhere where maybe the strange things that were happening to her would make sense. To see what it was all about, learn new things. And she certainly couldn't just hang around and wait to set something else on fire. The fires were getting bigger, harder to extinguish, springing wilder. Plus, she was a big girl. If she didn't like something or was uncomfortable, she could leave. Jade had learned the hard way to trust her instincts. She could always go and if she got a weird or hinky vibe, she could ditch it.

It was so bizarre. Sure, she knew of the existence of witches, everyone did. But she hardly knew anything at all about covens. Was a coven of witches ten, twenty or one hundred people? Did they live in cities or have their own little village? What they would expect from her when she got there?

"For how long?" Jade asked. "How long would I have to stay?"

Paris hesitated and she saw it clearly. She narrowed her eyes.

"A month," he said finally. "Come back with us for a month."

She met his unblinking eyes across the space between them. "What will I have to do there?"

"You'll get a chance to meet more of us. Learn more. We can teach you a lot of things."

She pursed her lips. "What if I want to leave?"

"I think you'll like being part of a coven, being around others with magic."

She shook her head. "That's not an answer. What if I want to leave?" she said again, more forcefully.

His smile was tight and she didn't like the expression on his face. "We won't keep you prisoner. If you don't want to stay, we won't force you."

She was tempted, that was easy to admit it to herself. There was something about him that she wanted to trust. But he definitely was keeping something from her. He wasn't outright lying, she didn't get that sense from him, but he wasn't telling her the whole truth either. She took a deep breath.

"Let's see some magic first."

"Pardon me?" Paris asked. She could tell by his expression that she'd completely surprised him.

She made a 'come on' gesture with her hands. "Magic. Let's see some. I want to see some evidence or some incentive. So far it's all been blah-blah-blah, talk-talk-talk."

"Did you forget that I managed to contain the fire you had started on your coffee table?" he said, waving a hand toward the charred mess.

She gritted her teeth. "No," she said sharply. "But I want to see some other proof. You can't ask me to just ditch my life for a month because you managed one party trick."

"Party trick," he repeated.

"Yes. You say you've got magic, well apparently I do too. I've been setting shit on fire for weeks. I want to see something else, something different. If you want me to go with you because you say you can teach me, show me something that I can't already do. Something that doesn't involve just setting stuff on fire."

"How do you think we found you if not for magic?"

She shrugged. "I don't know, but I wasn't there to see it so it doesn't count. So, chop chop." She clapped her hands. "Let's get with the hocus-pocus."

He appeared honestly and genuinely flabbergasted that she was demanding magic from him. *Well, too goddamn bad*, she thought. If he wanted her to go with him, join a coven or whatever, she wanted to see something worth her time.

After another moment, Paris raised both his hands, palms facing each other, in front of him. He whispered something in a foreign language and white-blue sparks shot out, a miniature lightning storm arcing back and forth between his palms. The sparks hissed and popped, the stink of ozone in the air. She felt Paris watching her even as she stared down at his hands, watched the energy bouncing about. He wiggled his fingers slightly and the bright blue currents moved to his fingertips, arching the distance. He cupped his hands together, pushed the lightning into a ball which then rotated in between his hands, curving it into a beautiful plasma globe. Paris uttered another incomprehensible word and it disappeared with a crackle. He held his unscathed palms aloft, turning them over for her to see.

"That's it?" Jade blurted. It was very pretty, but she'd kind of been hoping for something... More.

He raised an eyebrow. "Controlling a small amount of electricity in that fashion takes an extraordinary amount of discipline and focus."

Jade shrugged. "If you say so."

Paris pursed his lips together and tried again to take a step toward her. Again she moved back.

"I'm not going to hurt you."

"You bet your ass you're not," she replied quickly. "What are you doing?"

"I was going to assist you in trying some of your magic. On purpose this time."

Her fingers twitched and fidgeted as she thought it over. Punching him in the head or hitting him with her toaster were both still viable options if things went south. She was in her own apartment so she could yell or holler and make a run for it. She glanced at the door and then back at him.

"Okay," she said grudgingly. He stepped over to her and even though she didn't move backward, she felt her whole body go on alert at his proximity.

"Hold out your hand," he said, presenting his own hand out in front of her.

"Why?"

"I won't hurt you," he repeated.

She hesitated a moment, watching his outstretched hand. He didn't move, stayed perfectly still, waiting for her to decide. She reached her right hand out slowly, holding it out, palm down. He took her fingertips gently and she flinched, snatching her hand back.

"I just want you to turn it over, palm up."

Paris' voice was quiet and steady, no judgment in his tone and Jade felt a little embarrassed. She turned her hand over and held it out again, this time with more confidence. His fingertips were slightly warm and she wondered if it was from the magic he'd just shown her. This close, he smelled outdoorsy and spicy - like the night air.

He cradled her hand in one of his and she kept shifting her gaze from her hand back to him and then back down again.

"I want you to think about your hand, and think about heat, about fire. Think about the other times you seemingly made it happen. What were you feeling then? Surprise? Anger? Fear? Imagine-"

They both flinched when a small flame burst out of the center of her palm. Paris saved his eyebrows by shielding his face from the sudden, tiny nova. It didn't burn her palms, but she could still feel the heat and the shock of it.

"Is that...?" she began haltingly. "Is that what you wanted?"

She stared at the flames but it didn't burn her retinas or make her see spots. It felt different than it had before, when she'd done it accidentally. She could actually sense the fire coming from deep within herself this time, as if it was attached to something there. She focused on the orange and yellow flame in her palm and had a sudden urge to twist it.

It curled into a strange spiral, uneven, with small licks and tails spilling out from the edges.

It felt... Fun. She laughed a bit and was delighted when the flame seemingly wobbled along with her laughter. She wanted to make it bigger, brighter, stronger, more.

"No, not today," Paris said, almost interrupting her thoughts, and her eyes snapped back to him. He was warily staring at the flame in her hand.

Disobeying him seemed like the only natural reaction. She wanted more, she could do more, she could feel it inside her, like it wanted *out*. The flame in her hand leapt up higher, shifting from yellow to blue as it burned hotter and it made something in her relax and unclench.

"No," he said again and she felt the awful pressure in her chest again, the sick feeling like something was reaching inside her and pulling.

"That's my magic pushing yours, Jade. I can push harder. Let it go."

This time, she did as he asked - anything to make that churning, queasy feeling inside her stop. She dropped her hand, thinking *stop stop stop* at the flames, at the fire. It winked out of existence with a soft sucking sound.

The pressure in her chest immediately eased, but left a lingering nausea behind. She pushed a palm against her sternum, trying to press back against the heaving thickness. Jade felt a surge of resentment toward Paris for causing it.

He stumbled back a step as though she had struck him and glared her sharply.

"What?" Jade asked.

"You hit me with your magic," he said, his face open and stunned.

She didn't realize she'd done that, didn't even know how she'd done it. "Oops?"

"We're obviously going to have to work on your impulse control."

She frowned, put off by his tone. "You don't have to get snippy. I didn't do it on purpose."

"I know. That's why it's a problem," he said, giving her a school-teacher look.

Anger boiled up in her at his words, his expression. "You know, I didn't ask you to come here. You're the one that showed up all 'come to my coven and let's do some magic.'" She crossed her arms over her chest and stared at him defiantly. This was exactly why she didn't like to meet new people or join groups. There always seemed to be rules or expectations that she wasn't aware of, and then she felt awkward, angry and weird about it. "I can learn about it on my own," she lied. "I don't have to come to your stupid coven anyway."

Okay, now she sounded like a petulant ten-year-old but it was too late, the words were out there and she couldn't snatch them back. So maybe, she might possibly have a slight problem with impulse control. She didn't need this guy to point it out.

Paris held up his hands in a placating gesture. "I apologize," he said and she was surprised. She had flown off the handle but here he was, apologizing to her like he'd done something wrong. "I didn't mean to upset you."

"I'm not upset," she shot back. Yep. Still sounding like a ten year-old. *Goddamn it.*

"Excellent. I'm glad you're not upset," he replied smoothly. Paris sounded like he did this kind of thing all time - ironing feathers and making amends. Maybe he did - it wasn't like she knew what his job really was, other than he was a witch from a coven. "I do want you to come to our Coven, Jade. I think you'll learn a lot. Maybe even find happiness there?"

She wanted to tell him he didn't know a thing about her, or what would make her happy, but she managed to engage her brain-mouth filter for once and keep quiet. He looked at her expectantly and a silence filled the air. When he didn't say anything else she gaped. "What? Now? It's ten o'clock at night. I'm not going anywhere tonight. I have work tomorrow."

He blinked like that was unexpected and checked his watch. "So it is. We could leave tomorrow. Call in sick or whatever you need to do."

She shook her head. "I have to think about this. I can't just..." She waved her hand and huffed. "You can't expect me to just take off with you after a few magic tricks. It's all a little woo woo," she said making crazy circling motions with her finger near her temple.

"But you know it's real," he said assuredly. "You saw it for yourself. You felt it within yourself."

Jade bit the inside of her lip and shook her head again. "I need to think about this. I want you to leave."

Paris fumbled into his pocket for a moment and she got the impression it was one of the few times in his life he wasn't assured and in command of himself.

"Just, take my card." Paris handed it over to her and she fingered the expensive cardstock and raised type that had his name, his number and an email address. "Call me if you have any questions. Or you can speak to Callie, she accompanied me here. She'll be happy to talk to you as well. Anytime, day or night."

"Okay, I'm getting a bit of *eau de desperation* here and it's creeping me out," Jade said flatly.

His eyes narrowed in confusion or befuddlement and he stared at her. "You're very peculiar."

She rolled her eyes. "Way to win me over. Goodnight." She jerked her thumb toward the door and followed a step behind him when he moved toward it.

"Please, consider it seriously."

"Creeping me out," she repeated, swinging the door open and gesturing towards the hallway.

"It was a pleasure to finally meet you," he said and he held his hand out for her to shake.

She stared at it for a moment and then slid her palm against his. His hand was warm and dry and she felt awkward knowing hers was slightly sweaty. She hated limp fish handshakes. They grossed her out so she was relieved when he clasped her hand firmly. Doing the same in return, she managed not to flinch when he cupped their hands in his other one. It was a strangely old world gesture and she wondered if it was a witch thing.

"I hope to see you soon, Jade. Goodnight."

"Um. Yeah. Whatever," she mumbled back.

He released her hand and nodded once more before turning and walking down the hallway. She closed the door firmly behind him and then bolted the lock. She looked down at the card in her hand and its simple, bold script, wondering what the hell she was going to do.

CHAPTER FOUR

Paris tried to focus on his computer, ignoring the tense posture in Callie's body as she stood at the window and stared at Jade's apartment across the street. His partner turned, looked over at him and back again out the window. Out of corner of his eyes, Paris saw Callie open her mouth to speak and then close it. She crossed her arms and drummed her fingers on her biceps.

"She'll call," he said not looking up from his email.

"I didn't say anything," she protested.

He looked up at her. "Not out loud, no. It's only been two hours. I wouldn't expect to hear from her until tomorrow morning at the earliest. You should just go to bed."

Callie chewed the inside of her lip. "Maybe you should have brought me with you when you went to go see her. Maybe-"

Pairs grinned unexpectedly as he recalled Jade's peculiarity. "I thought it went well."

"I know. I'm just saying. It's so weird. Ever since we realized someone was wielding magic outside a coven, I've been trolling through old volumes and grimoires and there's just no record of it – not spontaneously like this. Do you know what that means, Paris?" she asked rhetorically. "There's a long history of this never happening before. So why now? Why her?"

"There has to be a first time for everything," Paris replied, his words more even and calm than he felt about it. He knew exactly what Callie meant. For all that magic was elemental and based in nature, it still tended to follow certain rules and structures. When something happened outside the expected norms, it was generally one of two things: extraordinarily fortuitous or catastrophically disastrous.

Strangely, while his intuition scored a favorable reaction to Jade's magic, Paris found he was torn on the situation as a whole. And that unnerved him. The amount of power she already brandished was worrying. When he'd been in her apartment, trying put out the fire, she'd fought him. Her magic had fought his. Even after he realized what was happening, he hadn't expected it to effectively put up any kind of real resistance.

Yet her magic did.

If he hadn't been trained as well as he had, Jade could have easily bested him. She could trounce half their Coven as she was right now and she'd never had a day of formal training in her life. Paris wondered if it was her panic, her emotions fueling her power in that moment but later on, when he'd been trying to get her to coax a small flame out of her hand, she hadn't even needed a spell-word to set it off.

Jade had done it because she wanted to. She'd *willed* it to happen without casting a spell.

He didn't know anyone else in the Coven that could do that other than himself. He generally used spells because they were drilled into his memory by his mother, by his teachers, by his mentors. But in many cases, he didn't actually need the words to make the spell work. His intent was enough - but that was after years of study and growing up surrounded by magic.

Jade had done it on her first willful try.

That petrified him. He was worried she'd turn down the offer to come to the Coven, forcing him to *attempt* to break her. He could damage his own magic in the process, or worse, kill her trying to strip her of her power.

On the flip, he was worried she'd say yes, come to the Coven and he'd be responsible for training someone with arguably more power than they'd ever seen firsthand. He'd be responsible for containing her spell-work, if it ever went wrong, or counter-hexing it if it wasn't stoppable.

As Coven Leader, he was accustomed to keeping a tight rein on his emotions both to control his magic and to soothe the rest of the members, but this whole situation threatened to unravel him. He felt frayed at the edges, raw and uncertain.

Callie chewed on the edge of her thumb and for a moment he couldn't tell if it was her own distress or if he was bleeding uncertainty into the air.

He cast a quick *sight* spell to check and saw her aura spiking and swirling with worry.

"I thought you were trying to quit that," he said.

She pulled her thumb out of her mouth. "Nag."

"Jade will call when she is ready." He could hear the calm, sure tone in his voice and was glad for it. Even though Callie turned back to watch the window, she visibly relaxed at his words. He was glad to see that even if he felt uneasy, he wasn't projecting it onto her.

He turned back to his computer and tried to settle in and focus on some coven business. Paris was always amazed at the amount of administration and minutiae running the Coven entailed. Keeping in touch with other covens around the world was a big part of his job as well as informal contact with other supernaturals. There was also dealing with the human side of things where the Coven was based. It seemed the city was always asking the Coven for help with some minor crisis. The Coven was clearly able to help with some things, like keeping tabs on new supernaturals coming into the city. Other items were just outside their ability and expertise, like problems with the power distribution grid. Sure he could cast a spell to flush out the grid and override it if there was a need, but that didn't solve the long term problem of the city needing a better one.

Magic was not there to be used as a stopgap when humans didn't want to be bothered fixing something and a lot of his time was spent explaining that. Repeatedly.

The mundane tasks soothed his mind and before he knew it, he looked up to see the clock read two in the morning. Callie was no longer staring out the window. Paris cast his magic out quickly and located her sleeping on the sofa just out of his line of site. He shut his laptop and stepped over to the window.

The lights in Jade's apartment were still on, the first time he'd seen the place illuminated past ten o'clock. She was likely awake right now thinking about his offer.

He dared to hope she said yes.

#

After Paris left, Jade decided she probably wasn't going to sleep anyway and finished the pot of coffee she'd made.

She wasn't much of a drinker, but she seriously considered taking it up now.

A witch.

It made a sort of sense, she supposed. She couldn't deny that she'd been able to control the fire for the first time today once she'd gone ahead and tried to focus on it, as Paris had instructed her. Nor could she deny that she could feel something about him when he created his electricity ball. She hadn't mentioned it to him, but it was like she could hear his brain humming while he worked. It had been a calming, droning sound and something about it niggled at the back of her brain.

But picking up her whole life and just leaving was... Much. Not that she was overly attached to her apartment or her job. Sure, she liked her apartment, she didn't loathe her job, but she wasn't emotionally invested in either one. The idea of abandoning her life and starting a new one had a strange, romantic and carefree appeal to it.

But she also liked the structure of her life, the routine. She recalled, growing up, how chaotic things had been. Unstable and unsafe. Her mother had been emotionally absent from life in general and her father...

When it rained, Jade still felt every single one of her broken bones ache with the weather change.

She didn't like being out of control. She swore when she was younger that when she grew up, she would have a nice, steady life and she'd never be held captive by anyone else's terms again.

What would life with magic be like? What did it mean to live in a coven? Would people treat her like family and how would she react? Would she have a home, finally?

She'd always sensed she was different. When she was little, she wondered if that was why her mother had been so cold and indifferent, why her father hit her. As she grew, Jade realized those things weren't her fault, but she still couldn't help but wonder what it was about her that set her apart, even from her own parents.

Maybe this was it. Maybe the same way she'd known she was different, they'd known too.

But there was something that Paris wasn't telling her. He wasn't lying, not outright, but there'd been something hesitant in the way he spoke, something reluctant in his eyes. She didn't know what to make of it.

She could always go, she supposed, and see what she thought. If she didn't like it or it felt wrong, she would leave. Just walk away and come back to her steady, simple life.

Where she had no close friends and no contact with her family.

She didn't mind being alone. In fact, she generally preferred it. While there were times when she got lonely, it passed quickly enough. If there were other times when she felt the pang of loneliness deep in her chest, late at night, well, the sun always came up the next day and she lived. It wasn't like she was going to die from loneliness.

Jade looked around her apartment, wondering, if she went, what she would take with her. She wasn't surprised to realize there wasn't much she felt particularly attached to. She could list the possessions she absolutely couldn't live without on one hand. Her laptop, her phone, her special shoebox, her favorite sweater.

That was about it. Everything else, she could probably leave and decide to take it later.

She could take some vacation time at work as she had plenty banked. There was never really anywhere she wanted to go and staycations were already stale for her. She liked staying busy so she worked.

With some mirth on her lips, she wondered what she would say to her boss about finally going on vacation.

Hi, I'm having a personal emergency of the supernatural sort. Turns out I'm a witch, which I'm sure many of you already thought. So, I'm going to run off for a month with these people who say that they're witches too and figure things out. By the way, the stats for the chemical corporation account are on

*my hard drive, and I've configured my email to send a
vacation response. Buh-bye.*

She snorted to herself. Yeah, that'd be
awesome.

Jade was back on her computer, combing the
internet for information about covens and witches.
Unfortunately, her searches revealed the same things
repeated over and over again: witches were born into
covens, able to use magic for simple spells, generally
weren't too powerful but could band together for more
difficult and complex spells, were governed by a
coven which in turn answered to the representatives
that sat on the Council for Supernaturals. Articles and
information after that tended to devolve into political
mumbo-jumbo on how the Council worked and who
was involved.

As far as researching actual magic, Jade came
up empty. Constantly. Apparently, covens diligently
sniffed-out unsanctioned magic and blocked it - most
humans couldn't work a spell but there were some
who apparently had enough residual magic in them -
likely from ancestral witches - to wield a minor spell
or two. Covens around the world were dedicated to
detecting unsanctioned magic use and they cast
counter-hexes, essentially nullifying any residual
magic.

It seemed like a full time job for some covens.

Jade wondered if they'd tried that at all with
her. That Paris guy hadn't mentioned it but maybe she
should ask.

That thought implied she would be contacting
him. When she sat with that thought, it felt right. She
nodded to herself.

She didn't look at the clock until she'd already picked up the phone and dialed. Three o'clock? What was she doing? She considered hanging up but realized that if someone called her and woke her up in the middle of the night, they damn well better stay on the phone so she could curse them out at the very least. She toughed it out and stayed on the line.

When Paris answered, his voice wasn't sleep rough or unclear in any way. She wondered if he'd been awake still or if he always woke up so alert.

"Yes?" he asked.

"Uh, yeah. So it's me. Jade." She rolled her eyes at her own inanity.

"Hello, Jade," Paris intoned.

"So, I'll go. To your coven. I'll check it out."

"I'm glad to hear that."

She could hear some kind of rustling in the background but couldn't tell if it was paper or if it was bedclothes.

"Sooooo," she said, drawling, "when do we go?"

"How soon could you be ready to leave?"

She thought for a moment about packing, taking some leave from work, clearing out the perishables in her apartment. "Um, tomorrow afternoon, I think? Say, around three?"

"Callie and I will come by your apartment. I'll make the necessary arrangements."

"Sure. You do that." She tapped her fingers on the computer in front of her restlessly. "Okay. So tomorrow."

"See you tomorrow then."

She hung up without saying goodbye, tossing her cellphone onto the couch cushions.

It appeared, for the next month, she was visiting a coven.

#

Paris released a sigh of relief and felt the tension he'd been pretending he wasn't holding bleed out from his shoulders and neck.

Jade would come back with them to the Coven.

There was no guarantee she would stay, but it was a step in that direction; more than he had a day ago.

Of course, Jade coming to the Coven brought its own set of problems. Paris would be responsible for her magic. He couldn't think of anyone that would have remotely enough power to train her other than himself. He'd never taken on an apprentice - he'd never had to. There'd always been more suitable witches about - witches who were born to teach, to nurture. Paris wasn't sure how apt to the task he would be.

He supposed he had more than enough time to worry about that when they returned to the Coven. Now that Jade had called, now that she had agreed to return with them, he found he was finally getting sleepy. He had blamed his lack of desire to sleep on a need to get some work done but as soon as he hung up the phone, he could call it what it was. He'd been anxious she'd say no and he somehow ridiculously felt that as long as he stayed awake, waiting for her call, then she *would* call and it would all work out.

He powered down his computer and stumbled over to the couch where Callie slept. The apartment they'd leased had only come with a few items of furniture: a couch, an armchair, a coffee table. After a brief disagreement, he'd finally gotten Callie to accept the couch and he took the floor. While it wasn't as bad as sleeping in the forest for his training sessions when he was younger, he was glad this was the last night he'd been spending stretched out on the threadbare, suspect carpet.

He closed his eyes and settled his nerves, reciting a quick invocation to keep his dreams at bay. At least for the night.

#

Jade started her day at the normal time, went into work, booked four weeks' vacation, spoke quickly to her manager and conjured some story about a family emergency.

The fact that she'd never taken any time off for her 'family' before probably worked in her favor. She managed a few silent nods to the sympathetic head tilts she received from her boss, gave a few noncommittal answers to the gentle, if somewhat slightly invasive, questions and was back at her apartment by ten.

She cleaned the perishables out of her fridge, powered down and unplugged her appliances and packed a suitcase.

Jade laughed when she realized the majority of her packing consisted of a phone, laptop, e-reader and power supply cords for all of the above.

And, of course, her running shoes. Shoes always took up the worst amount of space when packing. Ugh. She changed into some more comfortable clothes, settling on blue jeans, a gaming t-shirt she'd gotten online with some prancing ponies and some tennis shoes.

Ready much sooner than she anticipated, she didn't quite know what to do with her extra time. She stretched out on the couch figuring even if she didn't sleep, she could rest her eyes for a bit.

She was asleep in about five minutes and woke up with a start, bleary eyed and confused when she heard knocking at her door. Her phone told her it was five minutes after three - she'd slept the rest of the morning and part of the afternoon away.

"Yeah," she hollered, pushing herself off the couch and toward the door. She yanked it open at the same time as she used the other hand to check her ponytail, feeling half of it escaping out of its rubber band.

Paris stood in the doorway with a petite blonde woman who smiled brightly.

"Did we wake you?" Paris asked politely.

She half-grunted in reply, pulling the door open and then stepping back to let them in. She yanked at her hair and undid the ponytail and quickly re-secured it.

"You must be Callie," Jade said with a nod toward the blonde as she finished pulling her hair through the knot.

"Yeah," Callie said with a smile, coming forward with her hand stretched out for a handshake. Jade took it and grasped it firmly and then had a sudden thought that she probably had mascara or drool all over her face.

Well, it wasn't like they wanted her for her looks, she thought dismissively. She was pleased with Callie's firm shake.

"I'm really happy to meet you," Callie said with a warm, friendly smile.

"Apologies for our tardiness," Paris said and then looked at Callie pointedly.

"You said three! I was ready at three!" Callie defended herself.

"Generally, when one says three, one means a little before the actual time." He gave her a slightly disapproving look.

"Then you should have said two-forty-five," Callie replied easily.

They were comfortable with each other, Jade thought. This was clearly a discussion they'd had before. For a brief flash she envied them - their ease with one another. Jade fidgeted a bit not quite knowing what to say or do in their company.

"I guess you were close by," Jade finally said, figuring they must have either made obscenely good time or been close enough to reach her apartment in five minutes.

"Just across the street," Callie said brightly. At Jade's sharp look, Paris cleared his throat awkwardly.

"That's not creepy at all," Jade replied sarcastically. "You guys really were watching me, huh?"

"Oh, it wasn't like that," Callie said quickly. "We just, wanted to... I mean, we didn't know anything about you and we figured... Well-"

Callie appeared to finally realize there really wasn't a graceful way to end that sentence and her voice trailed off. Instead of finishing her thought, she looked at Jade sheepishly and shrugged.

"Um, so are we going or what?" Jade asked, still feeling slightly awkward.

"Yes, we'll be taking the train so we should head out. Are those your things?" Paris asked, gesturing toward the small suitcase and carry-on bag Jade had by the front door.

Jade nodded, slinging the carry-on strap over her shoulder and grabbing the suitcase. When Paris stepped forward to take one of the bags, she moved a bit back. "I got it." She didn't like people touching her things. "I just need to stop for coffee and I'm good to go."

Paris looked at his watch. "Oh, I don't believe there is time for coffee."

Jade gave him an even stare. "Oh, there is always time for coffee."

"I could go for a coffee," Callie chimed.

"I've made travel arrangements for us already," Paris said. "And since one of us was late," he eyed Callie meaningfully again, "I'm afraid we really need to get going. If there's time once we reach the station, perhaps we can stop there."

"No, absolutely not. I know the train depot and the coffee there is - blergh." Jade shuddered. "We can hit the place around the corner. It'll take, like, five minutes."

"We really don't have time," Paris said simply and Callie sort of sighed, apparently resigning herself to a lost point.

Jade pushed past them toward the elevator. "I'm telling you, coffee break will take five minutes."

Paris turned with a strange look on his face and Callie looked stunned. Jade stared back at them as she stabbed the button for the elevator. She got the impression that no one had ever really argued with Paris before.

"I said we don't have time," said Paris plainly. He wasn't angry or rude. He seemed completely flabbergasted they were still having the conversation.

"We have tickets, don't we? And those things hardly ever leave on time. Who cares if we're late?"

"That is hardly the point," Paris said frowning.

Callie's face turned back and forth between them like a tennis match.

"It's totally the point," Jade replied, stepping into the elevator when it arrived. "Make the train late with magic or something."

"That is completely not allowed."

"Then what are the perks of being a witch?"

Paris looked stymied. "There are no perks."

Jade gave a snort. "Well, you got screwed over then, English."

Paris had nothing to say to that. It was like his brain had frozen at the irreverent tone of her argument.

The elevator gave a 'ding' and they were at the main lobby. Jade pulled her suitcase behind her, rolling it across the tiled floor with a *clack* at each groove.

Paris stepped up beside her. "I cannot believe you are arguing with me about this."

She stopped and turned to face him. "Me neither, I could have had coffee by now." At his blank look she rolled her eyes. "Just... Go without me, I'll meet you there. Honestly." She turned to Callie, "I can get you something if you want."

Callie's face lit up and she was about to speak when Paris interrupted her. "We'll go as a group." He strode out in front of the women and Jade took a second to look at Callie and smirked. She mouthed the word 'coffee' with a smile.

Callie looked like she was stifling a laugh as she fell alongside the other woman.

Twenty minutes later, Jade sipped her coffee, content and victorious. She eyed Paris, sitting across from her, stonily staring out the window of their train compartment.

"See, time to spare," she said as the train lurched forward and started rolling away from the station.

He turned his gaze on her. "If you count running through the train station in a most undignified manner 'time to spare.'"

Jade shrugged. "Yet here we are, on the train. With our coffee." Jade turned to Callie, sitting next to her, staring at the lid of her cup like it was the most interesting thing in the world.

Paris stood up as he took his phone out of his coat pocket.

"I'm going to call the Coven and let them know we will be on time."

"Unless we run into some dire straits that set our pristine schedule back," Jade said, barely hiding her grin. "Who knows, I may need to stop for a hamburger."

Paris ignored her tone and shot a glare that had Callie averting her eyes. Jade smiled at him and batted her eyelashes. She got the feeling he tried not to slam the door shut as he left.

He was somewhat unsuccessful.

"He's a little too easy to rile up," Jade said, pulling her e-reader out of her carry on and flicking it on.

"I probably should tell you," Callie said, fingering the rim of her cup, "that no one in the Coven talks to Paris like that."

"Like what?" Jade asked, taking sip from her coffee.

Callie blinked twice in succession. "Like they don't care if he gets angry."

Jade shrugged. "I don't care if he gets angry."

"It's just that he's the leader and he is the most powerful witch in the Coven."

Jade paused. "So when he kept saying 'come to my coven' he really meant *his* coven?"

Callie nodded. "Yep."

"Uh." Jade fumbled for something to say. "Isn't this kind of errand a little beneath him then? Shouldn't he be off doing... Coven running things?"

"Well, you're very unique," Callie said quickly. "This has never happened before."

Welcome back, discomfort – did you miss me?

Jade loathed continually hearing how much of a freak she was. Even if it was said with the nicest expression possible, it still made her tense and edgy.

"Yeah. So you said."

"He's just usually afforded a little more respect," Callie said, either not noticing Jade was awkward or trying to smooth it over. "He's sort of separate from us, you know?"

"You seem comfortable enough around him. Are you two...?" Jade trailed off and raised one of her eyebrows.

Callie gave her a confused look for a moment and then laughed. "No, oh God, no. We grew up together, so I'm probably a little more relaxed around him than other coven members. But," Callie said as she shook her head, blonde hair swinging around her face, "definitely no."

"Oh." Jade shrugged. "Well, it was only coffee. Frankly, I probably could have gone without it but the fact that he was telling me outright that I couldn't go... It pissed me off. I don't like being told what I can and cannot do."

Callie's smile was hidden behind her coffee cup. "Oh, you're going to love the Coven," she said sardonically.

"Why? Is everyone like that?"

Callie shook her head. "No, no, it's just that, we have rules. Our magic comes with strings attached, I guess you could say."

"What kind of strings?" Jade asked, eyes narrowing.

"It'll be easier to explain once we get there."

Jade made a noncommittal sound and watched Callie's face carefully. She didn't sense any malice - but the thought of going to a controlled environment, one where she didn't set the rules and limits, made her uneasy. She reminded herself again that if she didn't like it, she could leave. She wasn't a child.

If she wanted out of a situation, she could go.

Like a mantra, she repeated the words to herself. She didn't have to stay anywhere she didn't want to. She wasn't obligated to join their coven.

Even if she would be the only witch ever not to be part of a coven, she could do that. She could leave.

The more she reminded herself she wasn't trapped, she could leave any time she wanted, the better she felt.

"You must be curious about your powers," Callie said. "If you had any questions, I'm sure Paris would be happy to answer them for you. He might seem like a grouch, but when it comes to things about magic - he'll always help."

"Why Paris? Why not you?"

"Oh, I'm not nearly powerful enough to teach you. I mean, I could answer some questions for you sure, but as far as assisting you with your magic? Paris will be teaching you."

Jade fingered the sleeve of her coffee cup. "Isn't that a little bit of busy work for someone who runs the place?"

"Maybe," Callie said with a bit of a sheepish grin. "But, given what we knew about you, it seemed like you would, well, you know, need someone who was maybe a bit more, I don't know..." Callie fumbled for her words and Jade stiffened slightly. "You seem a little, intense," she finally finished. "It seemed like you would need someone more ..." again Callie fumbled and finally gave a little toss of her hands, like she was throwing caution to the wind. "Paris won't take a lot of shit."

Jade gave a sharp laugh at that. "I'll keep that in mind."

"We're not afraid of you," Callie said, placing a hand gently on Jade's arm. "I don't want you to think that or feel uncomfortable. It's just that your circumstances are really unusual. And frankly, sitting next to you, I can feel how powerful you already are. That's quite unusual."

Jade frowned. "What do you mean? What do you feel?"

Callie squinted her eyes a little. "It's almost like... You hum. The way electronic devices hum. Like a television or a computer-" she trailed off. "No, that's not quite right. Like a generator. That's it. You hum like you're an electrical generator."

Jade nodded. "Oh. So does Paris."

"You can feel that already?" Callie asked, surprise written on her face.

"Is that weird?"

Callie shook her head but Jade got the impression that it was weird and Callie was trying to make her feel better about it. "No, no. It's just... Surprising. You haven't been trained at all yet and it usually takes people a while to be able to sense that kind of thing."

"You and Paris have lived at the Coven your whole life, right?"

Callie nodded. "Yeah, I was born there. Paris' mother took over when Paris was about five or so."

"You've been able to do... Magic," Jade said almost hesitantly, "since you were little?"

"Yup. My parents are witches so they taught me some stuff and then I learned the rest at school."

"Like, *witch school*?"

Callie laughed softly and looked a little rueful. "Yeah, it's not like Harry Potter. We had regular classes - math, science, language arts. But we also had magic classes. It's a good way to make sure everyone learns good witchcraft habits. You know, like the best ingredients for stuff, or cleaning up after your spells, or how to counter-hex yourself if something goes wrong. Like one of the kids hexed their hair to grow faster because she wanted it long, but she didn't specify a length, so it kept growing and growing and it was over eight feet long before her parents counter-hexed it. We learn how to research spells, where to look stuff up. I work in the library and part of my job is cataloguing and indexing our spell-books."

"Big library?" Jade asked for lack of anything to add.

Callie sported pride on her face. "Yes, we have quite a collection of books. Spell-books, spell-bindings, talisman recognition, history collections, that sort of thing. There is also a small assortment of artifacts that must be kept under lock and key, and I am in charge of that also."

The compartment car door slid open and Paris entered, giving them both a brief glance before taking his seat. He didn't look like he'd been up until three in the morning, thought Jade, so maybe she had woken him up when he called. Or maybe he was just one of those people that always appeared put-together.

Bastard.

"I've made arrangements at the Coven for Dr. Gellar when we arrive," Paris said, pulling out his laptop and setting it up on a little tray in front of him.

Jade made a face. "Why?"

Paris didn't look up from his computer. "Everyone has to have a baseline physical on file. Just in case."

"In case of what?"

She saw Callie shrug next to her. "In case you walk down the street and get hit by a bus, I guess."

"I'm pretty good at avoiding buses. And I'm in perfect health. I don't need to see a doctor," Jade said.

"Dr. Gellar is the Coven doctor. She deals with all the witches and is cognizant of your magic, should anything happen to you. It's quite useful to have someone so aware of our unique needs on hand. You'll also be getting your baseline powers tested." Paris added.

"Is this the kind of test I should be studying for?" Jade asked.

Paris ignored her sarcasm. "We test all witches to see what their potential is. Then we can adequately provide mentorship for them."

"I hear I've already got an adequately provided mentor. You."

"By all indications it would appear that I am the only one in the Coven that will be powerful enough to train you tolerably."

She made a dramatic face, full of mocking awe. "You are such a charmer."

He gave her a disapproving look she chose to disregard. She gazed out the window for a few moments before speaking again. "So, then what?"

Callie answered her this time. "We'll probably have to spend the rest of the day processing your paperwork."

"Paperwork? What kind of paperwork?"

"Well, we'll have to register you in the system, assign you a coven email account, access to the intranet, fill in the papers for your accommodations, any necessities you require, issue your coven identification and spell-license. That sort of stuff."

"Whoa, whoa," Jade said with a shake of her head. "I might not be staying." The thought of getting tied up in all their administrivia had her feeling like she wanted to bolt. Paperwork meant attachment, attachment meant she couldn't leave as easily.

"Callie, we can bore Jade on the infrastructure of the Coven when we get there. There's no need to do it now."

Jade got the impression he knew exactly what she was thinking and was trying to keep her from freaking out about it.

"I'm just telling her what she can expect," Callie said in that annoyed tone people use with their friends. "And then you're probably going to want to get settled so the rest of the evening you can unpack, look around. Get the lay of the land."

"Huh. I might not unpack just yet. I don't know if I'll like it," she said simply.

"But you have to like it," Callie said earnestly, flashing her wide, innocent brown cow eyes. "You're one of us."

"Well, we've already established that I'm different. Maybe I won't. You said I didn't have to stay if I didn't want to." The last part of her statement was directed at Paris accusingly.

"And so you don't. But give it try first, Jade," Paris said.

She weighed his statement in her mind and then finally gave a small nod. "I said I would. I do what I say I will." She picked up her e-reader and held it up. She'd learned well how to make her posture clearly state *I'm done talking right now*.

"I'm sure you do," Paris said as he flicked his paper again and went back to reading.

Callie looked back and forth at the two of them intently. "You'll like it," she said, even though Jade had clearly exited the conversation. "I know you will."

CHAPTER FIVE

It was evening by the time they made it to the Coven proper. They picked up Paris' car at the train depot and, after an exercise in spatial relations which Jade won, they managed to fit their luggage into the trunk and three quarters of the back seat. Callie was jammed in between three bags full of books, her two suitcases and the side door, leaving Jade in the front seat with Paris, separated by two carry-on cases and Callie's makeup case. Paris muttered something under his breath as his elbow hit the makeup case hard while trying to negotiate a left turn.

"What was that?" Callie piped from the back seat.

"I said," Paris said in what Jade was now internally calling his 'I'm not happy about this' tone, "next time I'm leaving you at the Coven."

"Promises, promises," Callie replied, waving her hand dismissively.

"Are we there yet, English?" Jade asked with a bored tone.

"Almost. Another twenty minutes."

Paris made good on his word and almost exactly twenty minutes later, Jade saw the sign proclaiming the Coven was a couple kilometers ahead. She knew from what she'd read online that it was quite a touristy thing to check out what was called the Covenstead - the main coven building where the majority of the Coven would gather for events or for learning and practicing magic. There had been some pictures online of other covensteads, but Jade hadn't been able to find a pic for the one she was heading to now.

Jade wasn't sure what to make of that fact - did that mean that no one had cared enough to get a picture? Did it mean that the Coven was small and didn't have a notable covenstead? Or maybe the Coven was so large it had enough resources to keep photos of their covenstead from being published. At any rate, she had no idea what to expect.

The city, from what she'd seen out her window, resembled most others she'd visited: buildings, coffee shops, parks, people milling about doing their everyday business. They drove past the downtown and more populated areas and pulled up to a set of wrought iron gates that appeared to have nothing behind them but trees and a wide open expanse. Paris leaned out his window and punched a code into a security box. The gates swung open slowly with a loud creak and they drove slowly past the entry and then down a long, winding driveway. Finally, the trees broke and Jade was speechless.

The building they approached was postcard worthy. It was three stories high, made out of dark gray stone - weather-beaten and worn, but gothically imposing and impressive to behold. Windows lined each floor and statuary adorned the areas between the glass panes. As the car rolled up, Jade could *feel* the building, as if it had a presence, a personality of its own. It reminded her of buildings she'd seen only in movies or on TV. It stood as a monolith in front of her. Massive, dark, almost foreboding.

"Is this yours?" she asked quietly, afraid the building would hear her.

"Yes," Paris said with a hint of pride as he pulled up the long stone driveway to the double doors of the building. "This is our Covenstead. Built when the Coven first moved here, it was once our home. Back then, all the witches in the Coven would have lived in the one building. We now use the old bedrooms for our offices."

"The library takes up the entire cellar and former dungeon," Callie said, her tone equally prideful. They weren't arrogant about it, Jade thought. Both of them just seemed discreetly pleased, sitting up slightly straighter, proud of their covenstead.

"Dungeon?" Jade queried, unsure of herself for the millionth time that day.

"Well, it was built five hundred years ago," Callie explained. "They had use of a dungeon back then. There is also a great hall, a ball room, dining hall and a greenhouse."

"How many witches are in your coven?" she asked carefully.

"About two hundred."

"Holy shit." Jade breathed the curse; it was all she could manage.

Paris slowed the car to a stop and he and Callie stepped out. Jade was stuck frozen in her seat, wondering again what she was getting into. It was the sight of the building in front of her - solid and palpable, coupled with everything leading up to her arriving that had her thinking, *this is very real now*. The building made it tangible.

Jade looked up at Paris and Callie waiting patiently for her. She snapped off her seat belt and stepped slowly out of the car. She felt out of place, gauche. She smoothed her hands over her jeans and tried to shake off the feeling as she trailed after Callie and Paris, up the stone steps and into the building.

It was surprisingly modern on the inside with bright lights and a circular front reception desk. The desk dominated the middle of the marble foyer and there was a young man sitting behind it, talking on the phone. He looked up quickly at Paris.

"Got to go," he rasped into the phone. "She's here!"

He slammed the phone down and sat up straighter in his chair, fluffing his out of control hair. It was about as subtle as a brick through a window. Jade glanced over at Callie and saw her smiling fondly. Paris had an amused look on his face, like those generally reserved for clumsy puppies that ate your guests' shoes - slightly embarrassing, but still kind of cute.

"Henri," Paris said in greeting. "Working late?"

Henri grinned. "I wasn't about to leave until you showed up," he said quickly, leaning off to his left quite obviously attempting to get a better look at the newcomer. "Marcus wants you to call him."

"Marcus can wait. Is Dr. Gellar still here?"

"Yes, she said she would wait for you to arrive."

"Would you let her know we're on our way up?"

"Yes, of course," Henri said, glancing quickly up at Paris and then back at Jade. It was obvious he was dying for an introduction and Paris didn't disappoint him.

"Jade," he said, turning toward her. "This is Henri, Henri, this is-"

"I cannot believe I am the first person in the Coven to meet you," Henri interrupted as he leaned up and over his desk, shoving his hand past Paris and in front of Jade for a handshake. She started slightly and then gave it a good grip. "I am the first person you've met right?" Henri added quizzically.

"Seeing as I just walked in, yes," Jade replied. Again she thought of a puppy as she regarded him. He was all excitable energy and enthusiasm, his dark eyes shining as he met her.

"Unreal!" he exclaimed. "I was just talking to my boyfriend on the phone and I was saying how I thought you would be here any minute and now, here you are!"

"Here I am," she repeated. He was still pumping her hand up and down in a vigorous handshake when she pulled it free with a slight tug.

"Unreal!" he said again. "Do you know, we've all been dying to see you? This is the most exciting thing to happen to the Coven since Jolene set her own house on fire. She wasn't in it at the time, thank God, but whoa, what a scene. But now there's you! It's been all very cryptic, you know. Very hush-hush. No one knows a damned thing about you, really. Except you're very neat."

"Neat?" she asked.

"You know. Tidy."

"What?!" she glanced from Henri to Callie to Paris, who wore equally matching confused faces, and back again.

"My boyfriend Daniel knows someone in Accounting who is dating someone who works with Nick, who's Callie's boyfriend and he said that he overheard Callie on the speakerphone with Nick and Callie said that the only thing that Paris had said about you was that you were very neat. Is it true?"

Jade gave her head a little shake. "What?" she repeated again.

Henri took a big breath, about to explain again how he had come by that little tidbit of information, but Paris cut him off.

"Henri," he said with his impressive tone. "Dr. Gellar?"

"Right," Henri said with a slight flick of his hand. "I'll tell her you're on your way."

Paris placed his hand on Jade's arm and gave her a slight pull to follow him. She let herself be led off to the left, circling around the welcome desk. Jade could hear Henri paging Dr. Gellar on the phone and then, seconds later, he was back on it with his boyfriend giving him all the dirt on her arrival, down to what she was wearing. Callie fell into step with Jade as they started up a large, sweeping staircase that climbed ten steps before it reached a landing, splitting there into two separate staircases, one for either wing of the Covenstead.

"And that was our head receptionist and lead coven gossip, Henri," Callie said with a smile. "If there is anything worth knowing going on in the Coven, Henri will know. And he'll be more than happy to tell you, your friend, your second cousin twice-removed, and anyone in earshot."

"I'll remember to watch what I say," Jade said.

Callie smiled. "I would do that. The strange thing is, he's really very trustworthy. If you tell him something's a secret, or if he thinks it's too malicious, he'll take it to the grave. However, if you tell him you think so-and-so has a crappy wind incantation, they'll hear it by lunch time."

As they walked up the staircase, Jade noticed that she was on the receiving end of just about every pair of eyes in the massive foyer. Surprisingly, they weren't dressed in gowns and witch hats – they appeared normal. Some people openly stared at her, others watched out of the corner of their eyes. She tried to meet all the glances head on and more than one person turned away sheepishly. She also noticed that there was a general hum of whispers trailing after her as they ascended the staircase and turned off at the second floor. Jade let her eyes sweep the hallway. It was easily ten feet wide with large doors on either side that stretched up eight feet. That made the ceiling twelve feet high, she thought. She guesstimated that there were about seven doors on either side of the hallway, that made fourteen for this side of the Covenstead and presumably fourteen on the other side made a total of twenty-eight. She multiplied that by three in her head for the three floors and then added in the library beneath the ground floor.

"Christ," she murmured.

"Pardon?" Paris asked, turning his head slightly.

Jade shook her head quickly. "Nothing." She didn't want to seem like the country cousin. If they could all walk around in such grand surroundings without blinking, so could she.

Paris turned into the second door on the left and she blinked twice in surprise.

Obviously it was some kind of hospital room. Medical machinery and paraphernalia filled the room, and several cots stretched out beside each cluster of equipment. The room was sterile and Spartan, only containing what it needed, while the marble floor's pristine sheen reflected the dying sunlight. It had that faint antiseptic smell familiar to hospitals and doctors' offices everywhere. She wrinkled her nose. Like most people, she had a dislike of hospitals or doctors' offices in general. They reminded her of painful bone breaks and deep cuts requiring stitches.

"This is the Covenstead medical unit," Paris said. "Obviously the city has its own hospital and we are more than welcome to use that. But most of our needs can be taken care of here at the coven. We generally only need to use the hospital in extreme circumstances."

"Like my whole 'getting hit by a bus' example," Callie said.

Paris' lips curved in a dry grin. "Yes, that may be a little much for even Dr. Gellar to work a miracle."

"I could work a miracle in a ditch with only a steak knife and a bottle of scotch."

Jade turned to her right to see a contemporarily gorgeous woman with short red hair and dark-framed glasses emerging from an interior door which she shut tightly behind her. She wore powder blue scrubs that effectively hid most of her shape but projected an air of professionalism and sterility that most medical facilities seemed fond of.

"You must be Jade," she said as she extended her hand. "I'm Elsabeth Gellar."

Jade shook her hand and was once again impressed to find a strong grip on the other end. She had yet to meet a limp fish in the bunch.

Dr. Gellar tucked her hands back into the pockets of her scrubs and turned to face Paris. "Did I just hear you doubting my medical skills?" she asked good-naturedly.

"I was merely explaining to Jade that while our medical facility is fully functional, it is not equipped to deal with larger scale emergencies."

"Well, that could change if you would approve my funding," Dr. Gellar said smoothly.

"I believe the accounting department laughed when they heard how much money you wanted." It was clearly a friendly disagreement they'd had many times if their easy banter was any indication.

"It wouldn't matter how much they laughed if you told them to do it. If you said yes, they would find the money."

"Yes, and then I would have Security after me for their share of the pie, and then Administration and then the other departments one by one. I can already see Callie's eyes lighting up as you and I stand here talking. She's probably calculating what new books she could purchase or track down if I gave her even half of your requested budget."

Callie didn't answer, but she swayed on her feet with a dreamy look in her eye.

Dr. Gellar smiled. "Well, I'll just keep harassing you then. I never know when I might get lucky." She turned back to Jade. "If you're like other witches, you'll want to get your physical and power testing the hell over with and never come back to the med lab again."

"I don't like doctors," Jade blurted evenly.

"Most people don't," Dr. Gellar replied without a trace of hurt feelings or malice. "No matter how many times I tell them we don't bite. But we must still complete your physical. Why don't you go into one of the examination rooms and change into a gown. I'll be in shortly."

Jade looked briefly at the doctor and then at Paris again, wondering if there was any way she could get out of the exam.

"Twenty minutes is all she'll need," Paris said. "Dr. Gellar is very efficient."

Jade moved begrudgingly towards one of the examination rooms at the back and then eyeballed the hideous green gown on the bed. She picked it up and waved it back at the group.

"Seriously? You guys have untold magic power and you can't do better than this?"

Without waiting for a response to her mostly rhetorical question, she shut the door behind her and started changing into the gown. At least it was one of the ones that fastened at the shoulder and not at the back or the side.

She detested the feel of hospital gowns. They looked like they should be soft but they never were. Then, there was the wonder at who'd been wearing it before her. She left her socks on and hopped up on the bed, swinging her feet. Two minutes later there was a knock and, at her assent, Dr. Gellar came into the cramped room.

It was a typical exam. A few blood vials drawn that Gellar did herself, an eye/ear/throat exam, blood pressure, heart rate, lungs, and some questions about medical history. The dreaded stirrups came out but thankfully, Gellar wasn't one of those chatty doctors that wanted to make small talk while she worked. It took less than three minutes before Jade was sitting upright again, answering more questions about her general health.

"Once Paris and Callie located you, I was able to request your medical files," Gellar said and Jade sensed the forced neutrality in her tone.

"Oh." Two could play the forced neutrality game, Jade thought.

"You seem to have had a few broken bones in your lifetime. A lot of trips to emergency rooms."

Jade shrugged. "I was a klutzy kid."

"Two or three trips, maybe. Seventeen? No."

Dr. Gellar waited for her to say something and Jade stared back in return. She'd out-waited and outwitted a lot of medical professionals in her time, most of them when she was a kid.

"Jade, I'm going to be your doctor here at the Coven and anything pertaining to your past medical history may be important."

"Just some broken bones; cuts and scrapes, doctor. I'm in pretty good health."

"Yes, you are. You're probably one of the healthiest people at the Coven. You exercise regularly and eat a balanced diet. But I would like to know how all those bones got broken."

Jesus, the woman was like a small, determined dog. Dr. Gellar kept her gaze steady and even, staring at Jade with her large green eyes, trying to look empathetic and professional at the same time.

"Who can remember all of their childhood? Kids fall down." Jade shrugged.

"I can remember exactly where I was when I broke my wrist." Gellar countered. "I was ten years old, biking half a block from home and I fell off. It was June. I think I even recall it was a Sunday."

"Well, I don't know what to tell you, doctor. I guess they just weren't as important to me."

Dr. Gellar stared at her again and the silence lengthened. She tapped her finger on the side of the chart.

"Well, perhaps after you've had time to settle in here, your memory will improve and you'll be able to tell me what happened."

Jade said nothing. After all this time, she wasn't going to become suddenly chatty about her childhood now.

"I would like for you to trust me, Jade. But I understand trust takes time. You can get dressed now. I'll meet you outside for your power tests."

The doctor seemed genuine and, while there was a part of Jade that wanted to trust her, there was a bigger part, the louder part, which reminded her that the only person she should ever trust was herself. Things just worked out better that way.

Jade dressed and walked back out, knowing from the way Paris and Dr. Gellar looked up that she'd walked in on a conversation about her. She tipped her head to the side and cracked her neck loudly. Several snaps echoed as her vertebrae slid along one another - it was a nervous habit, something she did without thinking about it. She saw Paris stiffen slightly and wince at the sound. Jade smiled, not at all trying to make it look like she wasn't baring her teeth.

"I'm sure I don't have to tell you - that isn't good for your neck," Dr. Gellar said.

Jade shrugged and looked around the medical area.

"I sent Callie home. Your testing is next and it's best to have no other witches about when it occurs." Paris answered her unspoken question.

"What about you guys?" Jade asked, gesturing to the doctor and the coven leader.

"Oh, I'm not a witch," Dr. Gellar said. "I just work for the Coven."

Jade looked at Paris as he spoke. "Part of the test involves your power being tested against another witch. I'll be testing your power with mine." He smiled benignly at her.

"Is it going to be like the other night, when you were trying to kill my fire?" she asked, wary. Thinking about the sick, heavy feeling that had permeated her chest and stomach made Jade wrinkle her nose in distaste. Paris made a waffling motion with his head and looked uncertain.

"Possibly," he admitted.

At least he's honest, she thought.

Dr. Gellar motioned Jade over to one of the chairs in the public area. "If you would like to have a seat over there, we can begin your power testing. I'm going to attach some electrodes to your head, neck and a few of your fingertips and then we can begin."

The room was silent as the doctor connected Jade to the monitoring equipment. Jade released her hair from her ponytail and shook it out, knowing it was probably in a huge halo around her head. She wasn't one of those women who could take their hair down and have it look like she stepped from the pages of a magazine. Out of the ponytail, her hair curved along a huge wave from where the elastic sat. It puffed from her head like a lion's mane. Gellar clipped more sensors to Jade's fingertips, and put a few on the side of her neck. Jade tugged at a few of the electrodes and poked at the machine they were attached to until Dr. Gellar rolled it out of her reach.

"Try to remain still, Jade," the doctor admonished.

Jade snatched her hand away and leaned back in her seat, tapping her foot on the marble floor.

"Completely still," Dr. Gellar said without even looking over at her.

Feeling churlish, Jade stuck her tongue out at her and then felt like an idiot for doing it, but it was too late. She slunk lower in her seat.

"Okay," Dr. Gellar said as she made one final adjustment to the machine, "now we can begin. Paris tells me that you've already been able to generate fire?"

"Yeah."

"I want you to try again now."

Jade held her hand out at elbow level and immediately a blue flame appeared in the center of it. Eyes wide, the doctor tilted her head sharply at Jade's palm and then glanced at Paris.

"I know," he said. "She has a knack for that one."

Dr. Gellar raised her eyebrows but didn't say anything as she made a few notes on a clipboard. Jade craned her head over to the side to see if she could read it but it was too far away.

The doctor returned her attention to Jade. "Can you extinguish it?"

As soon as she was done asking the question, the flame winked out with an audible *puff*. Dr. Gellar made additional notes.

"And bring it back."

The flame sprung up in front of Jade again, only this time, she didn't even raise her hand. The flame just floated softly in front of her at chest height.

"Jade, would you be able to change its shape?" asked Paris.

She shrugged. "I guess."

Thinking about the tiny flame caused it to dance a bit and she could feel the shape of it in her brain. She pulled at it, twisting it, getting a feel for it and then stretched it out and shaped it. She thought about a triangle and then discarded that idea immediately for a pyramid. The flame flickered into a flat triangle and then quickly folded in on itself and settled as a pyramid, keeping up with her thoughts. She rubbed her fingertips together and, feeling a rough edge along one of her cuticles, turned her focus away from the flame in front of her and looked down at her nail. When she glanced back up at the pyramid, it was rotating lazily in front of her, like a gyroscope, in three dimensions. She looked over at Dr. Gellar who was staring from Jade to the flame to the machines with interest.

"Anything else?" Jade asked.

Dr. Gellar came to stand in front of her. "You can extinguish your fire again, Jade." As it dissipated, she held out both hands toward Jade, a small object in each. Her right hand held a tiger eye stone, the left held a small gold coin.

"One of these objects has been charmed." Dr. Gellar stated plainly. "Can you tell which one?"

Jade looked at the items in the doctor's hands and although she didn't know why, she immediately pointed at the coin. Surprising herself, she raised her eyes to the doctor, who nodded and put the stone in her pocket.

She handed the coin to Jade. "What can you tell me about this?"

Jade took the coin and turned it over in her fingers. The top of her knuckles tingled slightly. She rested the coin on the top of her fingers, in the soft skin between her pinky and ring finger. The coin rolled easily from knuckle to knuckle, flipping itself over. She moved her fingers slightly, letting the coin flip itself over, running back and forth across the top of her hand.

"It was charmed so it won't fall off," she stared down at the flickering gold. Then, turning to Paris, she asked, "How do I know that?"

"Magic lingers, gives off an energy," he said as though it was a response she would fully understand.

Jade handed the coin back to Dr. Gellar, who in turn handed her another object. It was a solid clear ball, like a paperweight, only it had no flat surface to rest upon.

"Crystal ball," Jade said with a wry huff. "Can I pick out next week's lotto numbers with this thing?"

"It's actually filled with water," Dr. Gellar said as she stepped back slightly.

Jade shook the ball and, while there was no air in it for bubbles to appear, she could feel the sluggishness of it, the heavy weight that indicated it was full of liquid volume.

"What am I supposed to do with this?"

"You tell me," Gellar replied.

Jade eyed her dubiously, grey eyes clear and keen. She opened her mouth to ask a question.

"No fire," Paris said quickly, answering her unspoken words.

Jade's eyebrows drew together. "Well, gimme a word you want me to use or a hint."

He shook his head. "No hint. Either you can or you can't."

"Can or can't what?" Jade huffed, exasperated. "I still don't know what you want me to do."

"There's no right or wrong answer," Paris replied and Jade rolled her eyes. Oh. So it was one of *those* kinds of things. "Please try, Jade."

"Try what? I mean, I can chuck a pretty mean fastball." She hefted the ball in her hand and eyeballed the distance to Paris.

"No throwing," he said, amused. "You've shown me how you well handle fire. Show me what you can do with water."

Jade sighed and regarded the clear ball. She had no idea what to do. She tossed it from one hand to the other, juggling it while she thought. She rolled it between her hands and admired its simple qualities. Heavy and smooth. Heftier than a baseball, but almost soft, like if she pressed hard enough, she would be able to make a dent with her fingertips. She thought about how she could make it warm but without using fire the only thing that came to mind was to keep rolling it back and forth. She hummed softly to herself; her mind began to wander. Before she knew it, she was holding the ball in front of her chest, between her two palms. Without thinking, she let go, and was only moderately surprised when it hovered in midair instead of smashing to the ground. She could feel a slight pressure behind her eyes, a low key throbbing. She focused on the pressure and the ball began to rotate. Turning slowly, gyroscopically, it was mesmerizing to watch. It caught the light, and she could see objects in the lab through its crystalline surface. They became misshapen from the distortion of the light through the liquid. The globe spun faster and faster, giving off a slight humming noise. She found it soothing, and the more she thought about how pacifying it was, the louder it got. Watching it rotate madly in front of her, she became drowsy. Her breathing slowed, became more shallow. She felt like she was drifting to sleep, the white noise of the ball lulling her into a calm, serene state that she hadn't felt since...

She jerked up in her seat suddenly, and there was a loud cracking sound. She shut her eyes and threw her hands up in front of her face, waiting for the globe to explode and send glass and water all over her. After a few seconds, when she realized she wasn't wet, she cracked one eye open and peeked through her hands.

The globe hung in shattered pieces in front of her, but the water maintained its spherical shape and was rotating just as well as it had been before. There was no pressure behind her eyes this time.

"Am I doing that?" she asked.

"No," Paris said simply. "I am."

Jade slouched back in her seat. "Show off."

"I didn't think you meant for it to explode all over yourself."

She gave him a dirty look. "I thought I had something there for a moment."

"For a moment you did. But then you became distracted. Your power surged out and shattered the globe."

"That's why we have a mentor here when we run your tests." Dr. Gellar explained. "To contain anything that happens. Paris was able to take control as it exploded."

Jade eyed him a little sourly but couldn't hide her amazement when the broken glass drifted back together around the ball of water. She could still make out cracks where it had snapped into pieces, but then each crack glowed with a bright orange heat, and the glass sealed itself.

When he was done, Paris dropped it soundly in her lap. She jumped slightly and then picked it up, turning it over in her hands. It was seamless. Perfect.

"What made you lose your concentration?" Paris asked.

"I don't know." She shook her head. "Nothing."

"It must have been something. You were doing quite well. You seemed very relaxed, in control. Focused. And then-" he said, drifting his words off to let her continue.

It had reminded her of something, from when she was a child. A soothing feeling she used to get but it also made her nervous, sick. She didn't like to think about it. "I don't know, I got bored, I guess."

"Hmm," he said lowly, not taking his eyes off her.

She raised an eyebrow at him. "If you have something to say, you should just say it."

"Perhaps, like you, I am thinking of nothing," he said dryly.

"Smart ass."

She heard Dr. Gellar let out a loud snort at her remark. The doctor coughed, trying to cover it up, but it was useless. She made a slight show of making some notes on her clipboard as she composed herself.

Jade and Paris appeared to be locked in some kind of staring contest until Gellar moved in front of Jade, cutting her line of sight. She handed Jade a lump of coal. Jade wrinkled her nose slightly as she took it and sighed.

"What do you want me to do with this?"

"Whatever you wish," Paris answered.

Again with the guessing games. "Better be careful, English. I'd like to chuck it at your head."

He smiled. "You can try."

The coven leader clearly meant it only as a wry comment, so when she actually hauled her arm back and hurled it at him, he was frozen momentarily in shock. Surprised further, she guessed, to find that she had put her magic behind it, and the coal was glowing red with heat. He stopped it simply by pushing his palm forward. The coal halted mid-air and he raised his eyebrow at her.

"Oh shit," she mumbled, hoping the coal wasn't coming back in her direction.

He flicked his wrist and the rock disintegrated into a small pile of dust, settling neatly at her feet.

"Dr. Gellar," Paris said calmly, "put her skills with earth down as ineffectual."

"Are we done yet?" Jade asked hotly. She felt slightly put out that the coal hadn't bounced soundly off Paris' head, although she had been grudgingly impressed by how simply he had stopped it. In all, she was tired, annoyed and feeling a little too much like she was on display. It was frustrating knowing she couldn't keep up - that everyone knew more than her.

Gellar made a hasty note on her clipboard. "Almost. Last one. Paris?"

Jade was about to open her mouth to ask what was going to happen next when she felt a cool wave of something press over her. It wasn't wholly unpleasant but it did make the back of her neck tingle. Her eyes snapped up to Paris and she realized that whatever it was, it was coming from him. The wave intensified and she began to get cold.

"Stop it," Jade demanded. "I don't like it." It wasn't like the sick feeling from before but it was uncomfortable, invasive. She shuddered and curled in on herself as the feeling intensified.

Paris ignored her and the cool tingle turned to a chill and then the chill to a lower temperature. As the temperature decreased, she could feel her anger rising. She didn't like being tricked and that's what this was. There seemed to be a loud humming sound in the room and it felt like it was coming from Paris. Jade fidgeted, unable to control herself from cracking her neck, like she'd done earlier, like she always did when she was nervous. Her fingers clenched and unclenched and she ground her teeth. Jade shot her eyes over to Dr. Gellar who stood there calmly, watching the machines and taking notes.

"I said stop!"

This time Jade's voice was raised. Paris ignored her. He was staring at her intently, leaning in slightly. She glared up at him and then the humming sound in the room intensified. She could feel some part of him trying to reach out and surround her, encircle her, press her, and in some strange way, squeeze her. She gripped the edge of the chair so rigidly her knuckles turned white. Whatever he was doing, he was starting to have a hard time with it. She could see a fine sheen of perspiration break out on his forehead. She could feel pressure building in her head and wondered how much longer this was going to go on. She couldn't open her mouth to speak, the humming sound in her head was too loud. She couldn't look away from Paris, if she averted her gaze, she had this ominous sense something bad would happen.

"She's still holding you off," Dr. Gellar murmured in amazement.

The machines attached to her screamed their alarms in some sort of electronic protest. Her chair began to tremble. No, not just the chair, it was the ground. The ground was shaking. Then, the air in the room began to swelter. She couldn't think. She just needed to think, just five seconds and she could figure this out, she knew she could. A sharp pain began to pierce her brain, behind her eyes, making her squint, blurring her vision. She needed to stop, she needed it all to stop.

"Fuck off!" she yelled. There was a loud popping sound and Paris stumbled backward, a stunned look on his face.

The ground stopped trembling and the temperature began to drop. The humming ceased immediately.

The pain in her head was still there, unfortunately. She yanked the sensors off her fingers and started ripping electrodes off her head, not caring that she was pulling out some hair with it. *Out, out, out.* She had to get out, get away.

"You pushed me back," he said with astonishment.

"And I'll do it again," she said, although she had no idea what she was talking about.

"No one has ever pushed my power back."

Paris turned from her to Dr. Gellar who could only shrug as she checked the machines.

"She got you," the doctor said.

Jade pushed herself up out of her seat and locked her knees when they threatened to buckle. Paris stepped forward to help her and she flinched back. "Don't touch me."

"I didn't mean to anger you. When we need to test witches, this is how we do it. We use the fire to test your conjuring power, then water, then earth and air. Then we have another witch try to wash their power over you, to glamour you, so to speak. Your power rating is based on a number of variables, who was testing you, how you responded, how long it takes before you lose."

"But you won," Dr. Gellar said.

"It wasn't meant to upset you, Jade. I apologize."

Jade swallowed hard as a wave of nausea rushed up her throat. She bent over a bit, taking in deep breaths.

"Are you okay?" Dr. Gellar asked, leaning in, making a motion to put a hand on her back. Jade stumbled again. She didn't want anyone touching her right now. She went around the back of the chair, putting it between her and the others.

The pain in her head was gathering momentum, spreading like a cold shard of ice melting through her grey matter. She felt a cold sweat break out on the top of her lip and she pressed her hand against it. Paris took a step toward her and she jerked back. He stopped, his hands in front of him in a non-threatening manner.

"Jade?"

She wiped her hand across her face, staring down at the bright streak of blood. She touched her fingers to her nose and they came back covered in red.

"Doctor," Paris said quietly as he reached over to one of the cupboards and pulled out a small towel, holding it out for Jade. Her hand shook as she snatched it from him and pressed it to her nose.

"I'm fine," Jade said finally, pressing the towel to her nose. She looked up and saw both of them staring at her. She didn't want them staring at her, watching her closely. She took another step back, hoping she'd hit a wall soon, any wall. Something to put her back against.

"You're not fine, you're bleeding," Paris said calmly as he looked over at the doctor as she studied the readings and jotted notes.

"Jade, you appear to be experiencing an atypical reaction to using magic. I'd like to run a few additional tests." She began to prep the machines again.

"No."

"What? Oh, it won't take long."

"The answer is still no. I'm tired of being poked and prodded today. Go get another trained monkey if you want to run more tests." Jade pulled the towel away from her nose, patting it back and checking for new blood. It appeared to be slowing. She swiped at her nose a few more times and then sniffed, tentatively certain it was done bleeding. In response to the lingering spike of pain throbbing in tune with her heart, she pressed the heel of her hand against the bridge of her nose.

"Does your head hurt?" Dr. Gellar asked.

Jade gave her a 'well duh' look. "Like someone stuck a fork in it."

"I really wish you'd let me run some more tests. I don't know what using magic is doing to your brain. I've never had a witch have a reaction like this before." Gellar looked over a Paris, uncertainty obvious on the sharp lines of her face.

"I said no more tests today," Jade repeated hotly.

It didn't matter what Paris said or didn't say. She didn't miss the slight shake of his head that Paris gave Gellar, nor Gellar's dejected shoulder slump. Gellar stepped away for a moment and came back with a bottle of water. Jade took the cold bottle and pressed it against her forehead. She saw a medical laundry basket and tossed her bloody towel in it from where she stood.

"Okay," she said finally. "What's next?"

"You can take a few more minutes."

Jade glared at him, her headache making her more churlish than usual. "I don't need a few minutes."

"It's been a long day. How about I take you to where you'll be living and we'll call it a night?"

That sounded like a fantastic idea to her. She was tired, she felt gritty and worn thin after the testing and whatever the hell had just happened. A hot shower, maybe some food and some sleep sounded awesome.

Gellar handed her a card and she took it with numb fingers. "I want you to call if your headache gets worse or you have any other problems," she said, stepping into Jade's space and placing a hand on her shoulder. Jade looked down at the doctor's hand and then up at her face. Gellar pulled her hand away quickly.

Paris held out a hand to gesture her out of the medical unit and Jade kept a wide berth around it as she moved. She got the impression that he would corral her by placing a hand on her lower back if she let him get close enough but he made no move to get closer and she didn't have to dodge out of the way of his touch.

He led her back down the long hallway to the stairs and didn't say anything when she took them slowly, leaning on the railing. She could feel his eyes on her the entire way, though, and his presence hovering close by. There weren't as many people about as there had been before but she still felt numerous eyes on her as she made her way back downstairs.

Paris stopped by Henri's empty desk and she heard him say something low and quiet in a language she didn't understand. A desk-drawer slid open and there was an envelope with her name sitting on top. Paris opened it, dumped out the keys inside and then slid the drawer shut. He murmured again and she heard the soft 'snick' of a lock sliding into place.

His car was still outside, parked right in front of the Covenstead and she wondered if he had some kind of special permission to park there as the leader or if it just didn't matter. She was so tired, her mind bounced from unimportant question to inane details like how she didn't even know where the closest grocery store was.

There was more room in the car than before and she noted that all of Callie's bags were gone, leaving only her luggage in the back seat and presumably Paris' bags in the trunk. She wanted to root around in her carry-on for a sweater, as a chill settled in on her shoulders - but she couldn't be bothered.

Whether he was feeling cold as well or noticed that she was, Jade wasn't sure, but Paris turned the heat on in the car as soon as they rolled away from the Covenstead. She leaned her head against the passenger window, eyes half open on the scenery outside but not really cataloging any details.

Paris thankfully didn't talk to her as he drove. She tried to pay attention to where they were going, the street names and the turns they took, but her eyes were drifting shut. She didn't know how much time had passed before she heard her name being called. There was a quick touch on her shoulder. She jerked awake and sat up in her seat.

"We're here," Paris said lowly.

She looked up and noticed they were in front of an old cottage-type house - two stories, but cozy. It appeared to have been painted within the last couple of years and while the door and the windows seemed worn, they looked sturdy enough.

"I thought I would be in a hotel?" she asked.

"If you're going to stay here, you'll need some place to live."

"I might not stay," she immediately replied.

"Then you may as well be as comfortable as you can be while you're here," Paris said smoothly. Before she could answer, he was out of the car and pulling her bags from the back seat, leaving her with nothing to carry. He unlocked the front door for her and then handed her the keys. She followed him as he stepped inside and set her bags down in the small entryway.

"Would you like me to stay for a bit? Show you around or answer any questions?"

A jaw-cracking yawn that she didn't even feel coming was her response. She blinked owlishly at him and he suppressed a laugh.

"I'll take that as a no," he said with an amused tone. "I believe there's food in the kitchen and an assortment of amenities about. But if you need anything, you have my card from before?"

She nodded.

"I'll be by in the morning to take you back to the Covenstead. Say around eight?"

She shrugged. "Okay." God she was tired. She might even skip food and just face-plant into the closest horizontal surface.

"You're not feeling any worse from before are you? Headache getting worse or anything else?"

Her head still hurt but it was lessening - more like a regular headache now than the icepick pain of before. "No. M'okay," she mumbled.

"Well," he said somewhat hesitatingly, "I'll leave you to it." He paused, awkwardly reached out and patted her once on the shoulder. He then left through the front door closing it quietly behind him.

She stood alone in the entry way and did a small, uncoordinated circle, looking about.

Her first impression of her place was that it was soft. Soft colors, soft fabrics, soft furniture. There was a large overstuffed chair and a matching sofa stationed in front of a voluminous fireplace. A shallow mantle ran over the fireplace and on it were some candles and a few innocuous knick-knacks. She could see the start of a kitchen through a partial doorway - kitchen table for two, subdued curtains, some appliances. She thought about heading that way and scrounging something to eat but it seemed far away and onerous. She grabbed her bags and started heading upstairs, hoping to find a bed in the first room she came across.

Success!

It was a small master bedroom with a little ensuite. She used the hand soap to wash her makeup off, not even caring that it made her face feel tight and dry. She fumbled in her carry-on for her toothbrush and toothpaste and, after the most cursory brushing, she stripped off her jeans and wiggled her bra out from underneath her t-shirt. She crawled onto the bed and sighed at how soft it was, wrestling the cover from underneath her and tucking herself in. At the last moment, her eyes snapped open and she found the nightstand and bedside clock, fumbling in the dark to set the alarm. Once that was done, she let out a sigh and then flopped over onto her side.

Jade's mind started racing as soon as she closed her eyes. Witches, covens, spells and magic. Her thoughts became disjointed and jumbled as fatigue dragged her down. The last conscious thought she had before she fell asleep was that she felt something tickling her brain. She wondered if it was all the magic in the air, clinging to the Covenstead and city.

CHAPTER SIX

The knock came at seven forty-five the next morning. Holding a hair elastic in her teeth and her coffee cup in the other hand, Jade opened the door. Paris stood there looking as immaculate as the day before – almost like he was spared the morning routine, with all its hustle.

She took the elastic from her mouth and handed him the coffee cup. He looked down at it.

"Don't drink it, just hold it," she said quickly, putting her hair up in a ponytail, smoothing over any stray bits. She took the mug back from him unceremoniously. "You said eight."

"It's nearly eight."

"Nearly eight and eight are two separate times." She knocked back the rest of her coffee in two big swallows. "Do I need anything for today?" she asked.

"Like what?"

"I don't know. That's why I'm asking."

"I had hoped to have someone show you around the Coven. I have some meetings to attend, so I can't do it myself. Then, perhaps, meet you for lunch or dinner to see how you are doing."

"I like Henri," she said immediately as she pushed her sunglasses on. Not that she knew anyone in the Coven or who he had in mind but Henri fell directly in her 'safe' category, like Francis at work did. He had been excitable like a puppy, but gave off an entirely harmless vibe.

"I'm sure he'll be delighted," Paris replied with a quirk of his lips. He gestured her outside and she grabbed her purse and key as she left, locking up. "He stayed at work for three extra hours just to get a glimpse of you, so he'll likely vibrate when I ask him if he can show you around."

"So tour and then maybe lunch and then maybe learn some magic?" Jade asked hopefully.

"I have some items picked out for you," Paris said as he opened the car door and slid in. She looked down at the passenger seat and saw a small notebook and some kind of scribbler already there. She picked them up as she sat down.

"What - is this homework?" she asked, flipping through the small book and seeing post-it notes with some messy scrawls. "Is this even English?" she pulled one off and rotated it thinking it was upside down.

"My handwriting is perfectly legible and of course it's English," he frowned.

She eyed him doubtfully. "If you say so."

"They are notes on which spells I'd like you try on your own first. And only those," he said, pausing to look at her while he said it even as he drove.

"Okay," she shrugged as she opened the scribbler. "What's this for?"

"For your notes."

"Oh my God! It's totally homework. On the first day! You're one of *those* teachers."

"What teachers?" he asked, frowning.

"The kind that give homework on the first day!" Jade said, shaking the books at him a little. She huffed and then flipped through the little book. "These seem kind of basic. When do I get to do big stuff?"

"When you're ready."

"What if I'm ready now?" she asked, thumbing through the book.

"You're ready when I say you're ready."

She bristled at the tone and although she didn't say it out loud, her immediate thought was *oh don't you take that tone with me*. "I see," she said, her voice clipped.

"It's for your safety as well as that of the Coven."

"Mmm-hmm."

The rest of the car ride was silent until they pulled up at the Covenstead where Paris stopped the car just short of the front entrance. Jade exited the car and gave herself a satisfying stretch, hearing some cartilage popping as she did. She tossed the notebook and spell-book in her purse and followed Paris into the building.

Henri was already at his desk, typing away furiously at his keyboard. She gave him a quick smile as she pulled her sunglasses off her face.

"Good morning, Jade," Henri said brightly. "Paris."

"Henri, it would seem that I am in need of your services," Paris said as Jade rolled her eyes.

"What he means is - what're you doing today?" Jade asked.

Henri looked from her to Paris and back again. "Uh, well, working. Why?"

"I need someone to show Jade around the Coven and she thought you might be able to do it."

"Oh my goodness, yes, a thousand times yes!" Henri said, already pushing back from his desk. "Someone else is going to have to man the desk. Or woman the desk, as the case may be."

"I'll have my assistant take care of it," Paris said.

Henri grabbed a sweater from one of the desk drawers and was already coming around the front. He slid his arm through one of Jade's and she didn't flinch at his friendly contact – she got a good vibe from him. And she wasn't ignorant to the reason why she felt safe around him. He'd mentioned a boyfriend the other day and he was openly gay. She didn't have to worry about him being attracted to her or wanting anything from her. Given her past...

No.

She pushed those thoughts away before they could take hold and drown her.

"Have you had coffee?" Henri asked, already pulling her away from the desk where Paris stood, looking a little steamrolled. "Because I need more coffee and we have to go to Cafe Crema and you need to try the Red Hot Latte, it's my favorite. God, you drink coffee, don't you?"

She laughed and it came out free and easy for the first time in days. "Yeah, I love it."

"Thank God."

She turned and looked over her shoulder and gave a little wave at Paris. He started to wave back before he seemingly caught himself and gave a terse nod instead. She turned back and focused on Henri, who was saying something about making reservations for lunch.

#

It was hard not to be won over by Henri's enthusiasm and open nature. He was so easygoing and affable that Jade found herself in a comfortable camaraderie with him. Plus, if there was gossip to know about the Coven, Henri knew it. If there was someone to see about something, Henri knew them and if there was something you wanted, Henri knew where to find it. They started off wandering around the grounds of the Covenstead, Henri pointing out sites of interest - both historically and contemporarily. She saw where the first stone had been laid for the building and also where Mitch from Supply Chain and Deb from Accounting had gotten in their very public screaming match over whether Deb was cheating on him or not (she was, with Chad - also from Accounting).

Henri asked if she'd applied yet for a coven credit card and then rolled his eyes at her when she replied, "I have money."

He grabbed one of the applications. "Yes, of course you have money, how else would you have lived? But what I'm saying is all coven members get a coven account. You'll end up working for the Coven and you'll get paid by the Coven. It'll be your job."

"I have a job," she said bluntly.

"Right, with Normals, but all witches work for the Coven. We're like a business too. I can get someone from Corporate Affairs to explain it better and show you really boring slides of stock dividends and shareholder agreements, but bottom line - we all work together. It's kind like, 'the Coven is mother the Coven is father,' only not as creepy. Back in the day, like real medieval times, all the witches in a coven lived and worked together and that practice sort of stuck. It makes for good coven bonds. Only now we can't all be blacksmiths or cobblers, so we're our own corporation."

"Mmm-hmm."

"Anyway," he said, continuing, "you'll get an allowance as a coven member and then Human Resources will set you up with some interviews and questionnaires and see where you fit best."

"What if someone wants to leave? What if I want to leave?"

Henri paused in mid-step and looked at her and it made something twitch at the back of her brain. "I... Well, I guess. I mean, if you really wanted to but...We're witches. We're like each other."

"Maybe I'm not like you guys," Jade said with a shrug. "Paris said I could leave if I wanted to," she added suspiciously.

Henri looked relieved. "Oh, well if Paris told you that then I'm sure he knows what he's talking about. But you should stay. The rest of the world is so... Ho-hum." He reached out and grabbed her hand in mock desperation. "Swear to me you won't go back to the ho-hum."

She chuckled, feeling some of the tension that had just sprung up start to bleed away. "I'll do my best."

"Good," Henri dropped her hand. "So, until we get you set up with a job, your coven allowance will pay for your incidentals. I mean, your house is owned by the Coven so that's covered, and it comes with furniture, but you still need to buy groceries and clothes and hair dye. Things like that."

"I don't dye my hair. This is my natural color."

He looked at her knowingly. There was a tense silence. She finally sighed.

"It was worth a shot," she said defensively.

He held up his hands in a gesture of surrender. "Don't sell it to me, sister. I think it looks good."

She punched him in the shoulder and he gave a mock 'oof' of pain. "Show me around town, you dork."

#

Later, Jade looked out the car window as Henri drove around town, pointing things out. They drove by the local market, city hall, the grocery store, the public library, the rec center and the coffee shop he'd mentioned. Henri pulled the car sharply over to the side and dashed out.

"I gotta grab a latte, you want?"

"Yeah, get me the one you said is your fave. Big," she said, holding her hands five inches apart.

He snorted. "That's what *he* said."

Jade laughed as Henri slammed the door and ran into the coffee shop. Minutes later, he returned with the coffee already talking up a storm as he opened the door and got back in.

"Let me tell you how popular I am with Miss Mysterious, first witch born outside a coven sitting out here, waiting around in my car." He handed over her coffee and she took an experimental sip, giving him the thumbs up.

"Everyone wants to know what you're like and where we're going, what you think so far et cetera."

She made 'mm-hmming' noises as she drank her coffee.

"But I said that you weren't too chatty, hadn't said much, and you didn't tell me what you think of our Coven so far."

Jade blew into the tiny lid hole trying to cool it down. It never worked but she did it all the time anyway. Henri cleared his throat.

"Nudge, nudge. That was your cue to tell me."

She swallowed her coffee and half of a laugh. "Subtle, Henri, very subtle."

"Subtle is my middle name. If I had a middle name. So spill."

She shrugged. "I dunno. I just got here."

"C'mon, first impressions, ideas, anything?"

"It's very... Picturesque."

"Picturesque?"

"Yes," she nodded firmly, liking the word. "Picturesque. And clean."

Henri rolled his eyes and made a 'hurumph' sound, pursing his lips together. "You aren't just playing hard to get are you? You know, shy girl?"

She lifted one shoulder in a shrug. "I dunno. It seems nice here," she said absently, trailing her fingers over the cool glass of the car window watching the scenery outside go by. "I... Maybe I could be happy here. I guess."

Henri didn't say anything at first and then a few moments later he pulled the car over into a parking lot. She looked over at him sharply.

"Look, one of the things I'm good at - like really good at - is people's auras. I'm ridiculously good at it. Honestly, I should teach a class."

"Stop," she deadpanned. "Your modesty is killing me."

"I'm serious! And yours is all..." He shook his head and she stiffened not liking where this was going. "It's all grays and browns and just, murky, dirty colors. I can take a pretty good guess at what some of it means, but I won't," he said quickly as she opened her mouth to start to fight him. "Just... Whatever you're doing now? You're not happy. You're not screamingly *un*happy, but you're definitely not happy. And you haven't been for a long time. A really long time."

She didn't look over at him. She wanted to call him a liar or a fraud, but in her experience hot denial always made things worse.

"And maybe no one's noticed before. Or maybe they have and something went wrong. I don't know. But I think you're right. You could be happy here at the Coven."

Even though she'd just said the same thing not two minutes ago she wanted to argue with him and tell him he didn't know her, he didn't know a thing about her past or how she felt. Jade bit down on her lip and kept her head turned away from him, staring out the window in the empty, nondescript parking lot like it was interesting.

"Well," he said with false lightness in his tone, like they hadn't just had a really awkward moment, "why don't we see what Callie's up to for lunch?"

#

Paris knocked on Jade's front door at six o'clock. He'd called during the day and found her busy with both Henri and Callie and fairly dismissive of needing any further handholding. Paris had managed to hold Jade's attention long enough to say he'd be by at around six and he would check up on her magic then.

Jade had barely let him finish before she told him she was fine, she was being a good girl at her first day of school and that she'd see him tonight.

Paris was coming to realize she was a bit of a brat.

After no response at her door, he waited a minute and then knocked again. He waited another minute and then pressed the doorbell. He was about to ring again when the door finally swung open to the sound of Jade's voice.

"I thought you said you weren't done till six, what did you do, fly here?"

"I made an effort to finish early," Paris answered. "How was your day?"

Jade stepped back out of the doorway and motioned for him to enter. "Fine, good, you know." She started walking toward the kitchen as he took his shoes off and placed them carefully by the front door. He stopped for a moment and looked around sharply.

"Are you doing magic in here right now?" he asked. He could feel magic in the air, a fine mixture of it, but nothing that he recalled from the book he gave her that morning.

"Just some little ones," she answered over her shoulder.

"You really shouldn't try anything I haven't looked at. Without me present, it could be..."

His words trailed off as he turned the corner to the kitchen. Sitting on the table was the beginner spell-book he'd given her and another book he didn't recognize, probably from the library. It was an advanced spell-casting ledger. Her cup of coffee sat beside the beginner books and he stopped dead in his tracks when he saw the spoon stirring the coffee under its own power. A flash of light caught the corner of his eye and he noticed a ball of flame the size of a basketball suspended over the sink. A pot of water sat on the counter and above the pot a fine swirl of mist was lazily swimming around in a double helix shape. There were also six rocks balanced impossibly in a stack, with a seventh rock hovering above them before setting itself down on the gravity defying pile. A miniature tornado in the corner of the kitchen tossed confetti up, down and around in an eddy of magicked air.

Jade had apparently been running all of them even as she left the room to speak with him at the door.

"That book you gave me seemed pretty boring, so I got another one from the library. Callie helped me pick it out," she said casually as she sat back down at the table. The rocks wavered slightly but held their balance. The ball of fire drifted perilously close to her hair but seemed to stop outside flammable distance. Jade appeared not to notice.

"It's been going pretty good, I think."

Wordlessly, Paris pulled up a chair. The fire drifted closer to him and paused in front of him, almost like a pet sniffing out a new person in the room. Paris leaned back slightly, anticipating it would burn him.

"What?" Jade asked absentmindedly, as if Paris had spoken. She looked up from her book. "Oh." She saw how close the flame was to him and without even saying a word the fireball drifted back toward her with a slight wave of her hand.

"You're doing all of them at once," Paris said, even though it was obvious.

"Yes, why? Oh, by the way, I need some help with something in the pantry."

"What have you got in the pantry?" he asked warily, eyeing the closed door with trepidation.

Jade stood and opened the pantry door. It looked perfectly normal. Jars and cans of food lined the shelves all in perfect order.

"Looks like a pantry," he said.

"Yes, looks like a pantry." She agreed as she stuck her hand in and it disappeared up to her elbow.

He pushed his chair back. "Jesus!" Paris exclaimed as he stood up abruptly and made a move to grab her.

She pulled her arm back out and shut the door with a shrug. "I don't know what that is. I can see all my stuff on the shelf but I tossed a few forks in there and they disappeared. Now watch this."

She grabbed a can of vegetables from another cupboard and tossed it in. The can disappeared without a sound. She looked up at the ceiling.

He looked up too. "What-?"

"Shhh," she hushed him. "Wait."

Two seconds later there was a loud thud from above. She looked at him. "It landed on the bedroom floor. Isn't that bizarre?" Again she shrugged. "It's been like that for the last hour. And I'm getting hungry."

Jade sat back down and looked at him like a nine year-old waiting for permission to ride her bike. He took his seat slowly. Once again the fireball drifted in close to him, but she waved her hand and it moved back again. The rocks started to wobble.

"You really shouldn't have started without me."

"It seemed pretty easy. I finished the other books before lunch." She was clearly excited and pleased with herself, practically vibrating with energy. The stack of rocks wobbled a bit from their perch.

"And so you took that one out from the library?" Paris said indicating the other one.

"Yeah, it's more interesting. And you can mix and match things. Callie said it was a good one."

"Callie," he said. It wasn't a question.

"I mentioned that my book was boring. So she picked this one out."

"And what did she say when she gave it to you?" Paris asked, growing annoyed.

Jade eyed him suspiciously. "She said, 'Here's that book I mentioned.'"

"And nothing about you not trying it on your own." It wasn't a question.

Jade waved a hand in mild dismissal. "Oh sure, she said that. But the other book went so well I figured it couldn't hurt."

"I see," Paris said unemotionally. There was a long silence before he spoke again. "Did it never occur to you that you were putting yourself in danger?" His voice was slow and careful as he spoke, wanting to ensure she understood.

"With this?" Jade asked, gesturing to the fire, water, rocks and mini tornado. "How?"

"Did it not occur to you that there is a reason we make new witches cast spells with a mentor?" Paris' voice had gotten slightly louder. Her precarious stack of rocks wobbled some more.

"I told you, it's been going fine."

"And what if what's in the pantry had swallowed you up?" Paris demanded.

"I would have landed on the bedroom floor next to the cans of vegetables I tossed in," she said matter-of-factly. "Probably," she added. "I mean, most likely." The top rock fell off its perch and clattered to the counter.

"You. Don't. Know. That." Every word was perfectly enunciated and resonant.

A small burst of confetti escaped from the tornado and sprayed across the kitchen, peppering the area with bits of colored paper.

"While I agree that you are powerful, you have not the skill nor the discipline to control your magic yet." Paris admonished. "You were to wait for supervision."

Jade held an affronted look on her face. "Are you using a 'tone' on me?" Her little ball of fire swirled up in front of her and she batted it away.

"What?"

"I hear a tone in your voice."

"If you mean am I angry with you then yes, I am using a 'tone,' as you say."

"I have it all under control," she protested. Another rock slipped off the pile, the water mist fell back into the pot and another blast of confetti spat out of the eddy. The fireball grew larger. The coffee spoon wildly increased in velocity.

"That is hardly the point. We have rules in the Coven."

The third rock fell to the counter top.

"I said I had it under control."

Paris tried to contain his annoyance but wasn't successful. "You've no idea the kind of power you have."

"You said I was good at it!" Jade exclaimed hotly, gesturing wildly with her hands.

"When? When did I say that?"

"Well you didn't exactly say it but it was *implied*. There was an implication," she pointed her finger at him, "that first night at my apartment and then with Dr. Gellar."

"That doesn't mean that you have carte blanche to try things out on your own."

The ball of fire started to roll madly behind her and small flames licked out of the perfect sphere.

"I thought you would be glad that I had started without you. Being leader of the Coven probably doesn't leave you a lot of time for training me."

In a flash of irritation at the mass of things going on in the room, he waved his hand in a clean, sharp gesture, putting all her magic to a stop at once. It was a harsh and brutal spurt of power and Jade visibly flinched at it, curling in a bit on herself. The confetti fell to the ground, the rocks crumbled to sand on the counter. The spoon stopped spinning and the fireball was sucked to the ground where it disappeared.

"I will make time for you."

Rubbing her sternum, she gave him a petulant look. She probably felt a little sick from his magic. "Show off."

His responding look needed no words for her to interpret it. Exasperation.

Paris glanced towards the pantry and taking the spoon from her coffee cup, he tossed it in. It disappeared like the can of vegetables. There was a very soft thud as, seconds later, it landed on the upstairs floor.

"Would you please go upstairs and stand in your bedroom? I want to know where it falls out."

"Fine," she said in a tone of voice that somehow managed to convey a host of emotion with only one syllable. Jade pushed her chair back and left her kitchen.

After giving her enough time to get upstairs, Paris tossed another can of goods - chicken soup, this time - into the pantry. He waited for the impending thud and then headed upstairs.

Jade was standing with her arms crossed at the foot of the bed. She pointed to the ceiling directly above her.

"There," she said with no preamble.

A collection of foodstuffs and other items surrounded her on the floor. Several cans, some forks, the spoon Paris tossed in and an apple. He picked up one of the cans and shook it a bit. It still sounded like soup. He hefted its weight. It felt the same. Looked the same. He eyed the ceiling and pointed. "Right about here?" he asked.

"Yup," she followed his gaze.

Paris tossed the can up toward the ceiling. There was a loud *thunk* before the can came back down, bringing a chunk of the plaster and a fine shower of dust down with it.

He said nothing. Unfortunately, the same could not be said for his new student.

"Fucking brilliant, English," Jade said dryly, eyeing the dent in her ceiling. "Never would have thought of that."

He glared at the hole in the ceiling like everything was its fault.

"You've no idea what it is or what to do, do you?" Jade asked.

Paris let out a breath. "Absolutely none."

They stared up at the ceiling together.

"Do you think stuff will fall out of it on its own?" Jade finally asked.

"Hard to say."

They both nodded slightly to themselves as they craned their necks upward. Finally Paris clapped his hands together.

"Right," he said after a long silence. "I'm taking you out to dinner."

#

The restaurant Paris pulled the car up to boasted faux candelabras flickering on either side of the ornate door. Jade took one look and then turned to Paris.

"Absolutely not," she said flatly.

"What? Why not?" Paris asked, eyeing the restaurant with confusion.

"Just keep driving."

When she saw the golden arches of a fast food joint she slapped him on the arm with the back of her hand and pointed.

"You've got to be joking," he grumbled.

"Nope. I've got a mac-attack. Pull in."

It seemed as though the entire population of the restaurant turned and looked as they walked in and Jade was pleased to note that this time, no one was looking at her. They were all staring dumbfounded at Paris. He was clearly out of his element and stared at the menu as though he'd never seen it before.

Huh. Maybe he hadn't.

Jade ordered by number and then both she and the teller looked expectantly at Paris who winced a bit before his eyes found the salad menu and lit up. Jade rolled her eyes at his order.

"No one comes here for the salad. They're not even good salads. If you want lettuce, you can get it on your burger."

"We're at your choice of venue. You don't get to choose my meal as well."

She should be pissed at his tone but he was so affronted to be in the McDonalds, like it offended his very core, that all she could do was laugh. "Okay, English. We'll get you a salad."

He added a milkshake to his order and she raised an eyebrow.

"I've a sweet tooth," he confessed as though he were embarrassed.

"You've almost made up for ordering a salad," Jade replied back with a grin. She pulled out her wallet and paid for both of them before he could protest.

Their food arrived quickly and she snatched the tray with practiced ease, carrying it to the little condiment stand where she loaded up on salt, ketchup, pepper, napkins and straws. Paris seemed befuddled by the entire ritual, cataloguing her movements.

"Jesus, it's just a McDonalds. You've been in one before, right?"

"Not for a very long time. Not since I was a child, I believe."

"We're expanding your horizons," she said dryly. She picked a table and then ripped open a few packages of salt and pepper to sprinkle on her fries. Feeling his eyes on her, she looked up to his horrified expression.

"What?"

"I can hear your blood pressure rising."

"Pfft. Gellar says I'm one of the healthiest people she knows," Jade replied, dunking a fry in ketchup and cramming it in her mouth. "I mean, I'm not eating this every day for breakfast, lunch and dinner, so I think I'll be okay."

He made a noncommittal kind of sound and started sparingly putting dressing on his salad. After watching him struggle to toss it with the little plastic knife and fork, she took pity on him. Taking the plastic container from him, she sealed the lid and then shook it like maracas, presenting it back with a flourish.

"Ta-da."

He poked it with his fork and apparently found it satisfactory. "Thank you."

As they ate, he asked about her day at the Coven, obviously interested in where she and Henri had gone, and about her lunch date with her two new friends. She couldn't remember the last time someone had taken so much of an interest in her daily activities. It wasn't creepy or intrusive - he seemed genuinely interested in what she had done and her thoughts about the city and her tour. When she told him she had worked on her spells most of afternoon she inadvertently started up his lecturing again.

"What on earth possessed you to reach into your pantry? Your arm could have been lopped off at the elbow."

"I hardly knew that when I reached in there the first time, now did I? I was just trying to get some peanut butter and poof! Missing hand."

She thought about how it had happened and while she should have been scared or horrified, all she had felt was really excited by the development. Once she realized that she could simply pull her hand out and she was unharmed and still one piece, she'd spent the next several minutes playing the hokey-pokey with her pantry, putting her arm in and taking it out, putting her foot in and then she started throwing stuff in. She never quite worked up the hutzpah to crane her neck in.

Yet.

Paris made a sort of 'hmph' sound that came across as prissy and annoyed. "I want to have a look at the spells you performed."

"I can tell you exactly what I did."

He held up a hand. "Don't," he said warningly. "God only knows what would happen in a ... Restaurant," he used the word grudgingly, "full of people. I don't want to see anyone disappear from their table and reappear on the grill in the back. Besides, I need to see the spells verbatim."

"I know them verbatim," Jade declared. "I've a photographic memory."

"Truly?" he questioned in his oh-so-British way.

"For printed material, yeah. Not so much for stuff I see or hear. But if I read it, I'll remember it."

"You're just full of surprises, aren't you?"

Jade looked up from where she was trying to wrestle her burger into her hands without squishing the contents of the middle out and all over her tray and caught him staring at her. She sucked special sauce off one of her thumbs.

"I guess." She shrugged. "What did you do all day?"

She got the impression he was trying not to bore her as he told her about his day but it was kind of a total snore fest. She didn't know the people he was talking about, nor the departments, and couldn't tell if this was considered a normal day or was out of the ordinary in any fashion. The only thing that kept her from being completely bored was that Paris clearly loved his job. It was the most animated she had ever seen him and his passion for his work came across in his narrative, keeping her interested and invested. He seemed to realize half way through his explanation of the new accounting system for amortizing assets that he was getting a little carried away with the minutiae.

"Well, I suppose it sounds all very tedious and monotonous, but it's my job." Paris took a long pull on his milkshake.

"I get it," Jade offered. "My job is interesting to me too, but telling people you work in statistical analysis is usually a conversation killer."

He gave her a quick smile and she felt pleased that she had managed to pull one from him. Jade fiddled with the straw of her drink, at a loss for what to say next.

She jerked her chin at his empty salad bowl. "So, have I made you a fast food convert?"

"Absolutely not," he said. "I think the grease in the air is permeating its way into my bones as we speak."

She laughed at the distaste and disdain in his voice. "You just wait. It's like a drug. Now that I've dragged you in here once, sometime next week, in the middle of the day, you'll find yourself craving it." She leaned forward a bit, "The first time was free, but you'll have to pay for yourself from now on." Jade winked at him and felt rewarded when he laughed. She balled up her napkins and tossed them on the tray. "Okay, we better get you out of here before your delicate sensibilities become overwhelmed."

Paris folded his paper napkin carefully and placed it precisely on the tray, setting his plastic bowl on top. Jade wanted to take a picture of his pristine pile of garbage next to her mashed up wrappers and condiment packages. She made a move to grab his milkshake and put it on the tray as well but he quickly snatched it out of her reach.

"I'm not done with it yet," he said defensively and she held up her hands in surrender, taking the tray and pushing the rest of the garbage into the bin. She tried to hide her smile the whole way out of the restaurant as she watched him cradle his milkshake close, taking another long pull on the straw as they left.

He'd totally be back within the week.

#

Paris sat at the desk in his study and stared at the phone. He had dropped Jade off an hour ago and had been thinking about calling Hannah ever since.

Sometimes he didn't know why Hannah had parted ways with the Coven, leaving him in charge, to take a council seat when every time he had a sticky problem he ended up calling her.

Cursing under his breath, Paris picked up the phone and dialed. He needed her advice, needed her opinion.

"Hello, Paris."

Hannah had been saying his name the same way, with the same tone, for as long as he could remember. Even now, through the phone, over the distance, he was reminded of being a curious boy, watching her and his mother at the kitchen table, working spells, pretending they didn't notice him spying.

"Hello, Hannah."

"What seems to be bothering you?"

"Are you using your witchcraft on me?" Paris joked and she laughed.

"Hardly. I love you dearly but you tend to call only when something is wrong."

"That's not - Hannah..." He protested, feeling all of seven years old suddenly.

"You can feel bad about it later. Tell me your troubles."

Paris sighed, taking comfort in her matter of fact tone. He'd been relying on her since his mother died and turned the Coven over to him. He was too young and it should have gone to Hannah - she was the most powerful witch, the longest-lived of them all, but she'd always steadfastly refused the position. Instead, the Coven had fallen to Paris and at times he felt like he'd been fumbling his way through it ever since.

"Our new witch, Jade-" He began.

"Ah yes. Jade. I was wondering when you would call about her," Hannah said, her voice slightly teasing over the phone.

"Why? What do you know?"

"If it were up to you, I wouldn't know anything. You haven't called, haven't emailed, haven't so much as sent a smoke signal up to tell me about her. Lucky for me, it isn't up to you."

"I still don't know how you manage to stay so well informed, given the fact that you're never here."

Hannah snorted, a decidedly unladylike sound that he never got used to hearing from her. "I don't know why you think the entire coven isn't full of gossips. They're worse than schoolchildren at times - living in each other's back pockets and practically on top of one another."

"And what are the gossips saying?"

"A lot of talk about her power. And if Henri were straight, he'd marry her."

"I can name at least four other women he feels the same about," Paris replied.

"Yes, but this time I think he's serious," Hannah said lightly and then she paused. "But as I said, a lot of talk about power."

Paris sighed. It was what he called her to talk about so he supposed it was as good a segue as any. "I know. I'm... Worried."

Like his mother, Hannah knew when to stay silent and let him gather his thoughts. She didn't say anything, waiting patiently until he spoke again.

"If she decides not to stay, if she wants to leave, I don't think I can break her magic," he said finally. "Not without...," he trailed off, avoiding the potential, tragic truth.

"Not without killing her," Hannah finished for him, her words steady and even.

Paris blew out a breath. "No. Not without killing her. She's strong, Hannah. Stronger than I expected. Stronger than nearly everyone in the Coven, I think. I don't know how I would be able to break her magic without killing her."

"Does she not like the Coven?"

"I don't know," he answered truthfully. "She just arrived. She seems to like it enough but it's all still new and impressive."

"Has she said anything about not wanting to stay?"

"No," he hedged. "Nothing like that. She seems very interested and she's certainly shown an aptitude for magic. Although frankly, she's got so much power that it's like using an axe to cut cake. All she has to do is swing in the general direction and she's done." He shifted in his seat and pinched the bridge of his nose for a moment tightly. "I don't even know if I should be the one teaching her."

"If anyone can show her how to manage that magnitude of power, along with the measures of control and discipline it takes, it's you."

The confidence in Hannah's voice scared and calmed him simultaneously. He was humbled by her faith in him.

She continued, "And if you want to know how she feels about staying, as I've been telling you since you were little - when you want to know what someone's thinking, just ask. You'll save yourself a world of heartache and uncertainty."

"Yes, I know. You're right," he said, still feeling seven years old.

"I'm sorry, what was that?" Hannah chided. "You know I'm getting on in my years and I can't be sure I heard you correctly."

"You have better hearing than a bat and we both know it," Paris said, feeling a rush of warmth when she laughed. "But I will humor you. You are right."

"Thank you, dear. Now, on a more serious note, I will make some inquires with some powerful witches in other covens. Although frankly, I don't hold out much hope. Very few people can match you, and I doubt anyone can equal your conviction or your control. If you can't break her power without killing her, I don't know if anyone can."

"I thought as much," he said quietly.

"I'll see if I can do a little research as well. One of the more reclusive covens is angling to have their voice heard on the Council and they've a number of grimoires I've wanted to get a peek at. Perhaps I can bargain some kind of trade. You never know what may be hidden in those spell-books."

"Thank you, Hannah." Even though she hadn't been able to assuage his fears, he felt better for speaking with her.

"Of course the best option is simply to convince her to stay. As I said before, you can be quite charming when you try."

Paris held back a laugh. "It sounds a little disreputable when you say it like that."

"I'm not telling you to have sex with her, just be friendly," she admonished.

"Jesus, Hannah!" Paris choked, feeling a blush heat his face. He'd rather have dental work than have this conversation with her.

"I can hear you having an aneurysm from here."

"It's quite late, I should go."

Again she snorted. "Charming though you can be, you're a terrible liar. I won't hold you hostage on the phone and make you talk about unspeakable things."

"Thank you," he breathed with relief.

"I'll let you know if I find anything. Just... Don't borrow trouble thinking about what might happen. All it does it put a bug in the ear of the fates."

"All right, Hannah. Goodnight."

"Goodnight."

Paris hung up the phone and had a bit of a chuckle as he stared down at it. Only Hannah could make him blush like a schoolboy. He shook his head.

She was right. He was borrowing trouble where none existed, but he couldn't curb his apprehension. The entire situation was strange and bizarre. They could find no other references to a witch being born outside a coven. Yes, witches lived outside of covens, or left their covens, or lost their magic. But no one had heard of one being born outside of a coven.

The suspicious side of him wondered what else was lurking out there that they'd never heard of either.

CHAPTER SEVEN

She had to stop eating out.

Jade was sprawled on the couch with her laptop, where she'd been since Paris dropped her off. She looked down at her stomach and came to the realization: she really had to stop eating out. As much as she loved fast food, that had been her fifth meal out in two days. Not good.

Tomorrow! Tomorrow she would make her own food, pack a lunch.

When she realized what she'd just promised herself, she made a face. *I hate packing lunches.*

After kicking off her shoes, not caring that they went akimbo in the hallway, she made her way to the kitchen to check on the state of lunch-able groceries.

Her neck tingled slightly and she looked around at the remains of her earlier spell-casting. She cleaned up the confetti, the rocks, put the coffee cup in the dishwasher and emptied the pots of water.

Yes, she still felt magic in the air – like an overdose of cologne or perfume after their wearer had left the room.

She thought, perhaps, cleaning the mess would help disperse the after-scent, but apparently not. Jade studied her counter with a frown and then closed her eyes for a moment, trying to pinpoint where the energy originated from.

Oh, right. The pantry.

Now that she looked over at it, acknowledged it, she could easily sense it as the center of the magic she felt. Jade stepped closer and found she got a sharper, stronger feeling off the pantry the closer she got.

It felt heavy, dense. Thick. Like deep, dark molasses coming from the fridge. Sludgy. *It feels stronger than it did earlier*, she thought. Before it had been a little lighter, more airy. She had gone over all the spells she'd cast with Paris over dinner and he didn't have a clue how she'd managed to create... Whatever it was in her pantry. Paris had warned her sternly about performing magic on her own, a couple 'don't you dare's' and one 'I mean it, Jade' before stating that he would contact their Council witch, Hannah to see if she could sort it out.

Despite that, Jade found herself pulling the pantry door open and staring in. It still looked normal and innocuous enough, but the thick sensation intensified. Became unpleasant. She no longer had the urge to be curious and toss things in like she had before. Instead Jade found herself shutting the door firmly. She eyed one of the nearby chairs, thinking about putting it in front, jamming it up underneath the doorknob.

But that would be silly, wouldn't it?

She gave her shoulders a little shimmy. She was probably just unused to all the hoodoo. It was probably something she said or did, some slight variation in order or pronunciation. Paris would get a hold of that Hannah person and she would have some easy solution and Jade would feel foolish and probably have to endure another scolding - but that would be that.

Stupid pantry.

Jade forced herself to turn her back on her problem and check the contents of her fridge. She wasn't sure if she was pleased or disappointed to find she had the fixings for lunch.

Definitely no eating out tomorrow.

She headed upstairs and settled down with her computer to catch up on her blog reading, gossip sites and stream a couple of short sitcoms before settling in to sleep.

She wasn't sure how long she'd been asleep. Probably not long. Jade was a light sleeper, generally waking up to turn over. As she flipped and settled down again she felt it. A sense of *wrongness*. Of *otherness*.

She wasn't alone in her room.

Jade forced her body to relax, ears straining to hear a sound, any sound. She could hear the sudden pounding of her heart in her ears, hear her quiet breathing - a little faster than usual. She could hear the faint 'tick-tick-tick' from the antique clock on the dresser.

Nothing else.

But the air... It was almost as though the air were thicker, harder to breathe. Denser. Cloying.

Tension started curling into a tight ball in her stomach.

"Don't play possum. I can tell you're awake."

The voice came from beside her, *right* beside her - deep, thick and wrong. Without thinking she swung out with her open palm, hoping to clap it, him, *it* on the ear.

Her wrist was caught painfully, the bones squeezed so tight she felt them grind. She kicked her legs out, trying to writhe away and make contact at the same time. An arm went down across her throat like a stone wall - hard and painful and she made a strangled choking sound. She kicked, she clawed with her other hand, she bucked her hips up but in seconds she was flat on her back with it on top of her.

Correction - definitely a *him*.

From the ambient light in the room she could decipher black eyes, dark hair, smooth skin and prominent features. The first word that leaped into her head was a breathless '*beautiful*' and she felt frozen.

"Hello, possum."

His voice was impossibly stunning too, syrupy and deep and she had to force herself to look away from his face. She reached out with her free hand and managed to grab her alarm clock and with a mighty swing, she cracked it against his head.

It smashed, breaking into pieces and he barely flinched. The shock of it reverberated up her arm, making her joints ache.

"Tsk tsk, possum. I'm here to help you."

She immediately thought of her magic, pushing all her panic into calling up fire, like she'd done in her apartment, at her medical exam and just the day prior in her kitchen. A huge flaming sphere spat itself into existence in front of her face and she sent it screaming towards her attacker.

He flinched this time, but only for a moment before seeming to inhale the fire, taking a deep breath in and sucking it down.

"Very nice," he said. "But not enough control." He shook his head like he was disappointed. "You've definitely got the power, but not quite the focus yet."

Vibrating with fear, she conjured another fireball but it wasn't as big as the last one. She couldn't think clearly enough to make it as lethal. He jerked his head a little and the flames zipped off to the side before she could even try to burn him. He laughed at her and she let out a cry of distress, anger and just *fear*.

"You must have better than that," he said as though he were amused. "I had such high hopes for you." He leaned over her, putting his lips and nose in the column of her neck and he inhaled deeply, almost a sigh. "You smell wonderfully of power."

Jade turned her head, got his ear in her mouth and bit down as hard as she could, feeling the flesh split under the power of her jaw. Her mouth flooded with blood - salty, hot and awful with the faint taste of something else, something cloyingly sweet and thick mixed in.

He laughed, tearing himself away from her teeth and she gagged as she spat out part of his lobe. "You are fun," he said, his teeth long, sharp and inhuman, flashing in the half-light. "Unfortunately I'm not here for fun."

He circled her neck with one of his giant hands, cutting off most of her air, and she reactively clutched at his grip, trying to loosen it, to break free. She bucked her hips up and he tightened his fingers and dug his sharp, pointed nails into her flesh.

"I said I'm here to help you, stupid witch."

He was pressing her down and she panicked; all she could feel was fear - cold, prickly fear flooding her veins, making her shake, forcing her to struggle. She was trying to pay attention, trying to wait for a moment when she could... Do something. Try a spell, punch him in the throat, something, anything, instead of lying there paralyzed with fright.

"You're very powerful and I think you could be quite useful to me in the future. And you're not a screamer. Not that I don't love a good scream, but when you're trying to do business, screaming tends to hamper things a little. But, here's the thing," he leaned in a little closer and dropped his voice slightly. His lips were disgustingly close to hers, so close that she didn't really have anywhere else to look. But she couldn't look at his eyes - they made her stomach roll, made bile rise up in her throat. What the fuck was going on? She forced her eyes sideways, staring at the lamp on the nightstand with its strange pattern of vines and leaves, twisting and turning up the base, a glass lampshade with a leaf pattern on top. She'd thought it was so pretty when she first saw it. She stared at the glass, trying to find the pattern in the graceful twists and turns. "I'm not the only one that noticed how powerful you are. And more unfortunately, I wasn't even the first."

He was still pressing hard on her neck and *Jesus* she needed some more oxygen. She was seeing black creep along the edges of her vision, inky and more than a little tempting.

"I can't have you passing out so I'm going to let up a bit. Be a good little possum."

He eased back, his hand releasing some of the awful pressure on her neck and she took in a few hitching breaths. Her eyes flickered over at him a few times, but she resolutely forced herself to not look any higher than his nose after a quick glance at his irises left her with vertigo. He had one knee on either side of her hips and she tried to press her body backward, deeper into the mattress to minimize their contact. She felt slightly oily wherever he was touching her, even through the blankets and his clothes.

"The thing is, possum, I understand you're quite new to the Coven and you probably haven't had any lessons on demons yet so I'll cut you some slack and give you a few quick tips. You know, no one likes a cliché, but there are clichés for a reason and demons, myself included, do tend to be the bad boys of the supernatural world. Is it fair? Hey, no one likes labels. We are what we are." He shrugged, his shoulders and bones seemingly rolling over one another in a physics and nature-defying move. "And we'll do pretty much anything for the right price. Right, wrong. It's all pretty flexible."

He stared hard at her and she didn't know what he was looking for but he ended up easing back a little more, almost sitting down on her knees. With him off her chest, her hands drifted up, over herself, like an ineffectual shield. He eyed her again and then slithered down her legs and she scrambled to push herself up, away from him, pressed up against the headboard.

"See? It's not so bad. Now we can chat. Like friends. I'll dial it back some so you can actually look at me." He smiled and this time when she glanced up at his eyes, she didn't feel like she was falling from an impossible height.

"You've been noticed."

"By demons?" she finally managed to speak, her voice coming out low and raw, throat sore.

"By a lot of things. Everyone loves power. Although, right now, your biggest problem is another witch in your coven."

She blinked. "What?"

"I know, it's always the ones you least expect," he said, his voice sympathetic and melodic. "But there you have it. Someone wants your power. Someone is jealous."

"What?" she breathed again, confused.

He held up a hand. "I've given you an awful lot for free just now. Quick primer on demons," he said, one finger pointing up. "I didn't draw blood. Okay, not much." He amended as his second finger came up to be counted. She reached a hand up to touch the side of her neck and she felt a small, warm-sticky trail. "And I've hinted at someone, another witch, in your coven no less, being a little *too* interested in you. So before we go all the way, I'm going to need something from you."

She felt her stomach sink, a heavy stone in her body. "Like what?"

He doodled absent shapes on her duvet with his fingertip. "Like a deal."

Jade knew jack shit about demons and only the very basics of witchcraft but she knew without a doubt that a deal was a horrible thing. It was like her body immediately reacted to the wrongness of the idea - she went cold all over and felt her heart stammer a few beats.

"For what?" she couldn't stop herself from asking.

"I could be persuaded to tell you a few more details about what I know and you..." he trailed off, still dragging his fingertips over the light cotton.

"I what?"

"You would owe me."

There was no way in hell she was that stupid. She may have just learned she was a witch and had maybe only five minutes of training but that had to be the dumbest thing she'd ever heard of. It was all she needed to kickstart her brain.

"No."

"No?" he said, and for the first time she saw an honest reaction. He looked stunned.

"I don't know fuck all about demon deals but that sounds like just about the worst thing I could do - get into an open-ended, non-specific deal with some creature I just met and know nothing about."

His eyes shifted from the playful look they'd had a moment ago to something cold and dark. She got the sense of vertigo again but she forced herself to look him in the eye.

"I don't think you understand the situation you're in, possum."

She jutted her chin up, defiant. "Probably not. But I know that you want my power bad enough to show up here and start telling me things, things that maybe aren't even true-"

"Oh they're true all right." he ground out.

"So you say," she replied back, her voice wavering slightly. "But I'd be stupid to believe you without proof." Her words tumbled out of her mouth so quickly she was almost stuttering over them.

He tapped a finger against his knee. "Proof is a... Tricky thing. There's a law among demons. I can't tell you the details of any deals I know of, other than my own."

"Convenient." Jesus, she was in so much trouble here. She knew she was smart but she didn't know where the line was that would cross her over into insanity. He could smell the fear on her, so she couldn't pretend to be unafraid.

But just because she was scared didn't mean she was helpless.

"So you're turning me down," he said, giving her a look of incredulity.

"Looks like," she hitched in a breath.

"What's to stop me from killing you right now?"

Her mind raced. She almost got the feeling he was testing her. Playing with her. "If you wanted me dead, you would have already done it. But you want my power. You said so yourself. You think I'll be useful to you in the future." Her words were still coming out rapid fire, even as she quoted back his own words to him.

He looked... Proud? "Very nice." He inhaled strongly, pausing to consider the air. "I can still smell fear on you, but it's not the cold, naked terror that I'm accustomed to." He paused again sniffing. "But it's there, bubbling just under the surface. And yet, there you are, using your noodle." He tapped the side of his own head with his finger.

When she didn't say anything, he leaned in fast and close, his nose millimeters from her. He trapped her against the headboard with a hand on either side of her face. Her heart leapt hard and painfully against her sternum. She couldn't stop herself from gasping out loud. The curtains hanging from the window erupted in flames and her eyes darted to them quickly and then back to the demon.

"But there it is," he murmured as he closed his eyes slightly and inhaled again. "That sharp spike of adrenaline. Of fear." He hummed. "And power too." Her head was pressed hard against the frame of her bed. She tried to turn away from his face.

"Don't be shy," he breathed in her ear, a slithering whisper against her skin.

As the warm air from his voice whispered across her ear, she panicked. Her hands came up to push him away, he grabbed her wrists tightly, catching her flailing arms without trouble. She struggled for a moment until he tightened his fingers around her wrist and she felt the impending break of bone. The curtains crackled and sparked, flames licking up the side of the wall. He was going to break her wrist and she was setting the place on fire. She needed to get control of herself, of the situation. She forced herself to ignore the pressure he was putting her wrist, ignore the snap of the fire. She worked on pulling the fear back inside, making herself go perfectly still. Lifeless. She imagined she could see the fear in her body, like a slick, icy-blue oil, and she envisioned pulling the fine blue strands in from her extremities and coiling it into a small tight ball in the center of her chest. Out of the corner of her eye, she saw the flames die down. They flickered and dimmed, responding to her will. She pulled her feelings tighter and imagined squishing them, deep into the center of herself. She focused on the imagery, something she hadn't done since she was a child.

The fire was out and she was perfectly still.

"Playing possum again," he said softly, his voice tickling her ear. He let go of her quickly, and was across the room by the door before she could blink. "You think about what I said, possum. Even if I want you alive, someone else wants you dead. When you need help, you'll be ready to deal."

She didn't have a quick answer or snappy retort - just a heavy, sluggish weight in her stomach. He shimmered and then seemed to be sucked up into the ceiling.

Right near the hole Paris had dented in the plaster earlier.

What the hell did that mean?

Jade started shaking thirty seconds after he left. Her headboard knocked against the wall with the force of her tremors. She pushed out of bed and fell to the floor, fumbling for her phone. She got it in her hand and then crab walked to her closet, opened the door and crawled inside, pulling it shut behind her. She hadn't hid in the closet since she was a child but the inky darkness, the brush of clothes on her face and body was familiar. She pressed herself into the corner, pulling her knees up close to her and wrapping her arms around herself. She just needed to calm down enough to dial the phone, to talk, and it would be okay. She breathed in jerky fits and starts and forced herself to count to three on the way in and then again on the way out. The ritual soothed her, gave her control and she was able to unlock her phone and dial.

As soon as the phone rang once she had a horrible fear that Paris wouldn't answer, that he was one of those people who turned their phone off at night. She only had the one number. If he didn't answer, she'd... No. She was smart. If he didn't answer she'd go online and find another number for him, for the Coven, for the supernatural 9-1-1 they must have for awry magic or whatever. And she'd keep calling people until she found someone that would help her.

She wasn't a child anymore. She had options.

Still, she was really fucking glad when Paris answered in the middle of the second ring.

"Yes, this is Paris."

His voice had the low, rumbling timbre of a man who had just woken up. She panicked again and was pretty sure she heard a kind of *glick* escape her throat.

"Jesus, fuck," she blurted, all pretense of not being scared as hell chucked out the window as anger took the place of fear in her body. "You never fucking warned me about demons."

CHAPTER EIGHT

Paris shot upright in bed. "What?"

"Because I've been *listening* and I know sometimes you think I'm not but I *am* and there was nothing about demons. Not one goddamn thing." Her voice was a low hiss on the phone, like she was trying to keep quiet but couldn't quite help herself.

"What happened? Are you all right?" He scrambled out of bed, trying to hold his cell phone between his shoulder and his ear while he dragged some pants on. It was damn near impossible, but he managed to struggle into a pair of jeans.

Jade continued on like he hadn't asked her a question. "And if things, things like *demons,* are going to be waking me up in the middle of the night in my fucking bedroom then I want to know about it before it happens!" she hissed.

"What happened?" he repeated. "No, wait, where are you?"

"I'm in my goddamn closet is where I am, although I suppose you'll tell me that it's the worst place to be because the boogeyman lives in here." She paused and he swore he could hear the gears of her brain turning. "Holy Christ, tell me the boogeyman doesn't live in here."

"You're not hurt?" He was out his bedroom door and padding down the stairs, shoving his feet into shoes and grabbing a jacket to go over his t-shirt.

"I'm fucking traumatized. What the hell?" He heard glass breaking, loud and sharp over the phone.

"What was that? What's going on?"

"Fuck! Nothing, that was just... God, stupid light bulbs. I can't -" A nervous laugh bubbled out of her. "I gotta calm down before I wreck the place."

"I'm coming over." He grabbed his keys off the hook by the door and didn't bother locking up as he left. "Are you hurt?" he repeated, sliding into his car, slamming the door and starting the engine.

She hesitated and he felt his stomach flip a little. "No. Well... I'm a little -" He heard her take a deep breath and then let it out. "I'm okay."

"That answer does not make me happy." He was driving now and the motion, the physical sense of *doing something* settled his nerves. Slightly.

"Well that makes two of us!" she said, her voice still whisper-harsh.

"I'm on my way. I need you to tell me what happened."

"I don't know. Jesus, I just don't know." Her voice was shaky, but she didn't sound hysterical or desperately hurt. She breathed deeply and he could hear her shifting a bit.

"I was sleeping," she said quietly. "And I woke up and he was just... There. And he was strong and his eyes were... I couldn't look at them at first. And he held me down and I... I..."

He felt a cold sweat break out across his forehead and he didn't know what she was going to say next. He was afraid of what he assumed was coming. He didn't know what he would say, how he could help.

"But he just wanted to talk to me."

He felt grossly relieved at her words and had to take his own steadying breath. He hated the next question, but he had to ask, he had to know.

"Did you make a deal?"

"No!" she shot back. "Because even though no one bothered to fucking warn me about demons, I'm not a complete moron."

Relief coursed through his veins. "I'm almost at your place. Can you come downstairs and let me in?"

"Um," she sounded uncertain and small on the phone and for a moment he thought he was going to have to use magic to break her door down. He'd do it, but it would likely leave her without a door.

"Yes. I'm going downstairs right now. You're almost here, yeah?"

"Two minutes." He took a turn a little too hard and had to fight to keep the car on the road.

She cursed again. He didn't think he'd ever heard someone cuss so much in such a short amount of time.

Of course, he didn't directly know anyone that had ever met a demon before.

Demons were things witches were taught about as children, but for which they had no real concept. Like learning about saber-toothed tigers. Yes they were very frightening and could kill you, but it wasn't as though you had to worry about them - they were extinct.

Demons weren't extinct but for all the interaction they'd had with witches over the last two-hundred years, they might as well have been.

There was the odd story or anecdote. Urban legend. Someone knew a witch who knew a witch who knew someone who had brokered a deal with a demon. Tales whispered over campfires and told in hushed voices. Ghost stories for young witches. Some unfortunate or foolish witch who made a deal and came out on the losing end.

No one ever came out on the right end of a deal with a demon.

There had been history lessons in class. A teacher would bring in one of the demonology books and explain how they were forbidden texts, kept under lock and key and would then scare the living daylights out of the class by telling them what happened to witches who made deals. Forced to surrender their power, never allowed to die, enslaved to demons, some horrid combination of all of the above involving all members of a family or a coven.

Their teachers told them how they didn't have to worry about demons as long as they stayed clear of demon magic - no dark spells, no summoning, no trading magic for favors. Stay clear of demons and demons would stay clear of you.

Paris remembered asking his mother about it, feeling like his lessons in class had been a bit too theatrical and maybe over the top. He remembered her white-knuckled grip on her knife and fork at the dinner table, her blue eyes looking very sternly at him.

"I know that I don't always agree with your teachers and what you learn at school about magic, but in this case, they are right, Paris. Demon magic is... You can't... It never ends well. Even if you think you have all your angles covered, even if you're sure you've thought it all through and it's for the best, it won't work out. No matter what your intentions are, even if you are doing it for the most noble of reasons, demon dealing is too costly. And you don't know their full price. They'll never tell you the full price."

She'd pushed her dinner away, half-finished and he'd gone into the kitchen after a few minutes to apologize for upsetting her. He found her staring out the kitchen window, out into the forest that was behind their house, the dark winter evening making the trees seem like moving shapes of shadow and ink.

"You should ask questions. Always," she'd replied to his apology. *"It's better that you know everything up front. I will always answer your questions the best I can."*

As Paris finally pulled to a stop in front of Jade's cottage, his mother's voice was ringing in his ears. How brittle the tone of her words had sounded, how sharp her features had looked, how bright her eyes had seemed. He realized he'd been silent on the phone with Jade and she hadn't said anything in a while.

"Are you still there? Are you all right?" he asked.

"Yes."

"I'm here." He got out of the car and walked up to the door. It was closed.

"I'm coming."

He didn't hear any movement over the phone. No lights came on in the windows. He waited for a moment.

Still silence.

"Jade?"

"Fuckit, I'm coming, just - gimme a second," she blurted hotly and then swore again, three times quickly in succession, like she was steeling herself. He heard her move, identified the rustle of her clothes and then a light came on in the window above the door. Seconds later, the bolt was sliding back and Jade opened the door.

It was almost comical, the two of them staring at each other, holding their phones. He broke first, clicking his phone off and sliding it into his pocket. She fumbled awkwardly with hers, not having any pockets of her own in neither her shorts nor her t-shirt.

He stalled when he stepped closer and saw her in the light. She had angry, red marks around her throat, cuts at the end of each scratch, thin trails of dried blood on her neck. Bruising was already coming to the surface, sick blue and livid purple. She had matching bruising on her wrists - more vivid marks circling her bones. Her face was shockingly white, perhaps a little on the green side, her eyes a sharp pale grey with her narrowed dark black pupils.

He took a step toward her, reaching out slightly, he wasn't sure why. She stepped back instantly, holding a hand up to ward him off.

"There's been far too much touching already going on tonight. Keep your mitts to yourself."

"I'll call Dr. Gellar and see if she can come over and take a look at your-" He gestured to her neck and then to her wrists.

"Thanks, but no thanks. I'll live."

He blinked. "You really should be seen by a doctor."

"It's fine."

He slammed the door harder than he meant to as he finished stepping into the house. "It's not fine."

"Hey!" she snapped angrily. "You don't get to tell me what to do. If I don't want to see a doctor then I don't see a doctor."

"You've been injured-"

"Yeah, I have been," she agreed. "All a doctor will tell me is to put some ice on it and take it easy. I've had the shit kicked out of me enough that I know when I need help or not." She flinched at her own words, as though she'd surprised herself by saying them but then she jutted her chin out. "So don't start off by bossing me around."

He wanted to argue with her but she was right. She was a grown woman and if she didn't want to go, he certainly couldn't make her. He supposed he could also see how she'd want to assert authority over herself with him after being surprised by a demon that had hurt her.

"I'm sorry," he said quietly. "Would you tell me if you're hurt anywhere else?"

She shifted from one foot to the other. "I'm not."

Paris nodded. "Okay." He watched her for a moment. She was on edge, shaking slightly, her phone still clutched in her hand. "Could we sit? Either on the sofa or in the kitchen?"

"Not the kitchen," Jade said quickly. "I think-" She frowned. "I think it came in through the pantry."

"What?"

Her fingers twitched. "I mean, I don't know for sure but it felt really weird tonight. Like bad weird, but I didn't know that meant something. And then, when he was in my room, when he left, he disappeared through that spot. Where you'd tossed that can? And it left a dent?" Paris nodded at her and she continued. "He disappeared right there. I know it's not a lot but-"

"I trust your intuition."

"Really?" she blurted.

"Yes," he replied, taken aback that she was surprised. "You have shown a remarkable aptitude for magic. An innate sense. I was angry that you had tried so much because, unlike most witches, you could cause serious damage with the amount you'd be able to do on your own with no instruction."

She paused. "Uh, thanks."

"I want to take a look at the kitchen, if you prefer you can wait here."

She ground her teeth together. "I'll go," she said mulishly. "But I'm gonna stand behind you so, you know, if something does happen - it gets you first."

"Your concern is touching."

She shrugged. "I'm just being honest."

Paris tried to remember if he knew any anti-demon magic as he made his way to the kitchen, Jade right behind him, close enough for him to feel her exhale on his neck. He paused in the doorway and immediately felt what she had mentioned. A sense of wrongness pervaded the kitchen. It reminded him of getting carpets cleaned - the way the damp smell would linger for days or weeks afterward. It wasn't strong, but with his magic it didn't need to be. He could feel its otherness, pressing against his magic, worrying at his aura like a tongue at a sore tooth.

"Has anything changed since you were last in here?" he asked, not turning around, only angling his head slightly to speak to her.

He saw her shake her head out of the corner of his eye. "Nope."

Paris turned and made his way back toward the sofa, waiting for her to take a seat. She stayed standing, crossing her arms over her chest. He gestured for her to sit.

Jade shook her head. "I need to be standing up right now," she said simply, her face leaving no room for argument.

"Tell me what happened, from the beginning."

"I told you. I woke up, he was there."

"What did he say?"

She told Paris what happened, how the demon had strong-armed her, literally, into listening. How he'd implied Jade had been noticed by someone else in the Coven. How he'd been willing to offer her a deal for information.

How she'd turned him down.

Paris knew he must have looked visibly relieved when she said that. Jade had been watching him very carefully while she spoke and Paris got the impression that she was cataloguing all of his responses, filing each bit of information, trying to learn as much as she could without him speaking.

She ended with how the demon had disappeared, right in the same spot where the strange portal in her pantry had been dumping items onto the floor.

"So," she said, her voice more steady and even. "Verdict?"

"Pardon?"

"What I need to know is this: does this kind of shit happens around here on a regular basis?"

He shook his head, "No. Not hardly."

She gave him an incredulous look, her eyebrows arching up over her eyes. "Really? Because that demon made it sound like he already knew about another witch in a deal with one of his buddies."

Paris frowned. "Why do you say that?"

"Because he said he couldn't tell me the details of any other demon deals besides his own. That implied to me that there are other demon deals to know about. It's why I think he was dodgy on the proof part of his argument."

It made a certain sort of sense. Though it wasn't concrete evidence by any stretch of the imagination, given how dangerous demons were to deal with, he was fine going on circumstantial evidence and taking any and all precautions.

"So, it seems to me like you've all been showing me this shiny happy coven life and suddenly it turns out, hey! Seedy underbelly," she accused.

"It's nothing of the sort. I've never heard of a demon deal first hand. I swear."

She eyed him suspiciously and said, "I don't believe you."

He was surprised. She stated it so easily, so calmly. He opened his mouth to argue but she started speaking again before he had a chance.

"So unless you can tell me you've got a kick ass way to make this problem disappear," she said, stopping to take a deep breath, "I want out."

He was struck dumb for a moment. "Out of what?"

She gave him a look. "The Coven, you dumbass. If you've got some anti-demon mojo in your back pocket, then thumbs up! I wanna hear all about it." She gestured with her own thumbs sarcastically. "If not, I'm done. I don't want to be here anymore, I don't want to learn anything else. I'm packing my bags, I'll ride off into the sunset and you can all have a nice life or get sucked into a pit of flames. Whatever. Your choice."

"You can't just leave," he stammered.

She rolled her eyes. "The hell I can't. Listen, I lived for years without you guys and sure, it wasn't all shits and giggles, but I did okay. So," she said as she shrugged, "there were some fires, some weird shit, whatever. I think I have that worked out. You know, mostly. But this? This is nuts."

He cleared his throat, knowing that he had to tell her the truth and desperately wishing he didn't have to. There were bad times to tell people things and then there were *really* awful times to tell people things. This was a really awful time. Demons, veiled threats about other witches and now he was going to have to tell her the terms of the council. He took a deep breath and squared his shoulders.

"No, I mean, you really can't just leave."

CHAPTER NINE

Jade narrowed her eyes at him. She had a sudden urge to say, *'Oh no you didn't!'* to his statement that she couldn't just leave the Coven.

She could leave. She would leave.

She didn't stay places against her will. Not anymore.

"Watch me," she said coldly. She turned and, keeping her pace steady and calm, headed for the stairs. She would pack right that moment and leave.

"Jade."

She ignored him, one foot already on the stairs.

"Jade," he repeated, louder. "You don't understand."

"I don't need to understand," she said, halting her progress but not turning around. "You told me I didn't have to stay. I'm exercising my right to leave now."

"You can't-"

She whirled around and stomped over to him, pointing her finger and jabbing it in his chest so hard it made her joints ache. "You don't get to tell me what to do!"

"It's not like that-"

"I don't care what it's like. I make decisions for me, you make decisions for you. That's how my world works. Now, I don't know what kind of bullshit you have going on here at your 'coven,'" she said as she made air quotes around the word, snarling a bit as she did, "but you have no authority over me."

"A witch can't exist outside the Coven."

"That's bullshit. Henri told me there are witches who leave and you said," she said, jabbing him with her finger again, "that I could leave."

He took a small step backwards. "I should clarify. A witch cannot exist outside the Coven with their magic."

She paused. "So? What does that mean?"

"You know of the Supernatural Council, yes?"

Vaguely, she thought. It was like a United Nations thing for supernatural creatures. There wasn't really a lot of publicity about it and even if there had been, she hadn't been interested. It was the same as any other government conglomeration from what she gathered - a lot of politics, red tape and double talk but nothing actually *happened*.

"I guess. I know they exist and they have some kind of authority over all you freaks."

"Us freaks," he said, clarifying. "You're a witch too."

"Not by choice," she said loudly. "And not for much longer."

"The Council," he said, his voice carrying over hers, "was informed of your existence when you started using unsanctioned magic."

"It's not like I was doing it on purpose."

"It doesn't matter," he said fiercely.

She was getting nervous. She didn't like where this was going. Paris was obviously angry or upset or... Something. She didn't know him well enough to be sure exactly what he was feeling but he was more worked up than she'd ever seen him in the short time she'd known him.

"We do not allow magic to be performed outside a coven."

"Then I won't perform it. I have control over it," she argued, knowing that she was lying. She didn't have control over it, not totally. She'd learned a lot in a really short time but it was like music lessons in a way. Learning to read music was a hell of a lot different from actually playing the piano.

Paris looked like he was having a hard time not shouting at her. His eyes were bright blue, brighter than she thought was possible and she wondered, not for the first time, if it was his magic that made them that way. "That's not how it works. If a witch chooses to leave the Coven he or she is stripped of their power. We break their magic."

She felt something twist in her stomach. Well, that was fine. She didn't care. She'd only found out about her magic. She could give it up.

It didn't matter, she told herself.

She still found the words hard to say. "Fine. Take it."

Paris shook his head, appearing... Distraught.

His voice was soft now, quiet and she was more uneasy than when he was almost shouting at her. "I don't think I can."

"I don't want it," she lied, knowing as soon as the words fell from her mouth that she didn't mean them. "Just..." she flapped her hands, "Do it. Whatever it is."

"I really don't think I can. Not-" His eyes were sharp and clear. Like with the demon earlier, she wanted to look away but couldn't. "It's messy work, breaking someone's magic. There's a lot of variables involved. My magic, your magic, the type of magic we both have. How powerful we are. You're very strong, Jade."

"I won't fight it," she said weakly. "I know that I've said that and I did anyway, but I didn't know! I know more now. I won't."

"I'm strong but I don't think I can break your magic. Not without... Hurting you."

She felt a shock of fear go through her. "What do you mean, hurting me?"

Paris looked conflicted, his eyes never leaving hers, even as she took a small step backward. She glanced quickly at the door and his eyes tracked hers.

"I wouldn't mean to. I don't want to," he said quickly. "But I don't think I can break your magic without harming you. It might even kill you."

She was struck silent and she couldn't take her eyes off him as he met her stare. Her mind raced as she tried to put everything that had happened together in one, cohesive package she could study.

She held up her hands, as though she could ward him off. She jerked her thumb out, starting to enumerate her points on her fingers. "So you're saying that you don't have any anti-demon magic handy," she eyeballed him waiting for an answer.

He shook his head. "None that I know of. But we'll start looking immediately."

"And two," she said, interrupting him sharply. "I can't leave. You won't let me leave."

"It's not exactly that, but yes, I suppose-"

Jade cut him off again. "Because if I want to leave," she said as she held up a third finger, "you'd have to take my magic. And you can't do that without possibly killing me." A fourth finger came up.

"Yes."

"So get someone else," she said harshly, curling her fingers into a fist.

"There is no one else!" Paris shouted and she felt a shock of cold brush over her, slightly painful in its intensity and it felt... Familiar. It hit her suddenly that she'd just felt a bolt of his magic. He appeared to be struggling for a moment, clenching his jaw and his fists. He took a deep breath.

"I don't want to take your magic but if I let you leave the Council will send someone else and I... If they can't do it, I don't know what them trying would do to you. They could damage you terribly. We're looking to see if there's someone else more powerful, but I don't know."

That's when it hit her that he'd known this was always a possibility. That she would want to leave and they might kill her breaking her magic. Logically, it made perfect sense that he'd already known and maybe everyone she'd met had known, but hearing him say the words, hearing him talk about plans that were made, knowing he'd thought this through... That was when she really *felt* the full impact of his words.

It felt like being kicked in the chest.

They'd lied to her. Not so much in their words but in their welcoming smiles and their friendly actions, all the while knowing this was a possibility and not telling her from the start.

And then she remembered the demon. It wasn't like she truly forgot about him, but standing there, arguing with Paris, finding out that she couldn't just leave, the demon had fallen to the back of her mind for a minute. He returned to the front of her brain with a vengeance. She thought about his words - half-told stories about another witch in the Coven who was *interested* in her, whatever that meant.

Given everything she'd just found out, she was going to assume it was a very, very depraved thing.

She'd been stupid. God she'd been so stupid to think that it would all work out. That she could be happy here. That maybe she'd finally found a place she belonged. Found some people who could maybe someday be a sort of family.

She was so fucking stupid.

It was her against... Everything. Everyone. It always had been. Ever since...

No.

She was not going to start dredging up things that needed to stay dead and buried. Not now. She had a metric fuck-ton of problems, here in the present, without borrowing from her past. She needed to think, she needed to get her shit together and figure this out.

Step one: she needed to know if there was a way to keep a demon out of the house.

She suppressed her feelings. There was no time to feel sorry for herself.

She looked Paris dead in the eye. "Is there some kind of spell or, I don't know," she fumbled for the right words, "a ward to keep that demon out of here? A way to close the portal, if that's what he's using? Crazy glue it shut, anything?"

"What?" Paris asked, brows furrowed in confusion. "Jade, we were talking about your magic."

"I know what we were talking about," she snapped. "But I have to fucking triage this mess and keeping that demon out is priority number one. I'll think about you witchy lot and your lies," she said, spitting the words, "in a moment. First things first. Spells to keep the demon away?"

"I don't know."

"Then make yourself useful and figure one out." She remembered what Callie had told her on the train here. "You're supposed to be the most powerful witch in this goddamn coven, so pony up and show me some magic."

He swallowed hard, "I will try."

His words sounded like it was a promise to her, some kind of vow. She could see the guilt and regret written on his face but she didn't care what his intentions were.

"You'd better do more than try," Jade warned.

She squared her shoulders. Now for item two. The best defense is a good offense. She was usually a fair judge of people, sizing them up right away. Maybe she'd let herself be blinded by the bright, shiny baubles of magic and belonging, but no more.

"Next. I want to know everything there is to know about every one of you witchy freaks. I mean it. I want the gossip from Henri, I want files from your little coven business, I want you to sit down and tell me everything you know about everybody. I don't care if I have to sit in a room and have everyone come by one at a time. I want to look each one of you in the eye. If one of you is out to get me, I'll get you first."

"We don't know that the demon is telling the truth."

"Don't!" Jade shouted. "The only thing I know for sure is that you're a liar. You lied to me and I'm painting the rest of your coven with that brush."

"I didn't lie to you, Jade. I didn't know how powerful you would be when we first met. I didn't know it was going to be an issue."

"And when you did?"

Paris swallowed thickly but didn't break her gaze. "I should have told you but I never lied to you. I just didn't have all the facts."

She cocked her head slightly. "Yeah, when you catch people lying, they always have all kinds of excuses." Her tone was biting, acerbic.

He took her words like they were a blow, stiffening at them. He finally nodded. "I'll help you any way I can."

"I don't want your help. I just want to know what you know."

He nodded again, his face somber.

Jade felt calmer, more steady. She could do this. She had a plan. She was smart and apparently so powerful that they couldn't take her magic. She was stronger than them. She took a moment to try and feel that power, let that knowledge sit in her bones, fill in the spaces and holes inside her. Though she didn't have mastery over her magic, she could learn.

And maybe, once she understood her power, it wouldn't matter what their rules or agreements or governments said. If she was strong enough, powerful enough, they wouldn't be able to tell her what to do.

She would tell them.

"Jade, I -"

"You've said more than enough tonight. So unless you've got something useful to tell me, some other bombshell you've been saving for a special moment, zip it. Your platitudes don't do me any good."

He pursed his lips tightly and nodded formally. "I'll contact Hannah. She's the most knowledgeable witch I know. If there's a spell or a ward to be found, she'll know it. She'll be able to work it as well. She can teach me."

"Teach *us*." Jade clarified. "You," she said as she made a circular motion with her pointed finger, "just became a full disclosure spell-teacher. If you learn it, I learn it."

He opened his mouth as if he was going to argue and then shut it very quickly. "Very well."

She felt a rush of strength. Not magic or supernatural, just personal power. She was telling him things, dictating things and he was agreeing. It made her feel steadier, more in control. Whether he was doing it because he was afraid, regretful or just wanting to make amends, she didn't care.

All that mattered was she was in control now.

And she was going to keep it that way.

Information. She needed more information. All the information she could get her hands on. What did she already know?

"You keep the majority of your spell-books in your library, correct?" she asked, remembering what

Callie had said on her first day at the Coven. "In the old dungeon?"

Jesus, the fact they'd needed a dungeon at some point in their history really should have tipped her off that this was all going to go pear-shaped.

He blinked at her change in topic again. "Yes."

"Then we're going," she said, heading upstairs to change.

"Right now? It's the middle of the night."

She paused on the stairway, turning back to face him. "You got something better to do than keep me safe from a demon? 'Cause I sure as hell don't."

"If you'd like to get some rest, I can stay here. On the sofa." He added the last bit at her incredulous face. "And keep watch."

"Pass," she said harshly. "Funny how I don't feel particularly sleepy after being woken up by a demon and then finding out I've been lied to. I'm feeling a bit riled up. I'm just a delicate fucking flower."

"You'll have to sleep sometime."

His words could have been interpreted as a threat, but the look on his face, the tone of his voice was compassionate, kind.

It just worked as a bellows to her rage and she refused to buy into it.

Jade smirked. "Based on prior experience, not for at least twenty more hours. So I guess that's how long you have to come up with a demon-warding spell that will keep me safe while I sleep."

"I won't let anyone or anything hurt you."

She turned her back on his earnest eyes and committed tone and stalked up the stairs, calling over her shoulder as she did.

"Again, pass. *I* won't let anyone or anything hurt me. You're just along for the ride."

#

Paris was astonished at the speed at which she moved. Jade came back down the stairs not three minutes after she left, hair in a messy ponytail, wearing jeans and a dark grey hoodie that managed to cover the blossoming bruises on her wrists but barely concealed the ones encircling her neck. With her hair pulled up out of the way, the puncture wounds stood out, bright red and angry.

He wanted to suggest calling Gellar again but Jade caught him looking and narrowed her eyes. A laptop bag was already slung over her shoulder and she stuffed her power cord in it at the same time as she unceremoniously pushed her feet into tennis shoes and then looked at him askance.

"Pitter-patter," she said and she actually snapped her fingers harshly at him. "Let's get at 'er."

While she'd not been overly friendly before, this sharper, harder Jade was surprising.

And disappointing.

He'd known that not telling her the whole truth had been a gamble but he never expected anything remotely as serious or foreboding as a demon attack. Also, being the Coven Leader had him accustomed to not sharing the full details of issues when it wasn't necessary or when it would lead to more complications.

A fact he was sorely regretting at that moment.

She had only just come to the Coven, only just discovered she was a witch. If she got it in her head to try to leave, the Council could send someone to break her magic and end up killing her. If he did end up finding a way to break her power, she would absolutely take that option, never believing any of the benefits the Coven could offer.

If they couldn't find a way to break her power and she had to stay with them, it was the worst possible beginning for her to join their coven family. Her first foray into their world was now filled with deception and fear.

Paris didn't know if they could get over that.

If she could get over that.

She grabbed a few more things - her purse and her phone and then she was out the door, not checking behind her to see if he followed.

He followed.

"Do you have your keys?" Paris asked. "To lock up?"

She turned back and gave him an edged look. "I don't think the demon cares if I bolt the front door. And I don't trust that someone else in your coven doesn't already have a key. But if it makes you feel better..." She rummaged around in her purse and then lobbed the keys at him. "Knock yourself out, English."

It did make him feel better. He knew no one else in the Coven should have a key, even if Jade didn't believe it. He locked the front door and then went to his car, where she already waited by the passenger side, foot tapping.

It was cool outside, crisp in the late night/early morning air. She didn't say anything as she slid into the seat and settled her bags on her lap.

He couldn't think of a thing to say to break the silence that she wouldn't throw back in his face.

Paris drove quickly through the dead and quiet streets, making excellent time to the Covenstead. Once there, he let them in, getting past the large gates and then into the Covenstead proper, stopping to speak briefly to Security and let them know that he and Jade were on the grounds and to be aware of their presence.

Jade was a grim shape at his side - arms crossed over her chest, jaw set. She only used the absolute minimum effort to move - legs forward, feet rolling on the ground, then back up for the next step. She didn't twitch, didn't fidget.

Didn't look his way.

He led her down the circular stone staircase to the dungeon. It was cramped and slightly damp. If not for magic, a sizeable bulldozer and backhoe, they would have never been able to get all the furniture down to the depths.

The coven library was most kindly described as 'atmospheric.'

But no matter how many dark cherry book shelves covered most of the old brick and mortar, no matter how many electric candelabra they installed to help with the lack of large windows or how many radiators they installed to ward off the pervasive and permeating damp chill, it was still clearly a former dungeon through and through.

Paris switched on all the lights and waited while Jade glanced around. He tried to see it through her eyes. It made no difference what kind of bulbs they installed, the slight green cast of the stone always gave the entire area a sickly pallor. He saw her nose twitch and knew she was sniffing, inhaling the smell of incense and old paper that lingered like a corporeal being. She looked at the long rows of shelving, crammed into such a small space, her eyes going up and over the books lining each shelf.

She headed immediately for the main reception desk which jutted out awkwardly from the stairwell. There'd been no way in the dark, dank space to make anything picturesque or attractive. Everything was made to be functional. It didn't matter what it looked like. She booted up the computer at the main desk, standing in front of it and waiting till the screen lit up.

"I need a username and password that grants me admin rights to this and the rest of your network," she said, finally looking up at him.

"It's four in the morning," Paris replied.

Jade stared at him coolly. "No shit. Pick up a phone and make it happen." She turned her back on him and grabbed her own computer out of her bag, facing him again as she hooked it up to a power supply. "I want network access for my laptop too. Get your alpha geek on it. If he or she is any good, they don't even have to come down here to do it." Jade stopped for a moment and just looked... Defeated. She pressed the heels of her hands into her eye sockets and he took a step forward but before he could do anything, she was cracking her neck, pulling up a chair, sitting down and typing on her laptop.

Paris started making a series of obnoxious early morning calls.

He was the head of the Coven but that didn't mean he knew everyone's job descriptions and names. His first call was to his assistant, Suki, who blearily mumbled that she'd get on it and that he owed her a gratuitous gift that better include season tickets the local lacrosse team and a bottle of gin.

His next call was to Callie, asking only that she come to the Covenstead and he would fill her in when she arrived. She also sleepily mumbled that she was on her way but didn't extract any promises of gifts or favors.

Then, Hannah. He laid out everything he knew quickly, trying to give her all the information she would need, without getting too far into the minutiae of what had happened.

"There's got to be a spell," he said, summing-up, "that will keep a demon out of an area. I just don't know what it is." He paced behind one of the bookshelves, keeping an eye on Jade through a small break in the shelving. She was looking back and forth between the two computer screens, typing now and then on her keyboard and then back to the coven computer again, then keyboard. Back and forth.

Hannah was silent for a long minute on the phone and Paris checked his cell to ensure their call hadn't been dropped due to bad reception in the dungeon.

"Did your mother give you her grimoires?"

He was surprised by the question. "Yes. Several. I know them quite well. I don't recall anything about demon magic," he said assuredly. "My mother didn't pursue dark magic, Hannah, you know that."

Another long silence and he felt something in his stomach turn. "Did she?" he asked, suddenly unsure.

"I never saw her practice dark magic," Hannah replied and while it was an answer, it wasn't the definitive 'no, of course not' he'd been expecting.

Doubt surged up in him. "That's not a 'no.'"

"If you say there is nothing in her books then it's of no consequence right now," Hannah said smoothly.

"Hannah..." Paris began, feeling his stomach twist.

She cut him off before he could continue. "I'll start researching immediately. I know several... Avenues I can pursue. I should have something for you by tonight." He could hear her hedging over the phone. "It probably won't be as clean as the magic you're accustomed to."

He didn't like the sound of that but he was low on options. "Alright. I'll wait for your call."

"Paris," she said quickly. "You might want to... Think about looking through your mother's things."

He set his jaw. That sounded ominous. "I'll do that," he said, already making plans.

He hung up with Hannah and made his way quietly back over to where Jade sat behind the main information desk. She glanced up briefly as he came into her line of sight.

"If you're looking for something to do, I need breakfast," she said dismissively.

While he generally wasn't a proud man, he *was* Coven Leader and being instructed like some kind of lackey was galling. Jade hadn't been raised in the Coven and didn't realize that he had always been treated a little distantly, separately, than the rest of the witches. With his mother as Coven Leader and the suspicion that he would someday take over, he'd been somewhat segregated his whole life. Now, as the leader, he had to keep himself set apart. Paris was friendly, polite and tried to foster a spirit of camaraderie but always managed to keep himself a little isolated from everyone else.

Jade didn't know that and what's more, he realized even if she did, she wouldn't care. To her, he was someone who had shown up in her life, turned it upside down and then lied to her to boot.

And now he was little more than a glorified attendant - there to assist her in what she wanted, but nothing more.

"I can help you, whatever it is that you're doing," he offered.

She looked up at him, her cool grey eyes like mirrors. "No thanks."

He managed to catch Callie before she made it all the way to the Covenstead and she promised to stop off and get something for them all to eat. She arrived ten minutes later, coming down the steps to the library quietly, carrying a tray of coffees and a brown paper sack. Her blonde hair was in a messy bun, pieces and strands falling out of it already and she was dressed in slightly wrinkled dress pants and a shirt that had what looked like a pasta sauce stain on the front.

She caught him staring.

"When you call at four in the morning, you don't get to judge," she said, looking up and down at his jeans and sleep-mussed shirt. "I bet you don't even know what your hair is doing right now."

He patted the top of his head with a frown, feeling his hair sticking up. Callie took a nervous stance next to him and glanced over at Jade who had made herself at home in Callie's usual spot at the information desk.

"So what the fuck is going on?" she asked quietly.

Paris motioned toward the bag and coffee. Callie handed them over wordlessly and he stepped over to the desk.

"Callie brought breakfast," he said inanely, handing over a cup.

Jade took the drink without looking at him and then snatched the bag out of his hands and started rooting around, coming out with a muffin. "Your indexing system is crap," she mumbled around a large bite.

"Pardon me?" he asked.

Jade looked over his shoulder at Callie. "You're running your database on title and author searches but that implies the user knows the title and author of the book they want. It looks like you started adding dates but you're doing it inconsistently. You've got some summaries but they read like book reviews instead of a table of contents. It tells me if the spell-book is good, if the spells are neat and organized, but gives me no idea what they are *about*. You haven't even begun to tag your collection by keywords or metadata, so unless someone helpfully titled their book *How to Keep Demons at Bay*, I'm never going to find it."

Callie was in his line of sight now and Paris saw her turn toward him. *Demons*, she mouthed. He gave a gesture back that he hoped conveyed, *in a minute*.

Callie turned back to Jade. "I can help you search for whatever you want. I know the collection. We haven't had a chance to start indexing it. We were hoping to finish the scanning first."

"Bad priority. You've got the physical location of your books and your database isn't online. Anyone who's searching has to be here. You should have indexed it first."

Paris could see Callie bristle slightly. The library was her baby. She loved the books and the organization, treasured cataloguing and reading them. He willed her not to get into this now, before she knew the full details of the situation. Callie gave Paris another look and his thoughts must've been written on his face because she nodded and turned back to Jade.

"I'll get on that." Callie jerked her head at Paris toward the back shelves of the dungeon. He shook his head and indicated a spot closer to Jade, where he would still be able to see her, but be out of earshot.

"So?" Callie's eyebrows both went up. "Talk."

Her eyebrows became a barometer as told her what had happened. He told her about the demon and they went impossibly high, creeping up her forehead and making her eyes look bigger than he'd ever seen them. He told her what the demon had told Jade and her eyebrows came back down, frowning as she realized the implications - that there was someone in the Coven with a decidedly unfriendly interest in Jade. When he told her about Jade finding out the details of her wanting to leave the Coven, how breaking her magic would probably kill her or at the very least damage her, Callie's eyebrows softened into regret and remorse.

"Oh, shit," she murmured as she shook her head. "I don't understand. Why would someone be after her?"

He said the first thing that came to mind, the obvious thing. "She's powerful, Callie. More powerful than anyone else in the Coven. That kind of magic... We shouldn't be surprised someone wants it. We should probably be surprised that more people don't."

Callie pursed her lips in disappointment. "Look, I know that not every witch is a bastion of warm, fuzzy feelings and goodwill, but a certain amount of our power relies on our intentions being in-line with nature and the natural order of things. If Jade, or anyone, has a lot of power then they were meant to have a lot of power."

"You're a good witch and a good person," Paris said gently. "But magic is power. Someone is always going to want it. Someone is always going to be jealous." He paused, waiting for his words to sink in, watching Callie's face fall. He gave voice to the things he'd been thinking for the last few hours, wondering how this happened, why this had happened. "Jade's got a lot of power and no training, no control. She's like a big, waving beacon to anyone who ever felt cheated or like they deserved more."

Callie sighed, head tipping back, more hair falling out of her bun. "Okay, fine. I know you're right. I don't like it or want it to be true but I get it. But how would someone even get her power? I didn't even know that was possible?"

"That's what we also need to find out," Paris said darkly. "I need you to start doing research on that. But discreetly. If other witches or other covens find out what we're looking into-"

Callie exhaled, pushing her hand through her hair, getting stuck by her bun and undoing it, quickly wrapping it back up and securing it again. "Jesus, yeah. It doesn't matter why you tell someone you're researching that. No one will believe it's for altruistic motives." She huffed, "I guess that explains why our jealous witch went to a demon. A lot less questions that way. I just... I just don't want to believe that someone in our coven is like that. I know we're a big coven and it's not like we're all buddy-buddy, but still."

He agreed with her to some extent - their coven was a family of sorts, albeit a large, extended one.

But every family had their black sheep. He didn't know every witch in the Coven personally. His mother had known most of the families, and he tried to keep the same system she'd had - knowing a few family members and then knowing the rest by extension. Most everyone in the Coven was like that - close to a few people, acquaintances with the rest, like a small town.

He wondered how many more witches had slipped through the cracks. What if this one witch was only a symptom of problems in the Coven?

His coven.

Paris wondered if he was the best leader for the Coven. He didn't want to be a tyrant, to police other witches, nor did he want to be a sentimental leader - offering smiles and hugs to everyone. He just wanted everyone to work within the system, to use magic fairly and justly. To adhere to their most basic rule - do what you will, though it harm none.

If that didn't work, if witches didn't want to follow that rule, couldn't follow that rule, Paris didn't know what kind of a leader he would have to be to fix it. Or rather, he knew what kind of leader he'd have to become and didn't know if he could stomach it.

"I know," he finally replied, agreeing with Callie's sentiments but not willing to express the rest of his thoughts. "I know it's unpleasant work, but if you can find out about how to steal another witch's magic, maybe we can predict what will happen."

Callie nodded. "Speaking of prediction..." She began, trailing off and raising her eyebrows expressively. He wondered if it was just that he'd known her for so many years, but he really thought he could have an entire conversation with her eyebrows, without her saying a word.

"Yes?"

"Have you thought about prognostication?"

Paris immediately shook his head. "No," he said quickly. "I don't deal with the future. No one should. It's too dangerous."

Callie hesitated, licking her lips. "I know, but this could be the time when it's worth it."

"It's dangerous magic. No one should know the future. It's too... Convoluted. There are too many variables. Are you seeing what's going to happen? Or what's going to happen because you know it's going to happen? Do you do something to change it? Or is based on you doing something you never would have done if you hadn't tried to view the future in the first place? It's too complex, too fluid. Everything we do, every action is a bit of the puzzle and our brains just aren't meant for it. We'll only end up making it worse or driving ourselves mad."

Callie chewed on her thumb, worrying the hangnail. "Stop that," he said gently and she yanked it out of her mouth.

"Fine," she said grudgingly. "I know you're right. About future-telling, it's just... This is a really big fucking mess, Paris."

"I know. But we'll figure it out." Jesus, he hoped his voice conveyed 'strong, confident leader' because he sure as hell wasn't entirely certain.

His tone must have been reassuring because Callie was nodding and looking a little relieved. "Okay, I'm going to see what I can find and if I can help Jade with what she's doing." Callie looked over her shoulder at where Jade sat working away. "What *is* she doing?"

Paris shook his head. "I've no idea. She's not exactly the most trusting right now. She wants to see all the paperwork we have on everyone in the Coven and I don't know what I'm going to do about that. I can't just hand over that kind of personal, confidential information. It has everything - names, social security, power levels." He sighed and rubbed his forehead. "But I don't want to tell her 'no' either. She doesn't trust us. Frankly, she's got no reason to trust us."

"Fuck I'm glad I'm not coven leader," Callie muttered under her breath. She clapped him on the shoulder. "Well, that's why they pay you the big bucks, I guess." She made her way back to Jade, approaching cautiously and asking if she could work alongside her.

Jade looked Callie up and down, waited a cool beat and then shrugged. Callie offered a small smile and then went around behind the desk, sitting down at another computer. She gave Paris a little thumbs-up.

At any rate, he was going to have to pull files on coven members, even if he didn't hand them over to Jade.

He needed to go through the files himself and see if he could figure out who in his coven would want Jade's power badly enough to deal with demons. His conversation with Hannah also had his mind turning. She'd seemed skeptical when he'd professed his mother didn't deal in dark magic. Though she hadn't said anything outright - indeed, Hannah rarely did - her tone and answer had implied that she believed his mother had practiced darker magic and possibly even dealt with demons.

But surely that was impossible.

Wasn't it?

He knew his mother's magic. He'd felt it often enough, brushing up against his own, assisting his spells when he was younger, counter-hexing them if he made a mistake. It wasn't dark or sinister, malicious or malevolent. He remembered it being warm and fierce. Protective and safe.

Then again, he'd never had it directed at him in any way other than helpful - fixing his magic, teaching him spells, soothing his injuries.

Paris needed to go back and look at her spell-books. See if there was something, anything he had missed that could be helpful.

He wasn't sure if he was hoping to find something or not.

#

Jade found it hard not to be distracted by Callie.

She sat at the computer next to Jade, her diminutive form in the corner of Jade's eye. Jade was pretty sure she'd taken what was usually Callie's spot, and her chair. She'd had to adjust it considerably so she could sit at the computer and work. Callie hadn't said anything since she'd asked Jade if she could work next to her, doing some further research into the library. But she kept glancing at Jade, biting her lip and then going back to her own screen. She tensed like she was going to speak a few times and then would slump slightly, going back to what she was doing.

By the fifth time, Jade had enough. She was tired, the coffee had been weak and too sweet and she'd only had the muffin to eat.

"Jesus, if you have something to say, just fucking say it already!"

Callie flinched and tucked a few errant strands of hair behind an ear before speaking. "I just... I wanted to apologize."

Jade turned back to her laptop, typing in some notes she wanted to remember into her text file. "For what?" she asked, disinterested.

"I know you feel like we lied to you-"

"You *did* lie to me," Jade interrupted, turning back to look at Callie. Callie flushed slightly at the accusation and Jade felt vindicated.

"We didn't... I mean, we thought you'd want to join the Coven and it wouldn't be an issue. Everyone is happy here."

Jade snorted. "Yeah, someone's so fucking happy they want to steal my power. Keep it for themselves. Happy, happy, happy."

"This is the first time something like this has happened!"

"That you know about," Jade said.

"We're good people. Good witches," Callie said stubbornly with an affronted expression. "We want to help you. I want to help you. I don't want you to use this to judge all of us."

Jade shrugged. "Too late."

The kicker was, she had liked Callie. She thought she was growing closer to Callie, Henri and even Paris in a weird, distanced and aloof way. She had warmed to the idea of being a witch and joining their coven.

Now – she pushed those tainted thoughts from her mind. She had to focus. She was trying to get a feel for their database, for how it was structured, trying to figure out the kinds of books they had and if they could help her. She already had a list of ten. At some point, she was going to have to trust Callie, she supposed. She didn't know enough about magic yet to be able to judge if the books she was selecting were going to be helpful or not. She was trying to focus on defensive magic - anything that might help her protect herself. She likely wouldn't be able to read every book she wanted so she'd have to rely on some help at some point.

Jade was manipulative enough to realize that Callie would try harder to assist her if she thought Jade didn't trust her. It wasn't a pleasant thing to know about yourself - that you were good at manipulating people - but it wasn't something Jade had the luxury of ignoring right now either. She'd set the stage by telling Callie flat out she didn't trust her. Now she was going to offer Callie a chance to help.

Jade turned her computer toward Callie.

"If you really want to help, I want to look at these books."

Callie immediately leaned over, lips moving slightly as she read the titles. She frowned. "What are you looking for?"

Jade hesitated, wondering how much of the truth she wanted to reveal. She didn't want to lay all her cards on the table, but then she thought about how she'd felt when the demon was in her room, trapping her, holding her tightly, making her heart pound. Leaving marks on her body.

"I want to be able to defend myself. I'm best with fire."

Callie nodded, still looking at Jade's list. "Okay, well two of these are probably no good to you. They're higher level magic and you won't be able to learn them quick enough. I'll grab them so you can take a look, but-" She made a seesaw motion with her hand. "Probably not helpful. I can pull the other ones and there's another that's not on your list that might be useful too. It has some protective charms and wards in it. We can see if we can fiddle with them to get something more." Callie was already pushing herself out of her chair, pausing close to Jade. She put a hand on Jade's shoulders and Jade tensed up.

Callie immediately pulled her hand back. "I do want to help. We'll figure this out, Jade."

She was doing the cow-eye thing again, her big brown eyes staring down at her, like some kind of fairytale heroine - earnest and heartfelt. This was probably a woman who'd had a loving mother, a father who told jokes at the dinner table, friends that had sleepovers with pillow fights, giggling and too much junk food. All things foreign and unknown to Jade.

Callie had probably never known what it was like to be scared in her own home, of her own family, and overall disinterested in or invisible to the world at large; able to keep everyone at a distance while secretly resenting them for doing exactly what she wanted.

Jade wanted to have Callie as a friend but also resented her for having all the things that Jade was denied. Jade managed a tight-lipped nod, jerking her head once as she looked away. Callie put her hand back on Jade's shoulder as if the gesture had emboldened her, squeezing once in a reassuring manner.

It was probably the most genuine gesture Jade had received in years and it made her eyes suddenly water.

She blamed it on her fatigue and the bad coffee, nothing more.

CHAPTER TEN

By the time evening rolled around, Jade felt like someone had taken sandpaper to both her eyeballs and then sprayed lemon juice in her face.

She and Callie had moved to another area of the dungeon, the large wooden table strewn with books along with Jade's computer and some notebooks for Callie. Jade assumed that, at some point, Callie had texted or called Henri because he arrived with lunch salads, snacks and beverages, and presented it all without fanfare - which she would bet was a first for him - and then sat down at the table and started to dig in.

Jade ate some chicken Caesar salad, washing it down with three pieces of garlic bread and some carbonated drink. She hoped the sugar, caffeine and carbs would keep her going.

Not surprisingly, she felt sloshy in the stomach, although that could have been the subject matter. Callie had dug up some older books on demons. And by dug up, Jade was nearly certain she'd actually put shovel to earth somewhere because the books were dank, ancient and had a grimy feel to them. They were difficult to decipher as they were written in Latin or Old World English with scrawling handwriting using formal and ancient vocabulary, accompanied by hand drawn illustrations which Jade really wished left more to the imagination.

The first portrayal she came across took her a while to figure out. She had to turn the book sideways, then upside down, then sideways again to figure out what she was looking at and when the picture finally made sense, she dropped the book and scooted back a bit in surprise.

Henri and Callie had drawn up chairs next to her, on either side, and started reading over her shoulder after that incident. She should have told them to go away, give her space, but the ick-factor of the book had her grateful for the warmth of both their bodies, flanking either side of her.

She flipped another page over. The three of them each tilted their heads to the left, trying to make sense of the image that presented itself on the brittle paper.

"That's not even possible," Callie said as she stared at the drawing, a portrait of a female demon with her male servant lover.

Jade narrowed her eyes, studying the scene. "Well, I think she's doing most of the bending, so I guess it depends on how flexible demons are."

"It doesn't look like he's enjoying it much." Callie indicated the man in the drawing. His lips were pulled back from his teeth in a skin-snapping grimace of pain.

"Somehow, I kinda think that's the point," Henri said. "It's not helpful, move on." He made flappy motions with his hand and Jade got the impression he was eager for her to turn the page so they wouldn't have to look at the unsettling image.

The remainder of the book, while sexually disturbing and horrifically enlightening on the many ways the human body was breakable and bendable, wasn't helpful to their cause. Jade wished she could take a shower after looking at it. She settled for finding a washroom and scrubbing her hands three times and then using a healthy dollop of hand sanitizer.

Paris was absent for most of the day, disappearing a short time after Callie had sat down next to Jade. She definitely got the impression that while Callie and Henri were there to help, they were also keeping some kind of watch or vigil on her. Jade wasn't sure exactly what they were supposed to do if she had another hellish visitor, since it didn't seem like they knew a whole lot about demons.

But the company was kind of... Nice.

She needed to take a break from demons after that last book, so she flipped through one of the spell-tomes that Callie had brought over. Callie and Henri, still flanking her, began pointing out spells that would be good for Jade to start studying. Henri ran out and got them some coffee, bringing them all the biggest lattes with extra shots in each.

She found it frustrating at first, casting spells where nothing happened. Henri and Callie kept at her, giving her unhelpful advice that consisted of 'don't force it' and 'you're trying too hard.'

What was she supposed to do, try less? How did anyone ever get anywhere by trying less?

The spells weren't like the ones she'd tried earlier. She hadn't really even thought about those ones - she just read the instructions, imagined what she wanted and it happened. Callie tried to explain how beginner's magic was like drawing with crayons. You grabbed a crayon and you scratched it across the page - you had a line. You made a blue bubble and called it a cloud. You drew a yellow circle with spikes and called it the sun.

As you got deeper into magic, you started using finer tools - pencils, pastels, watercolors. You didn't just draw a picture, you shaded it in, adding depth and perspective.

Spells got harder, smarter, more intricate but their results also became stronger, woven into reality, more resilient. More able to stand up to other magic.

It wasn't until she got the first spell to work that she realized what they'd been trying to tell her. She'd been pushing at her power inside her - feeling it like a large rubber ball, pressing down against it, trying to force it to work, to move, to do something.

But what she really needed to do was *pull* at it. Coax it toward her, beckon it out, like a rabbit in a hole.

After that, it came a lot quicker. The fire spells she'd been working on before were easily extinguished by Henri and Callie which had made Jade sullen and angry. Now, Callie and Henri had to work a little harder to break Jade's magic. They had to think about it more, take more time.

But it was exhausting. She felt wrung out - like a thin, worn washcloth - twisted, frayed and left flapping in the wind.

She dropped her head with a *thunk* on the table, needing to close her eyes for a moment.

"What happened?" Callie asked.

"I think her latte just ran out," Henri said.

Jade sat back up and stretched, reaching her arms behind her, feeling her spine crack and pop. She slouched down in her chair again, good posture be damned. She shook her paper coffee cup, hoping there was a little swallow left or something.

Nothing. Godammit.

"Let's go eat," whined Henri, sounding like a plaintive child. He slumped over the table. Callie closed the book she was researching, a waft of air smelling like pine and sage puffing up from the pages as she did.

"Agreed." Callie pushed back from the table and Henri stood up. They both looked expectantly down at their companion.

Jade wasn't sure what to do. She was hungry. She wanted to get something to eat but she didn't entirely trust them either. They had been helping her all day with her magic but at the same time... She didn't really know them.

Her stomach rumbled. She did need to eat.

"C'mon," Henri wheeled around the table and jiggled Jade's chair a bit. "You've got to eat. We're not asking you to marry us or anything."

She fiddled with her pen, rolling it between her fingers. He was right but she was so tired and she didn't want him to be right. It was stupid and childish.

She couldn't afford to be stupid and childish right now, she reminded herself.

"Okay," she breathed. "Let's go eat."

#

They ended up at a place called 'The Chop Shop' where Jade waved her hand and let Callie and Henri order whatever they recommended for her. Jade leaned back against the deep red velvet booth and tried to roll some of the kinks out of her neck. Hunching over her laptop and old books all day left her feeling like Quasimodo.

There was a pinch in between her vertebrae, right at the point where her shoulder blades met. Jade tried to crack her back by opening and closing her wingspan to no avail. She rubbed at her neck, feeling a slight tingling sensation at the base of her skull where she probably had some kind of pinched nerve.

If this kept up, she was going to start walking with a lurch.

She glanced at Callie and Henri who were sipping their green tea and discussing a spell that neither one of them had been able to work today. They both appeared tired and worn - slightly red-rimmed eyes and fatigue-lined faces.

Jade should thank them for helping her, for staying with her at the library, for being patient and teaching her some magic.

But she still felt twisted up about them - unsure what their motives really were. They seemed genuine but she just couldn't make herself believe it.

In the end, she said nothing.

The food arrived and they all dug in, scooping servings off the communal plates and then later on, snagging pieces with their chopsticks. Callie and

Henri managed to keep the conversation going between themselves throughout, attempting to engage Jade but she kept her replies minimal, giving them enough so that she wasn't outright ignoring them but not adding anything substantial.

Callie's cell phone rang while she and Henri were in the middle of talking themselves into dessert. It was the ominous *Imperial March* from *Star Wars* and Jade wondered if that was always Callie's ringtone or if it meant someone in particular was calling. Callie answered, her eyes flicking immediately over to Jade.

"Yes, we're with her, having dinner." *It's Paris,* she mouthed at Jade. Callie listened intently for a moment, eyes moving from Jade to Henri and then randomly around the table.

Jade's interest perked up but she continued her lazy perusal of the cashew chicken, searching for the last lonely cashews in the mix of vegetables. Their waiter came by, dropping off the check and a bunch of fortune cookies. Henri quickly snatched the bill up, sliding his credit card into the little slot. Callie said a few more things into the phone - some non-verbal 'mmhmms', one 'yes, I know where that is' and then a few more assents before she signed off with a quick goodbye.

Jade tried not to look expectant as soon as Callie hung up the phone. The tingling feeling at the base of her skull was turning into a shard of pain. She wondered if she'd overdone the magic today at the dungeon. She hadn't done anything nearly as powerful as when she'd first arrived, when Paris' power had been pushing at her, but she still felt the beginnings of a headache creeping up into her grey matter and she couldn't tell if it was from the tight muscles in her neck or from magic.

Neither Henri nor Callie seemed affected, other than being tired, but Jade remembered Gellar saying she was having an atypical reaction to magic, so it's likely that they wouldn't be bothered using their powers.

Maybe Jade should have agreed to more testing, maybe should have pursued that line of knowledge but she hated being touched, poked and prodded. In her current situation, feeling vulnerable and out of her element, she just didn't think she could do it.

Callie tucked her phone back into her purse. "Obviously," she said, rolling her eyes self-deprecatingly, "that was Paris. He just wanted to check on you, make sure you were still doing okay and to let you know he's made arrangements for you to have somewhere else to sleep tonight. He figures your place is out of commission until we can-" Callie glanced around like someone might hear, "get that thing taken care of."

"You mean the demon portal that is my pantry?" Jade said dryly. The restaurant wasn't exactly teeming with people, there wasn't anyone around to hear.

"Um. Yeah. That." Callie winced. "Anyway, he's going to swing by and meet us outside and then we can head on over to the place he's got sorted. We can hang out, do some more research. Watch a movie. We'll stay with you." Callie tentatively reached a hand out over the table but when Jade didn't move to take it, she pulled it back, trying to smile a bit, reassuringly.

Jade was grateful she wouldn't be alone but at the same time, dreaded being surrounded all night. She'd never gotten used to being around others for long periods of time, and although she knew herself well enough to admit she was scared stiff about trying to fall asleep alone, she also didn't want to be crowded by people who, while very nice, were essentially strangers.

No matter how much she kind of liked them.

Henri snagged a fortune cookie and snapped it open, reading his fortune.

"You will be afforded a great opportunity," he read, smirking. "You know, you're supposed to add 'in bed' to the end of all fortune cookies."

"I've seen your boyfriend," Callie said, latching on to the chance to break some of the tension. "And that *is* a great opportunity." She winked at Henri and he grinned, nose crinkling in laughter.

"You don't know the half of it," Henri leered lasciviously and Callie laughed, making a totally loud and obvious snorting sound, a little shriek of surprise escaping her right after. This set Henri off laughing and Callie snorted even harder; the overly-tired, strung out laughs of people who were exhausted and probably couldn't even tell you why they were laughing.

Jade cracked a thin smile watching them, Callie's fine hair a nest around her face, Henri's choppy haircut no longer artfully arranged but just messy and overworked. Callie split open her fortune cookie and then resumed her laughter as she gasped the words out.

"Right now there is an energy pushing you," she said as she waggled her eyebrows and then gave an over the top wink, "in a new direction."

"In bed!" Callie and Henri finished together.

Jade rolled her eyes at the two of them but couldn't help the smile on her face widen a bit at their antics.

"Your turn!"

Like usual, there were far more cookies than needed, leaving an array of choices for Jade to pick from. She randomly grabbed one, ripping off the plastic and snapping it in half. She quickly glanced over the words and even she had to chuckle at this one.

"You will discover your hidden talents."

"In bed!"

Callie and Henri nearly shouted it this time and the waiter coming back to pick up Henri's credit card flinched at the volume.

By the time the beleaguered waiter came back and Henri signed the little slip, Callie was wiping tears from the corner of her eyes. "I don't even know why I'm still laughing," she protested, using a napkin to swipe at her eyes. Henri stood and pulled Callie's chair back for her as she groped for her purse.

"We need, like, twelve hours of unconsciousness and a decontamination shower after being stuck in the dungeon all day," Henri said.

"Speaking of," Jade said quietly, both Henri and Callie turning to look at her at the same time. "I'm just gonna pop into the bathroom really quickly." *And take twelve ibuprofen*, she added to herself, feeling her headache start to attack with a vengeance. Her skin had a strange, creepy-crawling feeling to it and she really just wanted to start scratching at the back of her neck. With a fork.

"You okay?" Callie asked, eyebrows coming together. "You look like I feel."

Jade quirked her lips. "Yeah, just too much coffee followed by three glasses of water." She gestured at the table.

Callie's phone rang again, a different ringtone than before, this time a pop song about being a sexy beast and Jade smirked as she heard Callie answer and start talking to her boyfriend.

She wondered if everyone who called Callie got a personalized ringtone and then tried not to guess what ringtone Callie would assign to her. If Jade even got her own on tone Callie's phone. She shook her head and started rooting around in her purse for painkillers even as she headed to the bathroom.

After finishing up in the stall, Jade took one look at herself in the mirror and decided she didn't own enough makeup all together, never mind the few items she kept in her purse, to make a dent in her disheveled visage. She knocked back four ibuprofen with a swallow of tap water and then redid her ponytail.

Still dismal but at least it was neat again.

Despite the hopelessness of the situation, she couldn't help but dust some pressed powder on her face, which turned her shiny, pasty white skin into matte pasty white skin.

Awesome.

She picked up and rejected six lipsticks from the bottom of her purse before finding her favorite. *And goddamn, why did they make a shade if they were just going to discontinue it at the end of a season?* Before pitching it forever, she attempted to coax another use from the blunted stump. Jade assessed herself again in the mirror, glad she had picked a lighter shade of lipstick. With her dark brown hair, pale eyes and sickly skin, anything too deep and she would've looked like Snow White's less attractive evil twin.

A really bitchy evil twin.

Who could hurl fireballs.

She caught sight of a stain on her hoodie and didn't even care all that much. It just completed the look - she may as well start wearing pyjama pants and just pretend to still be a university student if she was going to walk around on no sleep and criminal blood-caffeine levels.

She was just giving up when the mirror shimmered.

It was quick; so swift she blinked a bit and rubbed her eyes wondering if it was one of those floaty halos she sometimes got after too much computer work. Jade blinked a few more times and looked around, checking her eyesight.

Nothing.

Then, the mirror wobbled again, almost like the surface wasn't entirely solid. Semi-solid? She noticed something pressing on it from the other side. Her fingers itched to reach up and touch, but that seemed like a terrible idea. She leaned back slightly.

Her reflection didn't move.

Like a photograph, her reflection stayed perfectly still and Jade felt her stomach lurch at the physical impossibility of what she was seeing. The bathroom suddenly seemed too small, too silent, too still.

And then it wasn't.

Like it was molten, the mirror lurched up in a wave and appendages that only approximated the shape of hands pressed out of the mercurial surface. Jade jerked back, but not quick enough and the appendages grabbed around her ears and yanked her hard toward the mirror.

Her head cracked against what still felt like a very solid surface despite what she saw. Jade heard the firm *whack*, felt it reverberate through her skull and bit off a vicious curse. Disorientated and traumatized, her vision exploded into white-hot stars.

One of the hands fisted in her hoodie and *pulled*. She was forced to brace her arms on either side of the vanity to avoid getting clocked in the face again.

She could feel the sharp cold of split skin on her forehead, pain and blood following quickly after. Her reflection was active again, but delayed like a computer running too many programs - it didn't exactly match up to what she was doing. The hands tried to tug her closer, curling tightly in her hoodie and giving her a mighty yank. She couldn't hold herself back from the mirror and try to break the grip at the same time, so she tried to wedge one foot up on the wall and push back using the stronger muscles of her legs. With the extra leverage, she was able to take one of her hands off the wall and start tearing and beating at the silvered hands. One of them released her shirt, reached out and encircled her wrist. The powerful hand snapped her bone without any warning.

She shrieked at the hot spike of agony and stumbled, getting sucked in closer to the mirror where she didn't know what the fuck was going to happen. She grasped at the only magic she felt really comfortable with and thought *fire*.

The ceramic tile of the wall on which the mirror hung exploded in shards and spikes of clay and sparks of flame. There was a loud *whoomp* sound and the paper towel dispenser next to the sink went orange and hot, the flames licking up the side of the wall. The garbage can gave a loud pop and then its lid flew off, bright yellow and orange curls flickering up.

The fire alarm sounded and the sprinkler system blared. All she could think was *thank fuck, maybe I'll get a little help here,* as the hands turned sharp and clawed into her hoodie, pulling for all they were worth. She blinked the water out of her eyes, seeing red as it mixed with the blood on her forehead and ran down her face. The alarm was deafening in the small space and made her ears ring. As she struggled, she knew she was losing, the hands grew stronger, tighter, harder and she was getting closer to the mirror as her muscles weakened.

She repeatedly thought the word *fire fire fire fire,* trying to dredge up every last bit of her power. The room sweltered as flames surrounded her.

Then, the mirrored glass burst like an engorged water balloon, sending thick, soupy liquid all over her face and clothes. The mirrored hands fell apart like wet tissue, slipping through her own hands and spilling onto the floor. She stumbled against the immediate release and slipped on the moisture and goop on the bathroom floor. She fell hard on her ass and both her hands, crying out at the shock of pain that shot up her broken wrist.

The door to the ladies room burst open and Jade flinched. She pushed herself backward with her feet and her one good hand, throwing magic at the door, but she was tired, her magic weak and she felt it get deflected easily.

"Jesus Christ, what is going on in here?" Paris yelled to be heard over the fire alarm. His eyes were bright blue and he looked ready to spit nails, which for all she knew, he could actually do. Callie and Henri were right behind him looking shell-shocked and bewildered.

Jade blinked up at them through the water still raining down, and then looked around a bit at the mess. She pushed herself back against the wall and cradled her broken bone.

"Took you long enough," she said and she started to shake. She wasn't cold, but her teeth chattered and she could feel the big muscles of her legs trembling and weak.

Paris eyed the destruction in the small room, and came to kneel next to her, tipping her head back and looking at the cut on her head. She had to blink a few times to make him stay in focus. Her headache increased exponentially, nearly crossing her eyes with the sharp pain.

"What happened?" He looked around, presumably for something to stop the bleeding on her head and she laughed, a high-pitched, nearly hysterical giggle.

"I blew up the paper towels," she said.

Callie was in the bathroom suddenly, passing pristine white cloth napkins into Paris' hand and all Jade could think was, *they're never going to get that blood out. Head wounds bleed like a bitch.*

"They do, but it's not that deep," Paris said and Jade realized she'd been talking out loud.

He pressed the cloth against her forehead and she hissed, flinching back. Cupping the base of her skull to steady her, his hands felt like a vice around her brain, pressing into the pain. Callie crouched down on the other side, putting an arm around her shoulder and trying to tuck her in close. It was ridiculous because Callie was all of five-foot four and Jade was six inches taller than her and a bigger person to boot.

The alarm didn't seem so loud anymore, sounding more distant and she had a split second of perfect clarity.

"Fuck, I'm really sorry," she mumbled, leaning heavily against Callie's lighter bulk. "I think I'm passing out."

Then it all went dark.

CHAPTER ELEVEN

Paris stood silent, waiting just outside the medlab room where Dr. Gellar was examining Jade. Callie and Henri stayed behind at the restaurant to try to piece together what happened in the scant minutes Jade had been alone in the washroom. When his phone rang, he answered it immediately, hoping to get some answers.

"Hey," Callie said quickly. "I've got Josef and Yelena from Counter-Magic and they're saying something tried to punch through from another dimension."

Paris recognized the names of two of his coven members who worked with the Supernatural Council on tracking down unsanctioned magic performed by outsiders.

"Another demon?" Paris asked.

"Yeah," Callie said lowly. "But not very powerful if that makes sense?"

"I think it might," Paris said. "The first demon was warning Jade about someone, another witch, using magic to make a deal with demon in order to steal Jade's power. From what I know, it doesn't take a lot of magic to demon-deal, but the demons who respond do tend to sort of match the power of the person calling them. If someone without a lot of magic is trying to make a deal, he or she would call a lesser demon."

"So not the same one that Jade already saw?" Callie asked.

"No." Paris' tone was definitive. "I'm fairly certain that demon used a portal and it's the one in her kitchen. I'm thinking he somehow got whiff of this other deal going on and wanted to know what it was about. As far as I can figure out, witches don't regularly deal in demons, not here at our coven and not elsewhere. I'm assuming he got curious and once he realized how powerful Jade was, how powerful she is," he took a deep breath, "he saw an opportunity. If he wanted to come back, I think he'd just use that doorway again. He wants to deal with her." Cold fingers trailed down his back as he spoke, the idea of demon dealing distasteful and vile. "This must have been something else trying to come through."

"Well that's just it." Callie sighed. "Josef and Yelena say it's more of a one way kind of thing. It wasn't trying to come out, it was trying to pull her in."

Paris racked his brain trying to remember what he knew about demons and what he'd been speed-studying over the last few hours. "It probably has more power on its side. If it pulled her through, she would be easier to deal with." He suppressed a shudder, dreading the thought of one of his witches being pulled into another dimension.

"Lucky for her, she managed to stay on this side." Callie's voice was low and soft. "She's really powerful, Paris. She learns fast too. If she ever could use all her power, I don't think there's a spell she couldn't make work for her."

"She *is* powerful," Paris agreed.

"But she's untrained. How did she manage to stay on this side?"

Paris mused, more talking to himself than to Callie. "Yes, she's learning fast, but she still has very little knowledge. She must be tied to something here – like an anchor. Someone here, perhaps. She doesn't know any dimensional magic yet. I know a scant amount, but I've hardly ever had the chance to actually use it. If something wanted to pull her through, it should have been able to."

Paris had to find out more about her, about her past, her history, even her medical file. Anything that could tell him how it was she could do the things she could do.

"I'm never sleeping again," Callie said flatly. "I mean it. I've seen more scary shit in one day than I have in my entire life. Demons? Dimensions? I'm still creeped out by the stuff I was reading about today and I'm looking around this bathroom and this gunk on the floor? I think it used to be the mirror but I can't even tell. Honestly, I'm going to burn everything I'm wearing and bathe in bleach tonight. It stinks like death and rot and things that I don't want to think about."

"Speaking of sleep, you should go home. It's been a long day for you."

"Yeah," Callie said absently. "Has Gellar said anything yet?"

Paris looked over at the closed door. "No. Not yet. I'll let you know what I find out. Jade will probably be staying at the Covenstead tonight and I'll stay with her. Hannah is supposed to call me later with any news she's been able to gather and hopefully we'll have something. Until then, I'm the strongest witch in the Coven, so whatever happens, I've the best chance of dealing with it."

"We could... We could maybe call the Council and ask the Fae?"

"We could," Paris said, hedging. "But I'd rather avoid dealing with demons or with the Fae. You never know exactly what kind of help you'll be getting when you work with them. At least with demons, I'm fairly certain the motives are always magic and power. With the Fae, I wish I knew what they valued."

They spoke for a few more minutes before Paris finally convinced Callie to go home and go to sleep if she could. If not, at the very least, she could rest and be ready to help them with research again tomorrow. Paris promised to keep her updated on Jade's status, and she could pass those reports along to Henri.

Who could likely disseminate word to the rest of the Coven within twenty minutes.

Paris was hanging up with Callie when Dr. Gellar appeared in the hallway. He paused grimly, waiting for her report but she gave him a slight smile and she didn't have her 'this is serious news' face on, so he was moderately hopeful.

"As far as I can tell, she's sleeping right now," Gellar said, closing the door slightly behind her. Paris could see through the crack one of the nurses finishing up a cast on Jade's right arm.

"Are you certain? Her head and the fainting and- " He wasn't sure exactly what to call the mirror and the rest of incident.

"Head wounds often look worse than they are. Don't mistake me, she's got a rather nice goose-egg where she was hit and twelve stitches. It'll scar up into her hairline so she's lucky. She's also got a broken wrist and is looking at six weeks in that cast. But as for the rest of her brain-" Dr. Gellar frowned. "I think the problems she's having are related to her nature."

"How so?"

"Jade is very different from the rest of you. She's a witch and she has magic but I don't think..." Dr. Gellar trailed off, her hands moving around like she was searching for the right words. "I don't think her body is magic. I don't think she has the body of a witch."

"How can that be? She is a witch."

"I know." Gellar grimaced a bit. "I don't exactly know how or why, but I do know that when she was in here getting tested, she had that atypical reaction. The nosebleed, the headache. And then today. I know you're sketchy on the details but if you had to guess, would you guess she used magic? A lot of it?"

Paris thought back to the destruction of the small bathroom - the exploded tiles, the mirror, the fire, the hum in the air. He'd arrived at the restaurant and before he'd even gotten out of the car, he'd felt the magic in the air like downed power lines - thrumming with electricity. It had made the hair on the back of his neck raise and tingle. It had been furious and strong and he'd been able to follow it like a beacon to where she was. The fire alarm had sounded by the time he stepped inside the restaurant and he'd been pulled toward the back of the building like a moth to a flame.

"Yes. Quite a bit."

Dr. Gellar crossed her arms over her chest. "I'm only guessing at this point and without running more tests and consulting with some specialists, I may be speaking out of turn. But I think Jade's brain is trying to adapt her mortal body to her preternatural powers. But it's too much, too fast. And I don't know how much can be done."

"You mean, if you can do anything for her?" Paris asked.

"That and how much her brain can do for itself. The brain is an amazing organ and it can re-wire itself. We've seen it with patients who've sustained serious trauma. But there's a limit to how fast it can go and how much it can do. Yes, Jade has a lot of power. But I don't know if she'll ever be able to use all of it without consequence. If you think of it in terms of electricity, yes, you can keep increasing the load and sending more and more current down a wire. But the wire can only take so much. You can add more wires, more switches, more breakers, but you're going to run out of physical space. There's a finite limit to what you can do. There may be a very real, very finite limit to what Jade can do as well. No matter how much magic she has."

She ended with a gentle smile, the type of expression doctors reserve for people when they have bad news. "We can keep an eye on her medically tonight, but I think she'll probably sleep for a few hours more. I'll run some tests when she wakes up and I can discuss this with her, if you'd like."

He shook his head. "It's magic. Magic should come from me."

Gellar nodded as though it was expected. "Okay. There's a really busted up chair in my office that looks horrendous, but is actually pretty good for sleeping and there's some extra gurneys about if you want to catch some sleep yourself."

He thanked her and she popped her head in for one last check on Jade before she left. The technician finished up with Jade's cast and Paris took the opportunity to let himself into the room to check on her.

She had a large white bandage on her forehead and he could see little bits of stubble from the edges of where they'd shaved a bit into her hairline to expose the entire wound. Her clothes had been taken and she was dressed in a sickly green gown that gave her a sallow tone. A black cast encased her broken wrist, her pale fingers sticking out the top, long and pink. She had the completely relaxed and limp face of someone utterly asleep. On her good hand, her fingers twitched slightly and then settled again. He glanced around and saw one of the uncomfortable plastic chairs that was usually around in medical facilities and he pulled it up. He could sit for a few minutes and then think about his longer term plans.

Most notably, how to stop at least two demons and a witch.

#

Jade awoke with a start, jerking upright in bed which made her head pound like a freight train.

Ow. She went to press her hands against her temple and stopped short when she saw the fiberglass cast on her right wrist. She tapped it a bit with her left fingers. After having so many as a child, she felt like an expert on casts. She flexed her right fingers and rotated her arm a bit. Well done - snug but not tight. It wouldn't need a replacement when the swelling went down. She touched her fingers gingerly to the painful spot on her head, feeling gauze and bandage and then the prickle of shaved skin.

Motherfucker. That was her *hair*.

It wasn't like she was particularly vain, but a shaved patch wasn't going to be something that she could cover or that would even go away quickly. She'd be growing that out for months. She felt her eyes sting a bit with tears. It was such a stupid thing to cry over and she felt like an idiot for even caring. She'd survived - whatever the hell that was - relatively intact and if all she had to show for it was a cast and little bald spot, she should be grateful.

She would be grateful.

She'd be even more grateful once that patch grew in. *Ugh.*

In a ritual born from waking up after getting the shit kicked out of her by her dad, Jade closed her eyes and took a mental inventory of her body. Despite the cast, her arms and legs felt functional. Fingers and toes wiggled easily. She moved her neck a bit and her head throbbed as she did. Okay, so the head was a problem. She felt like her brain was bruised - not in the true medical sense but in the way that a headache or a migraine left parts of your head feeling tender and battered. Jade stretched her muscles a little bit. Nothing else broken or even cut up, just knocked around and sore. People in movies always got up and moved around after getting tossed about and they might have a busted up lip or a black eye but you hardly ever heard anyone complain that they just hurt all over.

But she *hurt* all over.

And she was in a hospital gown. *Yuck.* She glanced around for her clothes and didn't see anything.

Satisfied that she was going to live, but that it would really suck for the next week or so, Jade started taking an inventory of her surroundings. She recognized the medical area immediately from her first visit. She was in one of the small examination rooms - the area was uncluttered and neat.

Paris slept in a really hideous over-stuffed chair - head back, neck exposed, legs stretched out in front of him.

He'd be lucky if he could move his neck in the morning with the position he was in. An open laptop rested on his thighs and whatever was going for a screensaver made a strange pattern of light dance across his face.

"Paris," she said, her vocal chords feeling raspy and raw when she spoke, her voice coming out lower than normal.

He sat up immediately and looked directly at her, wincing as he tried to right his neck.

"You're awake," he said, blurting the obvious.

"What time is it?" she asked.

He checked his watch. "A little past two in the morning. How do you feel? Do you need the doctor?"

He made a move like he was going to get up but she stopped him with a little shake of her head, grimacing as the movement brought back the pounding.

"No, I'm okay. Where are my clothes?"

Paris looked somewhat apologetic. "I think your shirt was cut off because of your arm and it was fairly bloody from your head." He gestured to her head wound. "Your shoes and pants, I'm not sure."

She liked that hoodie. She'd spent three good years breaking it in. "Ugh, hospital types are always so eager with the snip-snip." She made a cutting motion with her good hand. "I've lost more clothes to scissor-happy nurses than you would believe."

He pulled the chair closer to the bed, coming up beside her.

"Jade, do you remember what happened?"

She swallowed, the events in the bathroom coming immediately to mind. She wasn't one of those people that had lapses in memory or pretended she didn't remember things. She may not want to talk about events, but she always remembered, no matter how hard she tried to forget.

"I don't know," she said quietly. "The mirror... It wobbled, or waved. Not like," she said, waving her hand to demonstrate, "but like a wave of water. Like it wasn't solid." She picked at some imaginary threads on the sheet of the bed and swallowed. "And there were these... Hands, I guess. They were strong. They came out of mirror like they were made of the mirror. Quicksilver. They grabbed me and they pulled."

He shifted a bit closer. "How did you fight back?"

A weak laugh escaped her. "Very badly. I just... Pulled backwards. Tried to keep from getting yanked in. It tried to yank me, whatever it was. But my head..." She touched the bandage. "When my head hit, the mirror was solid. I don't know if it could have pulled me in, but I wasn't about to find out. I called as much fire as I could and then..." She made an explosion motion with her fingertips. "Ka-boom. It all started burning." She looked down at her fingers. "The mirror took the longest. I wasn't sure it was going to go. I put everything I had in that." She shrugged. "I guess it worked."

"Some of our witches were examining the restroom and we think it was another demon. Different from the first one, but a demon nevertheless, trying to pull you through."

Another laugh punched out of her chest, thin and tight. "Fantastic. Another one."

Paris' hands rested on the bed, close to her hip but not touching. "This one wasn't nearly as powerful as the first. We think it's probably the one the first demon was talking about, the one who's working with a witch to take your power."

"We should really give them names," she said dryly. "You know, if there's going to be more than one, it's going to get tricky. Demon number one, demon number two." She rubbed at her eyes, feeling the grit of the long day and night settling in deep. "We can call them Bob and Doug." She snorted to herself. God she was tired.

"Well, 'Doug'," Paris said, and just from his tone, she could hear the air quotes around the name, "wasn't able to pull you through. From what I understand, that means you've got a very strong anchor here, in our dimension. Can you think of what that might be?"

She blinked at him. Her head throbbed, but the lights were dim so she didn't need to squint. "Like what? Like an object or my credit card bill?"

"I'm very serious," he admonished.

"So am I. You wouldn't believe how much I've got on that thing. Trust me, if anyone wants to keep me around, it's Visa."

"I was thinking more like a close family member. Your parents?"

"No." Jade probably answered him too quickly, too harshly but she couldn't take the word back now.

"You aren't close to-"

She cut him off as there was no way she was discussing her parents with him. "Just... No. Trust me. Unless a strong anchor can be born of mutual apathy, resentment and animosity, in which case, we're your family."

He studied her for a moment and she made herself hold his gaze, keeping her expression as neutral and bored as she could.

"No, it would be a deeper connection than that. No other family?"

Jade shook her head. "No. Not that I'm close to. Some cousins, but I don't know them really."

Paris *hmm'd* and she got the impression he didn't believe her. Well, she couldn't help that. It was the truth. She didn't have any close family and if she and her parents had their way, it would stay like that.

She rubbed at one of her shoulders, feeling a knot settling in and her stomach growled. She was too exhausted to think about getting food. But staying in bed wasn't going to solve her problems. If she wanted something done, she was going to have to do it herself.

Jade whipped back the covers, swinging her legs off to the side of the bed.

"What are you doing? Where are you going?" he asked, standing and crowding toward her.

"I'm getting up, I'm finding some pants and then..." She trailed off and looked around, feeling lost and unsure suddenly. "Oh fuck, I don't even know. Can I borrow a car or something?" She could hear the almost whining tone in her voice and she hated it. She just wanted to be able to do something, take care of herself.

Paris made a motion to push her back toward the bed. "You should go back to sleep. We can figure it all out in the morning."

Jade slumped in the bed. She hated hospitals. They smelled and they were uncomfortable and there was always some draft coming from somewhere. People moving about and then some nurse would be in three or four times to check your temperature or your stitches and chastise you for still being awake. But how could you sleep with people coming in and out?

She hugged her arms around herself. "This sucks," she said emphatically.

He stared at her intently for a moment, like he was measuring something.

"What?" she finally said, her tone snippy.

"If you're desperate, I can talk with Gellar and see if she'll release you tonight."

She wanted to jump at the chance, even if she was feeling like a sack of beaten potatoes. She just didn't know where she would go. Jade wondered if she'd get anymore sleep in a hotel, paranoid and worried over another demon attack or if she should just suck it up and try to sleep in the medical unit.

"Although," Paris said, continuing his thought, "it's probably not a good idea for you to be on your own and I'm not trying to be controlling or overbearing." He added the last bit quickly, somehow managing not to make it sound patronizing or disdainful.

"No. I know," she grudgingly admitted. He was totally right. She didn't *want* to be alone but she just didn't know what to do about it.

"If you're amenable, you may stay with me."

Jade glanced up sharply at him and gave him a suspicious look.

"I have a guest room," he said, clarifying.

She still eyeballed him a little sideways, gauging his intent. He seemed earnest and honest and she didn't get a sketchy vibe off him.

"I do have some anti-demon wards we can test out. Hannah found some success with her research."

That did sweeten the deal and she didn't know why she was wary - it was a good offer. She would be with the guy who was reportedly the most powerful witch in the Coven, she wouldn't be alone, and she might even get a real bed in which to sleep.

Jade pursed her lips. "Is there anything open this late? Can we get, like, drive thru or something?"

Paris smiled. "We should be able to rustle something up."

She watched him for another moment until she finally relented. "Okay."

"Okay," he repeated, his head nodding once.

"I'm still gonna need some pants."

#

Paris managed to find her some scrubs, convinced Gellar to release her and even found her shoes. They had a little bit of blood on them and were still a whole lot wet from the fire sprinklers, but they were *hers*. They were cold and clammy as she pushed her feet in and wiggled her toes against the wet canvas. She took a sweater he offered without protest, even though she felt a bit weird about putting on clothes that were obviously his. She kept wanting to insist *no, no, I'm fine,* but the truth was she was cold; the pervasive kind of chill that settles into your skin and bones when you're overly tired and need to sleep.

The ride home was silent, the low rumble of the engine and the constant hum of Paris' magic lulling her into a light doze until she heard the telltale squawk box of a drive-thru and she snapped immediately awake to order a bagel and a small coffee.

"It's not like a truckload of this would keep me awake at this point," she groused at his look, taking a sip of the hot beverage. Stuffing the bagel into her mouth in big bites that she had to really work her jaw around, she spotted her reflection in the passenger side window. *Shit.* Outside of *Animal Planet*, it was one of the most hideous things she'd seen - bandaged, exhausted, cast on the hand trying to hold a bagel and coffee in the other.

Fantastic. She'd be winning beauty competitions for sure.

They pulled up to Paris' house - a Tudor style home that completely suited him and would probably grace the covers of some magazine with an inane title like *Coven Witch Weekly* and feature a double spread of the manicured potting garden outside. It was beautiful even with all the greenery dying off in the fall air, the last stray bloom tucked close against the night.

The inside was very sparse.

No knick-knacks, no tchotchkes, no clutter anywhere. He seemed to prefer functional furniture made out of dark material - leather or some kind of substitute - and some end and sofa tables, also dark.

There were only three things hanging on the wall; one was a painting of the ocean - choppy waves and dark sky, like it was going to rain. It was large, framed in a deep cherry wood and she found herself staring at it as they walked in. She'd never liked water, never learned to swim, never wanted to go to a pool. Looking at this painting was exactly why. It was shadowy, treacherous and powerful. With a slight shiver, she turned away.

The next picture along the living room wall was a landscape of an open prairie sky - pale blue and wheat yellow stretching out in an unimaginable expanse. She liked that one better. There was so much space and no one and nothing around for miles.

The last picture was of winding tree roots, turning and churning into the earth, rolling over top of one another in a beautiful yet almost grotesque twist. There were some splotches of dark mossy growths on the ground, clinging to the tree roots desperately.

She looked along the wall, taking in the three paintings quickly again.

"You're missing fire," she said. Her voice echoed in the mostly empty space. There really wasn't enough furniture to fill the wide living room, and the hardwood floors did nothing but bounce the sound around.

"Pardon?" Paris asked, shutting and locking the door as he came in behind her.

She gestured with her good hand. "Water, air, earth. You're missing fire."

His eyes flickered over the paintings quickly. "They belonged to my mother. I don't know where she got them. I think they're all by the same artist, but I don't know why there isn't one for fire."

"Huh. Maybe she thought they looked better in threes," Jade mused. "But I would think for a witch, she'd want all four. Aren't you guys big on balance and representation?"

"If it's meant to be representative of magic, then yes, there should be a fourth painting. But perhaps she only meant it decoratively."

He led her up the stairs, hovering right behind her, too close for her liking. But the truth was, she did feel a little shaky and tired so she didn't say anything and she let herself be directed upwards and then along a short hallway to a quaint bedroom. He opened the door for her and flicked on the light.

"Extra blankets are in the closet, the bathroom's one door over on the left," he said, stepping back and leaving room for her to enter. It was sparse like the lower level, but the bed was a double and had a fat, white duvet. It looked like it would be ridiculously fluffy and soft and she wanted to weep just thinking about lying down and feeling it settle on her.

"Can I get you anything?"

She pointed awkwardly to the mirror above the room's dresser. "Does that... I mean, can it come down?"

He glanced over quickly and nodded once, striding over and pulling it from the wooden slats it rested in. He even flipped it away from her, facing his body.

"Uh, is there anything else that could suddenly grow hands or be in any way used as a portal to Demon Land?" She paused and looked hard at the bed. "Like under the bed?" She felt about six years old all over again staring at the dark, black space between the box-spring and the floor.

"No," his voice was assured, even. Everything she wanted to hear.

"Maybe I'll just live in this room. You guys can bring me food." Jade moved toward the bed and crawled on top, stretching out on her stomach. Even with all her aches and pains it felt *wonderful*. "And the internet," she added.

"For the rest of your life?" he asked. Through the corner of her eye she noticed him leaning in the doorframe, bulky mirror tucked awkwardly under his arm.

She pressed her face into the pillow, mashing it back and forth a bit, trying to find an angle that didn't aggravate the bruises on her neck or the bandage on her head. "I said food and the internet. What else do I really need?"

She could hear how slurred her words were. She really should push herself up, take his sweater off and get under the covers. And she would.

In five minutes.

"Do you need anything for tonight?"

Jade was going to say that no, she was fine, but if he had a spare t-shirt lying around, she wouldn't say no to using it for pyjamas and if he had a spare toothbrush, she'd take that too.

What came out of her mouth was a single syllable kind of grunt.

She had a vague notion of him stepping closer and then pulling part of the quilt over her, folding her in the soft white fabric like a croissant roll. The room went dark and she heard him pull the door shut quietly before she fell asleep.

CHAPTER TWELVE

Paris heard Jade wake up, her feet hitting the floor above him as he sat at the table, working on his laptop and sipping coffee. It was late, but she needed the rest so he'd let her sleep, deciding to do some work from home. Paris had eaten earlier in the morning but as it was almost noon now, he could stand to eat again.

Five minutes after he heard her feet on the ceiling above, she was poking her head around the corner, like a groundhog popping out of its hole in February. She looked horrible. She'd already had bruises around her neck and now more blossomed out from around her head bandage. She looked pale and stark, still wearing the sweater he had loaned her.

She sniffed the air cautiously, taking a few awkward steps into the kitchen. It was obvious from the way she moved that she was stiff and sore.

"What's that?"

"I'm making an omelet," he replied easily. "There's coffee as well. And some ibuprofen in the drawer by the fridge."

She made a beeline for the coffee pot, and hesitated slightly, turning to him and raising an eyebrow to ask for a mug. Paris jerked his chin toward the cupboard to her left. She deftly managed to pour herself a cup and then puttered over to the fridge to get the cream, using both hands despite one being in a cast. She found the ibuprofen and knocked back a few, washing them down with coffee as she headed for the table.

"You got enough eggs for two?"

He didn't miss how she turned his laptop toward her and looked over his screen, completely oblivious or indifferent to any privacy.

"There is enough for two." He gestured at the computer. "You should be able to check your webmail if you like."

She pulled the computer toward her and she was awkward with her broken wrist, unable to get her hand at the right angle to type. She hunted and pecked for the letters she wanted, studying the screen.

She pursed her lips. "Is there toast?"

He smirked at her nonchalant tone. "Since you don't smell any toast, you know the answer is no."

"Could there be toast?"

"There could be. Would you like toast, Jade?" Paris turned to meet her gaze as she peeked over the top of the laptop.

"I like to put the eggs on the toast," she said defensively.

"Well, I suppose it can be arranged," he was trying not to laugh at her expression, like she had to harass him into adding toast to her breakfast, or justify it. He plated the eggs and reached for the bread."But you have to turn the computer off."

She made a *pish* sound. "I usually just work and eat at the same time."

"Eating while working is vulgar."

"Who told you that?" her face had twisted itself up.

"My mother," he replied as he set her slices of bread into the toaster. The handle was sticky and he tried three times without success to get it to stay down. He pulled the slices back out, put them on the plate and waved his hand over them. They toasted instantly.

She was interested, her posture perking up as soon as she saw magic. "I didn't know you could toast like that."

"You've just arrived at the Coven. I've been doing magic since I was two."

She slouched dejectedly. "I'm never going to catch up."

He wouldn't set the plate down in front of her until she pushed the laptop off to the side. She rolled her eyes but complied nonetheless.

"Your mom big on manners?" she asked as she took a large bite of eggs.

"I had to follow proper etiquette at the table or I wouldn't get served." He scooted his chair slightly closer to the table.

"God, that explains a lot," she muttered around her mouthful of food. She washed it back with some coffee. "Uh, thanks for letting me stay here last night. And for the sleep-in this morning."

"You're welcome. If you feel up to it, I'd like to go back to your place and have a look around again and then back to the restaurant, see if there's any lingering magic." He paused, watching her push her food around on the plate.

"What're you hoping to find?" She stared down at her food, not looking up.

He shrugged. "Something that will lead us to our unknown witch. Something familiar to me, or perhaps some left over ingredients for any magic they may have performed in those locations."

"You guys found me easily enough, why not this person?"

"You were performing unsanctioned magic. Magic outside a coven and without any spells or incantations. It's quite distinct and sets off a sort of energy. We didn't track you, we tracked that. You were essentially bleeding out power and there were a few of us that could feel it. It's calmed down since you've started practicing magic. It's almost like you couldn't hold it all in and your magic was sending up a beacon for all witches to see."

She seemed to mull that over while she nibbled on the corner of her toast. "This unknown witch," Paris said, continuing, "is working within the system. We're all kind of desensitized to regulated magic, even if the spells aren't performed often, or are rare. It has its own kind of aura and it mixes and blends in well with other magic. Unless I can figure out something about it that's different, that sets it apart. Then we can track that."

"And the anti-demon magic? You said you had something last night."

He nodded, tossing back the rest of his coffee. "Yes, Hannah was able to procure me some wards and I used them last night to protect the house." He grimaced slightly. "Unfortunately, no one has firsthand knowledge of their effectiveness."

"So you can't tell if I'm safe or if I'm just not under attack right now."

He didn't want to say it straight out that way, but she had it in a nutshell. She ate most of her eggs and all of the toast, taking her plate to the sink on her way to get another cup of coffee.

"While we're at your place, you can pick up a few things and bring them back here. Some clothes, your electronics. I know you're fond of them."

She tried to smile at him from where she leaned against the counter. "Callie and Henri?" she asked.

He nodded. "Already back at the library researching. I think Callie is scanning some pages she wants you to look at. They have descriptions of demons and she was wondering if you could pick out the first demon from them."

"You mean Bob," Jade answered. "Bob's demon number one. Doug's number two."

"Yes. Bob."

She appeared uncertain and perhaps slightly scared, but she squared her shoulders. "Can do." She rubbed her eyes, careful to steer clear of the bandage over her stitches. "If we go back to the other place first, it should be safe to shower, right? I smell like hospital."

"I can set the wards there too. I'll stay with you." She gave him a sharp, incredulous look. "Not in the shower," he added quickly. "Obviously."

She started to give a full body stretch and then winced as soon as her arms were about to be extended. She curled back in on herself.

"Okay, I'm ready when you are."

#

Jade slept hard the night before, barely moving throughout the night, waking up hot, sweaty and feeling groggy and heavy. She had strange dreams that she couldn't really remember, only managing to get impressions of being chased, running and being afraid.

No big mystery there.

It was quiet as Paris drove to the small cottage which contained her stuff. Everyone kept referring to it as 'her place' but it wasn't. It was just the place where she was temporarily hanging her hat. Although, it was tempting to refer to it as 'hers.' It was cute, small, cozy.

She wasn't sure how she felt about staying at the Coven. Being under attack, feeling scared and paranoid was awful, but it could get resolved. Jade wasn't exactly an optimist, and would punch anyone who said she was in the throat, but she did think that most problems were solvable. Would she always like the solution or would it be easy? No, but there would be a solution. She just had to make it happen. She was practical.

So there had to be a solution to this mess, an endgame. After that, she'd have to decide what she wanted to do with her life.

Presuming, of course, that the solution to this problem included her making it out alive. If not, then the decision on staying at the Coven or not was pretty much made. The dead didn't move anywhere.

So, if Jade assumed that there was a way out of this, then she was going to have to decide what to do. Would they find someone to break her magic? If they did, would she want them to? Magic was pretty fucking cool, she admitted. She liked it. She liked it a lot, actually, and wanted to learn more. But it looked like being part of the Coven came with attachments to people.

She'd been studiously avoiding attachments for years.

But it had been nice that morning to have Paris make her breakfast, having someone there to talk to. She enjoyed Callie and Henri's company, and envied the easy way they had with one another. She hadn't felt like that around anyone else since...

Not going to think about that right now.

She turned her face to the window and rubbed her fingertips over her eyebrows, smoothing along with the short, tiny hairs, the gesture soothing the pain that was flaring up - a dull ache that she awoke with and would probably feel for a few days.

Once at the cottage, Paris took a quick look around upstairs, casting his wards, which he swore to teach her later, and declared the place 'safe.' She gathered some stuff from her luggage and then headed to the bathroom, pausing where he stood in front of the door.

"Would you hold out your cast?" he asked carefully.

She hesitated and then held it up in front of him. He passed his hand over it, reciting an incantation as he did and resting his fingertips lightly on the fiberglass mesh. She felt a strange tingling pass through her hand. Not painful, not unpleasant, but strange and slightly cool. He raised his hand and said the incantation again, touching the bandage on her forehead lightly, like a benediction.

"Now they're waterproof," he said, his voice quiet and low. "And I've warded the mirror in the bathroom both with the anti-demon wards and also an anti-hex ward that I'm confident in. My mother used it to keep items from... Becoming something they aren't. It keeps magic from touching them."

"Uh, thanks." She hurried into the bathroom and shut the door behind her, locking it with a flick of her wrist.

The mirror still gave her the willies and she avoided looking in it, both because she didn't want to take stock in how she looked but also because she was afraid that once she looked at it, she'd be too scared to look away and then she'd end up trapped in a bathroom, staring at herself in the mirror like a crazy person.

God her brain got the better of her sometimes. She sighed. Most times.

The water was hot on her skin and muscles and she washed every inch of herself, including the little stubbly patch where her hair had been shaved. It was amazing to watch the water divert its course, dodging her cast. She presumed the same thing was going on over her bandage and when she touched her fingertips to it, it was warm but dry. She spent a solid five minutes moving her cast around under the spray just to watch the water dance away, like a magnet being pushed by another magnet.

Totally one point on the 'stay with magical coven because they can do awesome stuff' list she was making in her head.

She remained in the shower a bit too long, her skin turning pink and the bathroom completely fogged up by the time she reluctantly shut the water off, dried and got dressed. She tossed some stuff in her smaller carry-on bag, leaving her suitcase in the bedroom. If she did end up staying at the Coven, she'd have to go back to her apartment, shut it all down and clear out.

Move everything.

For now, she was content to take a change of clothes, her toiletries and her little shoebox that she kept with her wherever she went. She felt foolish for always lugging it around when she left for holidays or business trips, but she'd tried to leave it behind and always ended up feeling sick about it. She'd had it since she was little. It was beaten up around the edges, covered in old magazine pictures, glued on, taped over, glittered from her teen-fueled glitter-glue phase. It was hideous but she kept it safe always. She put it in her bag, wrapping it in a t-shirt first.

After gathering her meager necessities, she headed downstairs again and had to call out to find Paris. Hearing him in the kitchen, she unenthusiastically made her way over. He'd said the place was safe, and he had it warded but he also said he wasn't one hundred percent sure.

He was hunched over the kitchen table when she went in, some things spread out in front of him. There was a piece of fabric, some small bits of debris, some powder, some glass. As she approached, she caught a whiff of something vile.

"Holy god, what is that?" Jade asked, covering her nose with her hand.

Paris was poking at the items on the table with a chopstick he must have liberated from the kitchen drawers.

"Hex bag. The kitchen was the source of the portal and our first demon, Bob, had to have had something that drew him here, to this precise location. Your magic would have been a beacon for him, but if it were only your magic, the portal should be in your bedroom - where you spend the most of your time, albeit asleep. After searching, I found it in a cupboard, against the wall that's shared between the cabinetry and the pantry. It must have been placed here by our unknown witch."

"What's it do?"

"I'm not sure. I believe it's some kind of a chaos spell. Likely to keep you confused or conflicted in general. Keep you off balance. It's a low level spell, but the intent behind it is negative. The negative intent would've assisted Bob in breaking through."

"Ugh, how did I miss it?" She gagged a little bit and then pulled her shirt up over her nose, breathing in the scent of her shower gel and deodorant instead. Paris' wrinkled his nose slightly but wasn't as dramatic.

She didn't care. Blergh. It was revolting.

Paris hovered over the hex bag like a medical examiner over a body in the morgue - intense focus and no indication that what he was doing was a little distasteful and creepy. "It didn't have a smell until I took it apart to figure out the ingredients. When you break a hex bag up, the magic dissipates. It will take on the smell of the ingredients but also partly, from the intent of the magic."

"It's filthy mcnasty," she said, her voice muffled from the cotton of her shirt. She was acting like a six-year-old and she didn't care. "That smell is going to linger, you know. I'll have to bleach everything."

She heard herself making commitments like she was planning on staying at the Coven.

Huh. Maybe she would.

"It should get better after the magic finishes decomposing."

"Yeah but I'll *know* it was there. It's going to need a full decontamination scrub down. How would I ever eat in here knowing that smell touched stuff?"

He looked up from the hex bag. "Smell doesn't touch things."

She knew she must look ridiculous, rolling her eyes when that was all he could see of her face. "Yes it does. Smell is in the air and air touches everything. Ergo, smell touches things and makes them gross."

He looked back at the ingredients, poking a small crystal with the chopstick. "I'll take your word on that."

"You do that, English." She craned her neck trying to see better without getting closer. "You got anything?"

He tilted his head and shrugged one of his shoulders. "Possibly. Some of these crystals are rarer than others. We can check the supply shops around town. I think our better bet though is to use the fabric from the bag and see if we can scry for the person that touched it last, other than me."

"We can do that?"

His eyes met her and she realized she'd used the term 'we' the same way he had, like they were a sort of team, or partnership. "Yes. We can." He found a plastic sandwich bag and using another chopstick, managed to fold the fabric up and slide it inside without touching it.

"First we need to do a little shopping."

#

They stopped off at a dollar store to purchase a mirror.

A dollar store.

"Don't you have some kind of witch-crafty store you can go to for stuff like this?" Jade asked, staring at the little drink umbrellas that were ten for a dollar by the front till. She picked up a packet of happy face stickers and then put them down wiping her hands a bit on her jeans.

They scared her. Bright yellow smiley faces. Creepy.

"It's not a magical item until we make it one. Until then, it's just a mirror." Paris declined a bag for the mirror, taking it as is.

"And an ugly one at that," she said. But for a buck-ninety-nine, she guessed it would do.

They headed back to Paris' place while he explained a bit about making a scrying mirror. Unlike a portal, which truly was a gateway to another dimension, a scrying mirror allowed a witch to see things on this side - lost things, missing things, unknown things. The idea of other dimensions wasn't as freaky as she would have thought and she felt a little vindicated in thinking about all the sci-fi she watched as a kid, believing in other worlds and far-off places.

Back at Paris' house, Jade watched with keen eyes and even pulled out a little notebook to record what she saw as Paris worked. Her hand was awkward and stiff around the pen, trying to work with her cast. She ended up with scratchy, uneven scribbles across the page, the point of the pen digging in hard and sharp, creasing the paper.

Paris explained what he was doing as he worked. He meticulously polished the entire surface with a pure cotton cloth, wiping away any touch of another person and then dabbed the whole thing down again with newspaper to take off any stray traces of lint. He brought out a tiny tool kit that held all sorts of implements - a small screwdriver, a wishbone, some pliers, a spool of copper wire, a drafting pencil and a few slivers of soap. He used one of the pieces of soap to trace runes over the edge of the mirror, cleaning up his lines with the polishing cloth when necessary. When he was satisfied with the placement and shape, Paris took a small etching pen and traced over his soap marks.

It was pristine, perfect work. He was silent as he traced the runes, brow furrowed in concentration, and she didn't interrupt with any questions. When he finished, he started polishing the soap off the mirror, leaving only the etching behind. He explained that while he worked, he tried to remain as focused as possible on what he was doing, imbuing the mirror with his magic. From his closet, he pulled out several cloth bags, checking the size until he selected one that looked like it would fit the mirror.

He glanced down at her tattered notebook and her scribbles.

"I'll have to get you a proper grimoire," he said, wiping his hands off and then sliding the mirror into the bag. He carefully opened the plastic bag that had the piece of cloth from the hex bag and slid it inside as well. "Every witch has at least one. A place to capture their studies, their thoughts, write new spells or copy down favorites."

She thought about it for a moment. "Could I use a tablet?" she asked.

He considered her words. "I don't actually know. Everyone I know uses a book. If you wanted, we could try. Although part of the process is letting the books be saturated with your magic. They travel with you, get handled by you, are surrounded by magic. It might not be the same if you kept replacing your tablet with the newest upgrade."

"Old school witches," Jade mused. "Maybe I'll figure out a way to get you into the technology age yet."

They headed back to the car, Paris grabbing a shovel and handed it to her on the way out. He drove for a few miles, leaving the population behind and entering some kind of park area with clay-red pathways and large trees that hovered dense and heavy overtop. It appeared to be a nature preserve with a few signs pointing out hiking trails and sites of interest. It was neat, but not manufactured. There wasn't any trash or clutter, but there were large, overgrown bushes pushing their way into the paths. Heavy foliage draped alongside the walkways, waiting for the chance to crawl across them and take over. The air cooled once they were a little deeper in the forest and Jade wished she brought a spare jacket or kept the sweater Paris had loaned her the other night. It was a little darker too, the sunlight choked off by the leaves up above their heads, only barely peeking through.

He stopped when they reached a crossroads of sorts - two pathways meeting at nearly right angles and then heading off again. He motioned her off to one side, giving her the mirror to hold onto while he took the shovel. He stood in the center of the crossroads and turned three times and then struck the shovel down hard into the packed dirt. It barely went in and he ended up putting his foot on it and leveraging most of his weight to start digging. He dug about a foot down and then motioned Jade forward with the mirror and directed her to put it in the ground.

"It's okay if I do it?" she asked, suddenly a bit nervous. She looked up at him with wide eyes even as she crouched near the ground. Though she disliked asking for his permission or his assurance, she wanted even less to mess it up.

"Your magic is quite powerful. It would be a great addition to the mirror," he said simply.

Jade laid it carefully in the small hole and then straightened up. He flicked out a Swiss army knife from his pocket and she smirked.

"You're a real boy scout, aren't you?"

He leveraged one of the blades open and nicked the fleshy part of his palm underneath his thumb, letting three drops of blood fall onto the cloth bag before stepping back and pulling a small handkerchief out of his pocket and pressing it against the wound quickly and hard until it stopped bleeding.

He covered the mirror with dirt, smoothing out the top layer of earth and then crouched to etch one more rune into the soil with a fingertip.

"How long does this take?" Jade asked, kicking herself for not asking before.

Paris seemed a little indecisive. "Well, that's a choice we have to make. For best results, three sunsets."

"What?" she said incredulously. "I'm a child of the internet and microwave ovens and fast food. I can't wait three days. How do we make it faster?"

"We can dig it up faster, but the less time we leave it, the less powerful it is," Paris answered. "It has to at least be one sunset but there's no way of knowing if it would be strong enough to work."

She looked at the soft mound in front of her and back at Paris. Three days seemed like a long time. In the grand scheme of things, she knew it wasn't, but she felt like everything had been happening so quickly that it had a kind of momentum to it, like a train going down a track. If she had three days to wait, that was three days to start thinking really hard about things. She generally did a lot better when she just reacted and didn't give herself too much time to let her brain fuck her over.

But she didn't want to screw it all up by not waiting the first time and then having to do it all over again and then wait three days. That would be even longer. Assuming it could be done again. She didn't know if it was a onetime only deal or not.

Three days. Ugh.

She groaned. "Fine. Three days. Oh my god, I'm totally going to figure out a way to make these things faster."

She looked over at Paris to see him smiling a little at her. Not a smirk or a snicker, just a pleased smile.

"What?"

He cleared his throat a bit. "That sounds like you're thinking about staying. In fact, you've said a few things that possibly imply you're staying with us."

She rolled her eyes to hide the slight embarrassment she felt. "Yeah, well, I gotta live through the week first and then we'll see." She shuffled her feet a bit. "Speaking of, is the offer of crashing at your very nicely anti-demon warded place still open?"

"Of course."

"Thanks."

"I do think you'll be happy at the Coven, Jade. Despite what you might think, you are a witch. You belong with a coven."

Jade worried at the inside of her lip with her teeth. She'd never really belonged anywhere but it would sound plaintive and small to say that out loud. "I'm thinking about it. I guess it depends on how this situation shakes out. And you guys really fucked up the welcome wagon. I might've listened if you'd told me the truth from the start, about not being able to keep my power if I didn't stay."

"I realize that. I should have told you the truth from the beginning."

Jade was surprised at his solemn and serious tone, the intensity of his gaze, the truthfulness she heard in his words.

"I can't change the past."

"No? Not one of your powers?" she said, a smile curling her lips.

"Not hardly." He looked up at the canopy of trees above them, the sun moving lazily across the cool sky. She glanced up, the light of the sun making her head hurt and her eyes squint even with the shade of the trees. She touched the bandage on her head lightly, still feeling the tight, hot pull of the stitches in her skin and the sharp prickle of stubble.

She caught Paris looking at her carefully. "We should head in. You look tired," he said.

"I'm fine."

He didn't argue with her but she could see he didn't believe her. She didn't know why she said it when she was obviously tired and beat-up from the day prior.

"We should head in anyway. We'll come back in three days. All right?"

She nodded. "Three days."

CHAPTER THIRTEEN

Jade was drained when she went to bed that night, but she wasn't as physically or emotionally exhausted as she had been the night before when she didn't so much 'go to sleep' as 'fall unconscious.' She lay in bed, staring up at the dark ceiling, listening to the unfamiliar sounds of the house. The furnace came on at regular intervals but had a soft click-click-click sound as it ran. It took her a while to get familiar with the rhythm and then, once identified, discount it. She heard Paris make a few phone calls and she caught snatches of words to do with what she assumed was coven business. She didn't hear her name, nor any mention of demons, so she managed to push that to the back of her mind as more white noise.

She could very faintly make out the sound of the train as it hoofed along the tracks about an hour after she turned out the lights. Its whistle sounded lonesome and far away. She heard the creak of the stairs as Paris came up to bed, heard him pause at the door to the room she was in, but he didn't knock or enter. She imagined him on the other side, listening to hear if she was asleep and, not hearing anything, assuming she was.

Like most people, Jade endured infrequent insomnia, but she didn't get worked up about it. She would just lie in bed, figuring either sleep would come or it wouldn't, attempting to focus her mind on easy topics like something she'd seen on the science and nature network or a book she was reading. Sometimes, even work. Her job was mundane enough to not cause a lot of stress, but challenging enough at times that it kept her mind occupied.

She studiously avoided thinking about the past.

That night, she was not only trying to avoid thinking about the past, she was also deigning not to think too much about the future. A few times she felt herself drifting to sleep only to jerk awake, feeling slightly nervous and vulnerable. Paris had said she was safe and although she was inclined to believe him, she couldn't quite make the leap of faith to just fall asleep.

Her wrist ached and felt tender and sore, even when she didn't move it. Her head still hurt and when she rolled onto her side, if she wasn't careful, she'd hit it against the pillow. Even the plush softness made her wince slightly. Her neck was still all bruised up and it too was tender. She tried not to move too much but found herself getting achy and fidgety in general.

Jade looked over at the closet, sizing it up. It was a good size. And there was nothing in it. She'd fit no problem.

But she was too old to be sleeping in closets.

Then again, if she couldn't sleep in a closet when she felt like it as an adult, then what was the point in being able to make all her own decisions? Besides, no one had to know that she was sleeping in the closet.

Mind made up, she grabbed two pillows by their cases in her unbroken hand and managed to snag the comforter with the fingers of her casted one, dragging it toward the closet. As soon as she opened the doors, she felt a bone-deep relief settle in. She tossed the pillows in and then followed, curling up on the side that didn't have stitches on her head. She dragged the soft comforter over her and managed to curl her fingers under the lip of the doors, pulling them shut.

She snuggled down into her little nest and blinked drowsily. It must be Pavlovian, she decided, as she felt sleep starting to tug at her immediately. Being in the closet made her relax in a way that was familiar and safe. She'd never been hurt any time she slept in one. It was like her own little cocoon.

Sighing a bit, she fell asleep.

She woke up with an aching shoulder and hip. Apparently, being an adult not only meant she could chose to sleep in a closet, but that she must also suffer consequences of doing so. Jade wasn't eight years old anymore and sleeping curled up on the floor had left her stiff and sore in addition to her bumps and bruises. She opened the doors a crack and peeked out, seeing the clock read five in the morning. A little too early for her but she could tell by the way her brain was already going that she wasn't getting any more sleep. She dragged all the bedclothes out and dumped them in a heap on the bed and figured she'd head downstairs and get some coffee.

She had to root around a bit in the kitchen to find filters and the coffee grounds but managed to get it all sorted out and brewing in ten minutes. Unfortunately, Paris didn't have one of those pots that you could take out half way through brewing and pour a cup, a fact she found out the hard way after hot coffee spilled across the counter. She hastily mopped it up with a dishtowel and resolved to ask Paris if there was some kind of spell to keep the coffee from flowing while she grabbed a cup. It was just water, there had to be magic for it.

And yes, Jade decided she would totally abuse magical powers if it meant she could make her everyday life easier. No question. No hesitation.

Mug in hand, she wandered around Paris' house. She saw his laptop set up in a small office and she ran her fingers over it and on a whim, tried out the username and password she'd been given at the library. It let her into the system and she poked around on the internet for a bit, checking her webmail and reading some of her favorite blogs. Paris' office was definitely the most 'witchy' with magical texts lining the bookshelves. She tilted her head to the side and read the titles along the spines. Many didn't have titles and she wondered if he just knew what they were; if he'd had them so long he recognized them by sight alone. On a whim, she reached out and touched one and was surprised by the tingle of magic that ran through her fingers and up her arm. She touched another and got a different tingle of magic. After touching about thirty books with each tingle being slightly different, she reasoned that was probably how he told them apart - running his hands along the shelf until he found what he wanted.

There was a photo tucked into a small corner of one of the shelves and Jade picked it up, staring at it for a moment. It was a young boy of about ten or twelve and a naturally beautiful woman with the same intense blue eyes and dark hair. Even as a boy, she recognized Paris' facial structure and figured it must be him and his mom. They had teeth-baring grins, smiling so big both sets of eyes crinkled at the corners. His mom had an arm around him tightly and he was pressed up against her, oblivious to any personal space either one of them might want.

They looked really happy.

She put the photo back hastily. It was the only thing she felt bad about touching so far.

Jade continued her perimeter walk of the room, looking out the window that gave a view of a large backyard with a tall mountain ash tree starting to go yellow and red with the fall. The backyard wasn't really manicured, but it looked somewhat tended to. The grass was long but there were no weeds, no obnoxious dandelions bursting forth. There were some annual plants around the edges - peonies with no blossoms, some rose bushes with the last stragglers trying to bloom.

Jade took another step and paused when she felt the same kind of tingle shoot up her bare foot as she had felt in her fingers from the books on the shelf. She looked down at the wood-paneled floor and rocked forward on her foot, feeling the tingle, and then back, feeling it dissipate. She crouched down, setting her mug on the ground and pressed against the floor boards with her fingers and found it loose.

It only took a little fiddling to get it to pop open and reveal a little cubbyhole. Inside were three dark covered books - similar to the ones on the shelf. She picked them up and wrinkled her nose. They felt slightly greasy, dirty, and she wanted to immediately rub her hands off on her pants but she resisted the urge.

She placed them down in front of her and picked up just one, opening it to the middle.

Magic spells and incantations were scrawled on the inside in a messy, but completely legible script. Also included were snippets of other books - pages torn out and fastened in with tape or paper clips.

Pictures of demons, demon spells, demon knowledge. Her heart twisted in her chest as she flipped through the book, not really understanding what she was reading. She flipped the book over, studying the outside cover again, looking for some identifying marks. She opened the cover and on the inside was a single word.

Sakkara.

"What've you got there?"

Her head snapped up to see Paris standing in the doorway of his office, holding a cup of coffee and gazing in her direction inquisitively.

Jade pushed herself to her feet, ignoring her body's protest. "You said you didn't know any demon magic. You said no one practiced it anymore." She jerked the book at him, shaking it a bit.

He frowned. "I don't. Except for what I learned in school when I was younger."

"Then what the hell is this?" She stomped over to him and thrust one of the volumes in his face.

He immediately recoiled, a look of distaste on his face, like the book offended him.

"What is that? Where did you get it?"

"From right there," she said pointing to the hole in the floor. "You're shit at hiding books, they gave off some 'woo-woo' just like the books on your shelf. I didn't even have to look for them, I just found them."

He set his mug down on one of the shelves and took the book from her gingerly. "I don't know what you're talking about, these aren't mine. I don't have any hidden books."

She looked at him disbelievingly. "This is your house, isn't it? Your office?"

Brow furrowed, he flipped open the book, pausing when he saw the word on the inside cover.

"What's that mean? *Sakkara*. What is that?"

He didn't say anything at first as he ran his fingers over the script. "That's my mother's name." As he flipped through the book, his face turned rigid as he perused the contents. "You said 'them.' There are more?"

Jade jerked her head towards the other two books that she'd pulled out. He went over to them and hunkered down, touching them gently and then recoiling.

"I've never seen these books before," he murmured.

"Really?" she said dryly.

"I'm telling the truth. I didn't know these were here. They're definitely my mother's. I recognize her handwriting and some of the magic, but..." He swallowed hard and looked solemn and grave. "I had no idea about these. She... I didn't think anyone practiced demon magic. And certainly not her."

He looked wrecked and she felt her anger chipped away by the lost, confused look on his face.

However, she pushed aside her useless sympathy. Paris peered down into the cubbyhole again and reached in deeper, pulling out a worn, water damaged envelope. He flipped it over in his hands.

"What's that?" she asked.

"It's addressed to me. I think it's from my mother."

She hustled over to him and made a 'hurry up' gesture with her hands. He stared at her.

"Don't you dare play the privacy card on this one. Full disclosure, English. I just found a secret cache of demon books in your house. You're telling me what that note says."

Paris turned it over in his hands a few times more and she made an impatient sound.

"I swear to god, I will rip it from your hands and tear it open with my teeth if I have to."

He slid one finger under the seal to force it open. He pulled out a single sheet of paper and read it, frowning as he did.

"What's it say?" she asked, poking him with a finger hard in the shoulder like a child.

"It's from my mother," he confirmed, his voice sounding a little dazed as he read from the note. "'*I'm sorry you're reading this. I hoped you'd never find these grimoires. They have been charmed to only respond to someone touched by demon magic, and if that's happened, I want you to have all the knowledge you can. All my knowledge. Whatever has happened, I hope it's not a consequence of my actions. It's so hard to tell with demons. They lie, they cheat. They'll do anything to get free of their world. But their tenacity, their immorality is sometimes what's needed. I'm sure you'll think less of me knowing I practiced demon magic. All I can say is, I did what needed to be done. My intentions were always the best, even if my methods were not. Be careful.'"*

He stopped and just stared down at the letter.

"That's it?"

Paris nodded not looking up at her, fingering the paper in his hands. He flipped through the first grimoire quickly, and then grabbed the other two and coursing through the pages, probably looking for any other stray notes.

Nothing.

He set the books on his desk carefully and didn't say anything for a few long moments.

"We'll need to study these," his voice was a little rough.

She eyed her coffee cup on the floor, nearly empty and then back at the grimoires. She still had the greasy, unclean feeling on her hands from when she handled the first one and she recalled the desire to take a shower after reading the demon books at the library. She sighed.

The task at hand would require more coffee.

#

Paris watched Jade out of the corner of his eye as she read through one of the grimoires.

She seemed to have none of his hesitation, none of his reluctance and was plowing into it, typing notes on her laptop in quick staccato bursts.

He didn't want to start reading the one in front of him.

He couldn't stop thinking about the letter, about what it meant, about the grimoires themselves. His mother dealt in demon magic and he'd never known.

As a child, he was like most others, not realizing his mother was an entirely separate person apart from being his parent.

He thought he left behind that childish notion after her death, when he became coven leader and struggled through his job the same way he assumed she must have. He thought he gained a deeper understanding of her as a witch, as a person, as a leader.

Now, Paris felt like a child again, like his mother was some aloof stranger and he didn't know her at all.

With a sigh, he forced himself to focus on the words in front of him, tried to force his brain to decipher the spells and hexes in the book, the notations, the history blurbs, and see what sense he could make of it. He immediately recognized some bits and pieces as part of the wards Hannah had provided to him to set around the house. He wondered if his mother had based her spells on them or if somehow, her spells were out there somewhere, and someone else was basing magic on her work.

At any rate, demon magic or not, he felt more confident and at ease with his mother's magic and he copied down her wards to set them against the house, protecting it from demons. He wished he had enough power to ward the entire coven but he'd settle for at least his house while Jade stayed with him.

Her fingers typed away again, tickety-tacking on the keys and then she paused and looked up at him.

"If the scrying mirror doesn't work, I still want to see the records of everyone in the Coven."

He was amazed at how much she was able to keep in her brain, juggling ideas and threads of conversations. After refreshing his mind on the topic, he remembered that she'd asked him for all the personal data on the Coven members.

"If the mirror doesn't work, I'll see what I can do."

She pursed her lips and looked back down at her laptop. "You know people say stuff like that when they don't really want to do something."

Jade had a sharp tongue and wasn't afraid to blurt out the uncomfortable truth. She was right, however. He didn't want to provide her with the Coven records and he'd hoped that the platitude would appease her for long enough for it to become a moot point.

"You're quite intelligent," he mused.

She looked up at him, unimpressed. "Is that supposed to be flattering? I don't need you to pet or stroke my ego."

"No, of course not."

Jade rolled her eyes. "Now you just sound patronizing. Stick to your book," she said, returning to one of his mother's grimoires. "You'll get a lot further with it than you will with me."

He studied her for a moment more. She'd make a strong addition to the Coven and not just for the power of her magic. Paris tapped his fingers against the table as he thought. She could possibly even work with Hannah on the council. Jade didn't seem the type to be intimidated or awed by anyone – why should werewolves, vampires, Fae or other magical beings be any different? Her natural inclination to be distrustful and suspicious would probably serve them well and he made a mental note to discuss it with Hannah.

Or she could work with the Counter-Magic Department - her magic was strong enough she could likely un-hex anything that had gone awry. She would likely be able to untangle most corrupted spells and charms without doing the damage that generally came from counter-magic.

She might do well in the Supernatural Defense Department, working with other witches and magical creatures when they had a rogue element on their hands. Tracking and capturing supernaturals was always a tricky business, but she was smart and again, her power gave her a lot of flexibility.

"Oh my god!" she exclaimed loudly, glaring at him. "You're not even being subtle. I can hear you thinking and your power is just humming along and it's all directed at me. Jesus, tone it down a notch, I'm trying to work here."

Paris was startled. He knew his power was a tangible force that most witches sensed, but no one had ever mentioned it being distracting or directed at them before. He made a conscious effort to rein his power in, focus his mind and look back down at the grimoire in front of him.

"Thank you," she said, sighing, though her tone nothing close to grateful. More like annoyance or chastisement.

"There are some wards here that I'd like to try instead of the ones that are currently on the house," he said, picking up the book.

She made shooing motions with her hands. "Go. Go do witchy things elsewhere. But do it quietly."

"You know, I'm considered the most powerful witch in the Coven," he muttered to himself wryly as he left the kitchen.

"Color me impressed," she replied sarcastically and he was surprised she'd heard him. "I'd be more impressed if you just focused on keeping me from dying a horrible demon-related death."

He ignored the feeling of being chased out of his own kitchen and stopped by his office to grab some chalk for the wards and sigils he wanted to try. He cleared his mind as he worked, focusing on the runes and symbols, trying to infuse them with as much magic as he could muster.

Unlike the other wards he erected, these felt like they drained him significantly. After only three of them, he felt worn and thin - his magic stretched; feeling tender and sore even as he pulled and pushed at it. He could feel the strength of the symbols - much more powerful than the ones he'd used before and he wondered just exactly what his mother had been dealing with demons for that necessitated her creating and using such strong wards.

After this crisis was over, he wanted to sit down with his mother's grimoires, the demon grimoires, and study them alongside her other books to see if he could construct any kind of timeline or design bits of history by charting the progression of her magic.

He wondered if he could gather up enough witches in the Coven to see if they could ward the Covenstead at least. On the other hand, he mused, introducing demon magic, and having to explain *why* to a group of witches was a horrible, ill-thought-out idea.

Though draining, the work was rhythmic and repetitive and lulled him into an almost meditative state. He was surprised as he cast the last rune on the last ward to see that it was past lunch. He'd spent all morning warding the house, time becoming fluid and inconsequential as he worked. He made his way back to the kitchen and found Jade still seated in the chair she'd been in when he left, but at some point she must have showered, her ponytail still wet and leaving faint damp spots on her t-shirt.

"There's a sandwich over there for you, if you want," she said, jerking her chin to the counter. It was a simple thing - some sliced meat he knew he had in the fridge, a slice of cheese and some mustard. An apple sat next to it and he appreciated the thought as his stomach growled at the first bite.

"Thank you."

She shrugged off his thanks. "No big deal. I made one for myself and figured it's just as easy to make two as one."

Paris ate the sandwich in a few quick bites, washing it down with a glass of water. She looked pointedly at the apple and then back at him and he bit into it, feeling like he'd just been guilted into eating his fruits and veggies.

"Do you feel up to a visit to the Covenstead? I'd like to get Callie's opinion on one of my mother's grimoires and check in with her to see what they've got. Also with the witches that were investigating your attack."

"You had people checking into it? Like detectives?"

The look on her face made him feel like he kicked puppies for a living. Like she didn't believe he had witches investigating what had happened.

"Of course."

"Oh." She blinked a few times and then swallowed. "Okay, sure. We can go to the Covenstead."

"All right. I'm going to take a quick shower and then we'll head out."

He left her still working in the kitchen and came back down twenty minutes later, his magic already feeling less bruised and sore than it had been when he finished the wards. She packed up her laptop and cords and made a fresh pot of coffee, finding a travel mug in his cupboards and filling it. She had a hard time trying to juggle the mug, her laptop and her purse so she handed him her laptop bag expectantly. He took it without comment and they were off.

He'd been taking care of some work from home, but as they arrived at the Covenstead, he was nearly overwhelmed with other witches wanting to speak to him, set up meetings with him, or get his opinion on things. Jade managed to grab her laptop bag awkwardly from him and head down to the library in the dungeon while he headed for his office to get a few things shuffled around and get his assistant's help on rescheduling the rest.

By the time Paris made it down to the basement of the library, Jade was already sitting with Callie and Henri in a quiet corner of the dungeon, talking in hushed voices over his mother's grimoire. Callie looked up at Paris with wide, expressive eyes as he came over, her entire face screaming at him how she felt about the revelation that his mother practiced demon magic. Sympathy, confusion, apprehension and concern all telegraphed in her eyes. Henri kept his eyes turned toward Jade and the grimoire, studiously avoiding Paris' gaze. He didn't seem afraid, more intimidated than anything else.

Jade looked up at him as well. Of the three of them, hers was the most uncomplicated expression. Clear, seemingly unbothered and focused. "You get the unwashed masses sorted out upstairs?"

"Yes," he said dryly, coming to sit with them, next to Callie and across from Jade and Henri.

Jade tilted her head at Callie. "Callie wants to know if you're going to try to ward the Covenstead with our shiny new demon wards."

Callie bit her lip. "It's just, I mean, should we ward everywhere Jade is? I don't know anything about demon wards so I didn't know if that meant that everyone would be able to sense them and that might lead to a whole bunch of questions." She looked at Paris.

"They were quite draining." Paris admitted slowly, watching surprise flicker over Jade's face as he said it. "I don't know if I could ward the entire Covenstead. Perhaps only the library? Most witches don't come down here very often, not that it's a commentary on the library, but most witches tend to stick to the spells they know."

Callie hesitated and Paris could see the internal debate going on in her head. He'd known her so long and so well he knew exactly what the problem was. She wanted to help, but was concerned about using demon magic herself.

She seemed to square her shoulders. "Can I help?"

"I should be all right," he replied, touched by her offer but not wanting her to practice any dark magic if she didn't have to.

"You can teach me," Jade said firmly, pushing herself to her feet.

"It was demanding, but I can do it alone." He didn't want Jade to have to practice it either.

She raised an eyebrow at him. "I'm not some shrinking violet." She looked at Callie, somewhat sheepishly. "Uh, not that you are either but..." She fidgeted for a moment. "Um. Sorry. Or whatever. But," she said as she turned back to Paris, confident again, "I'm helping."

"I can help too," Henri said suddenly and Jade turned to him and kind of patted him on the shoulder.

"Henri, I don't think your magic is... Mean enough for it."

Paris was surprised by her insight. She hadn't actually worked the wards herself but must have intuited that they did require a certain strength of intent behind them. Callie might have been able to manage it but from what he sensed of Henri's magic, he wouldn't have a chance.

"Oh thank god," Henri said quickly, his body relaxing from its tense state. "I want to help, I do, but demon magic scares the crap out of me."

Jade patted him again. "Yeah. But thanks." She looked back at Paris. "Let's do this."

He was sure her tone was meant to be firm and strong, but with her bruised and bandaged body and the dim, greenish ambient light in the dungeon, it only emphasized how fragile and very breakable she looked. If she hadn't been so insistent about learning, he would try to talk her out of it. As it was, all he could do was hope that with both of their magic combined, their wards would pack one hell of a punch.

CHAPTER FOURTEEN

Jade could never admit it out loud, could never even hint at it.

But demon magic? It was *fun*.

Okay, so it wasn't as much fun as it was interesting. Intriguing and twisted up, like a really big logic puzzle. As Paris taught her the symbology behind some of the warding and helped her focus her magic to work the runes, she found herself enjoying it. Even with her limited knowledge of magic and even more limited knowledge of demons, she knew it was a bad, bad thing.

She shouldn't like it. She should hate it, fear it, loathe it, mistrust it.

Instead she found herself eager to learn more. In a creepy way, demon magic made sense to her.

Callie and Henri had gotten spooked by it. Jade hardly made it halfway through her first ward when Callie shuddered and Henri turned a little green around the edges. Paris gently suggested they grab a bite to eat or some coffee and they'd hustled it out of the library like the place was on fire.

She could see what Paris meant about the warding being draining. She wasn't exactly in top notch condition with her stitches, bruising and cast, but she felt even more wiped out after only two wards. Her wrist throbbed with a cold ache that deepened and made her wince slightly when she started on the next rune. She didn't know how many she could complete until she would absolutely have to stop. Paris had indicated there were about five he'd like her to learn and they needed to be repeated over the library in various spots for maximum efficacy. She'd pestered him on why he was placing them where he was but he argued that learning the wards was taxing enough without learning about ward placement just yet.

She couldn't help it. She wanted to know *more*.

"Hello, possum."

She yelped and jumped back from the voice in her ear, pressing up against the damp stone wall.

The first demon, the one in her head she'd taken to calling 'Bob' stood a foot away from her, admiring her handiwork.

Her *anti-demon* handiwork.

"You can't... You shouldn't be here," she stammered, heart racing as she glanced at the ward and back at the demon.

Paris came around the corner quickly and muttered something, a spell, hex or incantation she couldn't tell. Something flew at the demon and he batted it away easily, sending it back toward Paris, like a wave of hot, compressed air. It seemingly blew through Paris and though he flinched, he didn't back down.

"I'm not here to hurt anyone," the demon said. "I just came to talk to my little possum." He turned his gaze back to Jade and she got a flash of the strange vertigo she felt the first time she'd met him. Blinking, she pressed harder against the wall for stability.

"You work the wards wonderfully," Bob said to her, studying a nearby rune. "Unfortunately, there's still a lot about demon magic you don't know."

'Bob' didn't really do him justice. It didn't convey the otherness of his presence or the frigid, almost cloying aura around him.

Like a flash, Jade remembered something she'd read in one of Sakkara's books just that morning. She pulled her magic around her and then flung it at Bob, the awkward and strange words spilling from her lips.

He flinched. Then, like acid had been poured over him, the skin of his face spat and hissed, pouring putrid smelling smoke into the area. She gagged at the smell but held her spot.

Bob shook himself like a dog, bits of flesh and gore spraying out from him. One of them hit her in the cheek and she swiped at it hastily, rubbing the hem of her shirt over her skin. *Yuck.*

"Very good," Bob said, not the least bit put out. He sniffed the air. "That was your first try at that one, correct? Quite nice. But I've been around the block a few more times than your common demon." He held up a hand toward Paris who'd been stalking closer and *tsk-tsk'd* his fingers at the coven leader. "Now, now. I don't mind if you stay, but I won't put up with your interruptions. Hush now. I'm only here to talk to her."

Jade gulped as he turned his full attention back to her. "Do the wards even work?" she asked, hating how her voice came out shaky.

"Quite well. On lower class demons. It's also tricky work to put them in a place like a Covenstead. The walls, the furniture, the witches all bleed a different kind of magic. Left over spells, the potential of future spells, charmed objects and different kinds of power all mixed up together in one place. Makes the wards dodgy. Riddled with holes and wobbly bits. Weak spots where things can still get through. Also, this much demon magic being used at once and in a place of magic as well?" He looked at her sympathetically, dark eyes flashing. "Oh possum, you may as well put a big spotlight on yourself saying 'interesting things going on here.'"

Her eyes flickered to Paris who stood still as a statue watching the demon with careful eyes.

Bob shrugged. "Not everyone will notice and not everyone will care. Witches are mostly beneath us. But there are some who'll pay attention. Like me. Because I like you, maybe as much as our little friend who has his eye on you."

"Who is he?" she asked immediately.

Bob looked at her knowingly. "You know I won't tell you. Not without a deal." Again his singsong tone was back. He inched closer to her and she side-walked away from him, keeping her back to the wall.

"I thought, perhaps, after your little taste of him the other night," he said as he tipped his head, indicating her cast and then her stitches, "you might be a bit more interested. Still think I might be lying?"

"No. But that doesn't mean I trust you. Or care to listen to you either."

Bob smiled, showing his sharp teeth and she leaned further away from him. She had a sudden image in her head of him poised over her, like a wolf, jaws ready to snap down and break her neck. "Clever possum. I like you more and more, you know."

"Gross," she blurted at his leering expression.

"Everyone deals, possum. Given the right leverage, everyone deals." He glanced over at Paris. "His mother could tell you that."

"You knew my mother?" Paris spat, horrified.

"I knew *of* your mother, though I never had the opportunity myself to deal with her personally. I know someone who did. Like she reportedly did, you positively reek of good intentions and noble magic." Bob sneered. "Although you don't quite have the stench of desperation about you that demon-dealers usually have." He turned back to Jade. "You, however... You just smell of power. Unfettered." He sniffed the air again. "And fear, but everyone who deals with demons smells of fear. It's mostly lost its *je ne sais quois*. We smell it all the time."

Jade debated trying the spell again, trying to push more magic behind it this time, as much as she could manage. But if it didn't work, she'd likely just make him angry.

And then she'd be really fucked.

"Blah blah blah it's all talk-talk-talk," she burst out, hoping she sounded more confident than she felt. "I can do without the monologue. What do you want?"

Bob shrugged. "I just thought I'd check in, see what all the hubbub was about. I could feel you warding this place from the other side. About as subtle as a bull in a china shop. I wanted to know if you were ready to deal yet."

"No."

"Ouch." He winced with mock pain, clutching at his chest. "Your tone hurts, possum. I tell you what-"

Blazingly fast, he was crowding her against the stone wall, his body a scant inch from hers. The overly thick, syrupy smell of him pressed against her. She saw Paris move out of the corner of her eye and she shook her head at him. She was okay, she was fine. She wasn't hurt. Yet. If Paris was going to try something, better he wait until they really needed it and not just when she was getting intimidated.

Goddamn she was petrified though. But if Bob wanted to hurt her, he would have already done it. That's what she kept telling herself. He wanted to deal with her.

He couldn't deal with her if she was dead.

Jesus, she hoped not.

"I'll give you one of my names. As soon as you change your mind, you call. Then we'll deal."

"Yeah, that's what all the boys say. Call me, I'll drop everything." Her voice came out thin and airy, like she was two breaths away from hyperventilating.

"For you? I will." He leaned in closer, his breath hot against her ear. "But don't call unless you mean it, possum," he whispered. She kept her eyes focused on Paris, on the solid, steady line of him, poised like a racer waiting to spring, waiting for her to twitch or beckon. She couldn't tell if he was afraid and that made her feel better, not as skin-stripping scared.

Bob continued to speak quietly in her ear. "Don't call unless you want to deal. Say my name, say it with intent, and I'll come running. But if you trick me..." He snapped his teeth shut, making loud biting sounds against her ear. She flinched and Paris took a step closer. She willed him back with her eyes. She wasn't hurt, she kept reminding herself. The demon was just like a bully, barking at her for a reaction.

She wouldn't give him a reaction.

She turned her face slightly, enough for her to whisper in his ear. "I can do without the theatrics. Your name," she said plainly.

He whispered it so quietly, so lowly in her ear, she wasn't sure she heard it.

And then he was gone. But the sticky-sweet scent lingered.

Jade started shaking and let herself slide down the wall. It was cold and she'd been pressed up against it for too long, the chill of the stone seeping into her bones.

Paris knelt beside her, one hand on her shoulder. "You're all right," he said calmly, repeating it a few times and she wasn't sure who he was talking to.

"Of course I'm all right. He didn't hurt me," she said, sharper than she intended. She didn't pull away from him. In fact, she leaned a bit into his side and almost sighed from relief when his arm, heavy and warm, encircled her shoulders protectively.

Neither one of them said anything for a long few minutes. Finally, she pulled away from him and he dropped his arm from her shoulders awkwardly. She pushed herself to her feet.

"So, I guess warding the library equals bad idea." She took a deep breath. "Fuck."

"What was his name, Jade?"

She turned incredulous eyes on him. "You're not thinking of calling him, are you?"

"Absolutely not," he replied. "But maybe we can find out more information about him with his name."

She opened her mouth to say it and then froze, suddenly afraid that would be akin to saying it out loud, with intent. After walking back to the table they'd been at earlier, she yanked open her laptop and launched a text-pad application. She typed the name out in four keystrokes, surprised at how innocuous it looked.

Seth.

#

After Seth's impromptu visit, they relocated to Paris' house, Callie and Henri joining them.

Along with a trunk full of Callie's books.

"These are my important ones!" Callie pleaded at Paris' affronted look as she dragged the trunk over his hardwood floors. Jade smirked and thought that they were like siblings in each other's company too much - always a little eager to pick at each other. They spread out across the large dining room table, Jade taking the head of it with her laptop, little notebook and one of Sakkara's grimoires. On a whim, the first thing she Googled was 'demons named Seth' and was surprised when she got some hits.

God, how she loved Google more than a little bit.

Her love affair with the search engine lasted only as long as it took her to read that Seth was an Egyptian god, although he generally went by Set. She dropped her head in her hands.

"I'm so fucked," she said to nobody specific.

Callie's head popped up from where she sat at her chair. "What is it?" She came over to where Jade sat, reading over Jade's shoulder. "Seth is the god of the desert, storms and foreigners. He may also be attributed to darkness and chaos." Callie's face was pale as she rested her hand on Jade's shoulder. "It... It might not be that bad."

"It says he killed and mutilated his own brother!"

Callie looked torn and Henri buried his head back into the book he was reading. Paris stood silently by the kitchen doorway, hovering.

When nobody offered any comfort, Callie patted Jade's shoulder. "Mythology is quite often only metaphors for the morals and values people wanted to instill. We don't know if that's true."

"Well next time he pops out of nowhere, I'll be sure to get him to confirm or deny." Jade rubbed at her face. "You know, I went a really long time without being on anyone's radar and now, all of a sudden, there're witches and demons all around and they want stuff and I've got this power and it actually kind of sucks."

Callie squeezed her shoulder and Jade wondered if this was the price she was paying for having people in her life. Like some weird kind of balance or scale, if she wanted to have friends - or whatever Callie, Paris and Henri were becoming - this was what she was going to have to deal with.

"At least it doesn't seem like he wants to hurt you," Callie said finally, still reading over Jade's shoulder. "I mean, he seems kind of invested in getting a deal out of you, but he needs you alive for that."

"Fantastic. I feel so much better already." Jade deadpanned.

"It just... It could be worse."

Jade eyeballed her. She didn't want to be fatalistic, but it was about as awful as she could imagine. She wanted to say she didn't see how it could be worse but she wasn't dumb enough to toss that out for fate to stomp all over with some fresh new hell she hadn't thought of yet.

Depressingly, this was only taking into account demon number one - he who was formally known as Bob. She had no info on demon number two, Doug - a lesser demon according to Seth. Not to mention their unknown witch who was the root of all this.

When she figured out who it was, she was going to punch them in the throat, she thought grimly. Really, really hard.

Callie moved all her stuff to be closer to Jade to offer moral support or something, Jade didn't really know. She wasn't exactly an expert on people skills. Paris sat at the other end of the table, studying two of his mother's books. Jade looked up at him every now and then and saw his dark, bleak face. She kind of felt sorry for him. She'd known from a young age her parents were grade-A class scuzzbags. It must be a real punch in the gut to find that kind of thing out later in life and have it take you completely by surprise.

She didn't have time to be sentimental for herself, let alone for someone else, so she pushed it aside for now and focused back on the demon grimoire in front of her. Jade had been keeping thorough notes as she read through books in the library - and now one of Sakkara's books - and she found it useful to go back and search bits and pieces of items she'd transcribed and compare it to what she was reading now. She wrote out some ideas as she worked, making additional notations and theories as she went. At some point, she vaguely overheard Paris telling Callie about their scrying mirror and asking if they could come by and borrow her cat when they dug it up. She wanted to ask about it but got distracted by another hex at the bottom of the page. It looked only partially finished but it had little tiny stars drawn around it, which Jade had learned was Paris' mother's way of indicating her interest in something. She took out her phone and snapped a picture of it, sending it to her laptop and pasting it in her growing document.

Bringing witchcraft into the twenty-first century, she thought, smirking. Whether it wanted to go or not.

They ordered delivery for dinner and she longingly stared at the menu online before settling on salad with grilled chicken, thinking about the state of her jeans. She thought about ordering a whole cheesecake since it very well could be the end of her world. But if it wasn't, she'd spend the rest of her life trying to get that cheesecake off her ass.

What she needed was a spell to make cheesecake calorie-free but taste exactly the same - now *that* would be useful.

Despite the dire circumstances, dinner was a fairly light affair. Henri and Callie supplied most of the conversation, both of them talking about their significant others and plans they were making for vacations or anniversaries. Callie invited Jade over for dinner with Callie's boyfriend Nick, Henri and Henri's boyfriend Daniel, 'once this whole mess was sorted out' which was a really nice way of saying 'you know, after we take care of your little demon problem.'

Callie also suggested bowling which started a fight over the last time the foursome of Callie, Henri and their significant others went bowling and apparently ended when Henri 'lost' the scorecard only to keep Callie and Daniel from coming to blows over who was the victor.

They were both quite competitive, it seemed, and Henri had decided then that all sporting events, board games and quiz shows were out of bounds for double dates.

By the time Henri and Callie called it a night at about nine o'clock, Jade was already yawning and wishing for a few more painkillers to take the edge off. But she felt a little bit lighter than she had all day.

"They're fun," she said simply as the door closed behind Callie and Henri.

Paris nodded.

She gave a big, jaw cracking yawn, feeling like her mouth needed to go just that extra bit wider to make it really satisfying.

"You should head to bed," Paris said and she nodded. It was early, but she was already beat. She looked almost longingly at the books spread out over the table.

"It will all be here tomorrow," he added.

"Yeah. Okay," she agreed and trudged up the stairs. Halfway up, she paused, watching Paris head back to the table. She surprised herself when she said, "Hey, Paris. I'm sorry about your mom." She felt immediately kind of lame until Paris offered her a weak smile.

"Thank you," he replied softly.

She stood on the stairs for a moment more, unsure if she should say something else. In the end she decided just to head on up. Like the night before, she heard him moving around downstairs for quite some time after she was already in bed. She managed a whole half hour in bed before she again jettisoned the idea of sleeping there and made her way to the closet and settled into the inky dark.

#

Jade practically vibrated through most of the next day, counting the hours till sunset when they could dig up the scrying mirror. They had spent the day at Paris' house again, Callie and Henri coming back over to offer moral and intellectual support. Plus, Henri brought food so that was a bonus. She was learning more about demon magic but Paris was unsurprisingly reluctant to let her try any out. She could admit to herself she was a little wary as well, given what Seth said the day before about her warding being like a beacon.

On the flip, she wanted to learn and the best way to learn was by doing. Callie argued that Jade would likely never have the opportunity to use demon magic again; it was rare and no one dealt with demons. Jade replied back that she'd been at the Coven less than a week and already had two demons on her back. Statistically speaking from her viewpoint, Jade would need it a *lot*.

She grew even more fidgety and restless as the day wore on, a combination of anticipation and cabin fever. Callie made a trip over to Jade's cottage and returned with the rest of her suitcase, which included her runners. While Jade ran for exercise, she couldn't say she actually enjoyed it. Well, she didn't hate it. It was something that needed to be done. But today, waiting around for sunset and being cooped up in Paris' house, she stared longingly at her runners and thought about a jog. She felt like a border collie without a job - full of bottled up energy, just waiting to be directed toward something.

Either it rubbed off on everyone else or they took pity on her. After lunch, Paris went outside to his backyard and warded the area. He dug up some badminton rackets from his attic and-

Seriously? Badminton rackets? She was never going to let him forget that.

At least she got the chance to burn off some excess energy by messing around with Callie and Henri. They were all equally awful at it, lunging and dodging for the shuttlecock and missing more often than not. The only thing they excelled at was making all kinds of innuendos and dirty jokes about the shuttlecock, all three of them snorting and guffawing with laughter at their horrible grade school mentality.

It was the most fun Jade had had in a long time. The air was cool and crisp and she felt red-cheeked and a little winded after all her inactivity over the last week. Callie and Henri were joking back and forth with each other, locked in a battle of double entendres regarding their boyfriends and the shuttlecock. It all had Jade thinking, again, *wow, I really could live here.*

By the time sunset came around, the sky blazing orange and pink, she felt calmer than she had in days, despite the circumstances. Callie and Henri headed off, Callie promising to see them shortly at her house so they could borrow her cat, and Henri saying he'd see them both tomorrow.

Jade and Paris drove back out to the nature preserve, Paris easily navigating back to where they had buried the mirror. She used her phone to verify the sun was well and truly set, since they couldn't see it directly with the tree coverage. Paris dug quicker than before, the ground softer from previously being disturbed. It occurred to her on the car ride back to Callie's that she'd never asked what the cat was for.

"We're not killing the cat, right?" Jade blurted.

The heavy weight of the scrying mirror and cloth bag was on her lap, inside a garbage bag to keep the loose dirt contained. The everydayness of Paris suggesting a household garbage bag to preserve cleanliness had struck her as funny and so simple. Of course they could put a scrying mirror in a garbage bag, he'd told her. Why couldn't they?

It had just seemed so... Normal.

"Of course we're not killing the cat," he said, like the notion was completely absurd. "We just need it to look in the mirror first."

"Oh, of course," her tone was sarcastic.

He turned to face her at a red light, slightly hindered by the slight bucket seats of his car and the steering wheel. "After we prep the mirror, we can't be the first to look at it or it will steal our soul."

She laughed at his ominous tone, figuring he was having a joke at her expense. "Right," she huffed.

He frowned. "I'm serious."

Jade stared at him, watching him for a smile or a hint of mischief and felt her own smile fade at his stillness. "Holy shit you *are* serious. Fuck me. Okay, don't look at the mirror. Got it." She shivered at the implication, not wanting to ever find out if it was really true or some kind of urban witch legend.

"Cats have always been close to witches, guardians of the underworld, associated with Hecate. She's the closest thing we have to a goddess. We make a scrying mirror and then a cat will look into it first. After that, it's safe for us to use."

"So, how many people do you lose to scrying mirror incidents yearly?" she asked, wondering if there was some kind of statistical recordkeeping for witchcraft related accidents.

"What? None," Paris replied, eyes looking forward as he drove.

"Seriously? With temptation like that, no one has done it?" She was flabbergasted, assuming it was like the warnings on everything else in life. Make it idiot-proof and someone will make a better idiot.

"We don't teach scrying to children. Everyone who does it is an adult. They know better than to look."

"So there's no kind of Darwin awards for those witches that just screw the rules, muck it up and get injured? Or dead?"

"I'd like to think we're a bit more civilized than that," Paris said wryly.

"So does everybody," she replied with a shrug.

They arrived at Callie's place, an older-styled duplex which reminded Jade of the 1940s. Stairs climbed over the car park and onto the patio where the front door was located. The house was painted a deep purple that conveyed the feeling of happy-welcome-frivolity all at once.

It suited Callie well, Jade thought, as Callie swung open the glass-paneled front door, her blond hair swaying with her movement.

"Hey, long time no see." Callie joked. "I put out some food for later but I figured you'd want to get the mirror done first."

Paris had taken the mirror from Jade as they left the car and he carried it to the kitchen, to a small island that was set apart from the rest of the area - clearly Callie's witchcraft station. The island featured runes and wards sketched into the surface and also carried a beat-up, well-used air which the rest of the kitchen lacked.

Paris felt along the bag for a moment and when he pulled the mirror out, it was reflective side down. He kept it like that the entire time, polishing it with a cotton cloth. After that, he produced the hex bag, this time seemingly not caring if he touched the contents or not. There was no longer a foul stench accompanying the hex bag and Jade remembered Paris saying the smell would dissipate as the magic did. Callie took the hex bag items and put them in a large stone mortar, setting them on fire with the touch of a match.

"You shouldn't use your magic to set the contents aflame," Callie said, looking over at Jade while the small fire burned in the mortar. "It's cleaner to use a match."

"Why?"

"If there's any lingering magic, this will kill it. Using your own magic just infuses it with more."

Callie then started making *kiss-kiss* sounds and calling for a cat named Stuart. After a few minutes, she gave a frustrated sigh and then went over to the electric can-opener on the counter. She ran it for five seconds and, almost immediately, the fattest cat Jade had ever seen lumbered into the room. Callie bent over and hefted him into her arms, putting significant strength into it.

"Jesus that's a fat cat," Jade blurted.

Callie looked scandalized. "He's big boned. And he has a lot of fur. He's really fluffy," she said, indicating his über-fluffy multi-colored coat. Jade met Paris' eyes and he shook his head minutely, seemingly warning her not to get into the fat-cat debate with Callie.

Stuart eyed Jade in that way cats have of judging and dismissing with their eyes in one, simple look of disdain.

"Ready?" Paris asked.

Callie nodded and placed Stuart down on her witch-counter as Paris flipped the mirror over, reflective side up. All three of them were looking askance, but Jade could see out of the corner of her eye, Stuart went directly to the mirror, towards his own reflection. The fur on his neck stood up and he puffed himself out, making him look even grander. He gave a sharp cat-hiss, teeth bared, before deftly jumping from the countertop. He then scowled back at Callie, cat-betrayal written all over his little, furred face.

"Sorry, Stu," Callie said, reaching for a can of tuna and opening it quickly.

Stuart hopped up on the counter and ignored Callie until she put the tuna in front of him. She dropped a quick pet on his head and he butted up into it. Apparently, all was forgiven.

Paris leaned over the mirror, Callie and Jade flanking him on either side. He took a deep breath and then said lowly, "Show me."

And nothing happened.

Jade fidgeted a bit. "Um, this isn't going to be like a tea leaf reading where you're telling me you see a tree or a number four and all I see is a bunch of soggy, wet leaves, is it?"

Paris turned to her, aggravation on his face. "Patience."

She leaned back a bit so she could see Callie on the other side of Paris. Callie quirked her lips at Jade and mouthed the word, 'patience,' her face going comically serious for a moment before her eyes started dancing with humor. Jade snickered and looked back at the mirror.

So far, all she saw was the ceiling of Callie's kitchen.

Then it shifted.

She started slightly, a shock of fear hitting her deep in the gut. It was like at the Chinese restaurant when the mirror rolled and shimmered, right before she'd been attacked. She flinched back slightly, fingers digging into Paris' forearm.

"It's fine. It's working," he said lowly, his tone reassuring. She managed to un-claw her fingertips from his arm.

The surface of the mirror wobbled and then clouded over, like foggy glass on a cool, damp day. Then, a vague shape appeared in the mirror, though it was obscured and strange, like she was seeing it from very far away.

"That's the Covenstead," Callie said and Paris made a sound of agreement.

"Yeah, but we already knew it was someone in the Coven," Jade said, a little disappointed.

"Yes, we knew it was someone in the Coven, but not everyone works or visits the Covenstead on a regular basis. For the mirror to show us this, our unknown witch must spend a lot of time there. Probably works there."

"So, that's good, right? That narrows it down?" Jade asked.

Paris studied the mirror carefully. "Yes."

As she watched, there was something else along the edge of the mirror, faint and wobbly. She studied it and thought it could be a rune, like the kind she'd been using in the wards. Yes, definitely a demonic rune of some sort. She tapped her finger next to the mirror.

"Is this indicative of this person making a demon deal?" she asked.

Paris frowned. "I can't see what you're looking at. What do you see?"

She glanced over at him and Callie, both of their expressions open and curious. "I see a rune here, like the ones I've been using in the wards. You don't see it?"

Callie shook her head. "I can't see anything."

Paris looked closer. "I can tell something's there, but I can't tell what."

Jade looked back. It seemed rather clear to her and she wondered if it was because she wanted to see it or...

"Maybe it's like your mother's grimoires. I can see it because I've been touched by demon magic. You can see it a little bit," she said to Paris, "because you've worked the wards. But Callie hasn't done anything so she can't see it at all."

Paris made a low *hmmm* sound, like he was agreeing with her.

Jade looked back at the mirror, looking for anything else. She wasn't sure how long this kind of thing lasted or what other things she would see. As she stared, she thought she could make out another shape, along the edge. Long and angular, it was like an obelisk with smooth sides and a pointed, pyramid-shaped end.

"Here," she said, again tapping at the edge of the mirror. "What's this?"

Paris leaned in closer, as did Callie, but from their faces they couldn't see it.

"You don't see this one either?" Jade asked, already knowing what the answer would be.

Callie shook her head and Paris turned to look at her. "What is it?"

Jade leaned towards the mirror. "It's like a long shape, with a pointed end." As she spoke, the mirror started to unfog, becoming clearer and she could see bits of Callie's ceiling poking through.

"What's going on? Is that it?" Jade asked.

"It's fading. Scrying mirrors don't last long," Paris said quietly.

Jade's eyes tried to flick over everything all at once, trying to take in as much as she could, see if there was anything else she was missing. In the center of the mirror, overlapping the image of the Covenstead, she thought she could see the beginning of something else; a shape, a letter... Something she couldn't decipher. She leaned closer, seeing a bit of her own reflection on the part of the mirror that was completely clear again.

She tilted her head, heard Paris ask her a question just as she also noticed, like before she was attacked in the restaurant, her reflection didn't move.

She reared back, pushing away from the mirror just as a set of claws, long, silver and sharp, erupted from the surface and swiped where her face had been. Callie screamed in surprise and Jade felt Paris pull at her good arm to yank her back even as she brought her cast down hard on the surface of the mirror, next to the claw, cracking it into pieces.

The three of them stood stock still for a moment, staring at the broken shards of the mirror in front of them.

Nothing else happened.

Jade looked up sharply at Paris who stared at the mirror and then to Jade.

"Good reflexes," he said, nodding his head toward her cast.

She cradled it a bit in her good arm, sore from the amount of force she'd put behind her strike.

"Thanks."

"Is that what happened before?" Callie asked, her brown eyes large and wide. "When you were attacked?"

"Yeah," Jade said, still unable to take her eyes off the shards. "There was this moment where the reflection didn't match what I was doing. It was like that before and then... It happened. I saw it happen this time and I just reacted."

"It's likely a combination of Callie's house not being warded and also the mirror being tied to the witch that called the demon. It made a convenient portal," Paris said. He took the cloth bag that the scrying mirror had been in previously and started sweeping the broken glass into it, using the sleeve of his shirt. "We should bury this just in case, put some runes over it for any magic that lingers."

"You can bury it out back," Callie said with a jerk of her head. "I've an area back there that's all fallow ground. I can't get anything to take there. It's probably just been overused."

"And then we'll head over to the Covenstead?" Jade asked.

"It's late, hardly anyone will be there. I suggest we take the evening and head over first thing tomorrow morning." Paris suggested.

Jade waffled. On the one hand she wanted to head over right now, shake some trees and see what fell out. But she could see the logic behind what Paris was saying. If it was people she was interested in, she had a better chance tomorrow once everyone showed up for work. Then she could finally get Paris to hand over some files and start meeting suspects to hopefully glean a vibe from them.

Jade also had this strange sense that, like the grimoires she'd found and the scrying mirror just now, she'd be able to somehow tell who'd been working demon magic because she'd been touched by it herself.

She bit her lip and finally agreed. "Okay. Tomorrow."

Paris nodded and headed out the back door of the kitchen to Callie's tiny yard.

Callie put her hand on Jade's arm to get her attention. "Wanna eat something?" she asked hesitantly.

"I could always eat," Jade joked shakily, still caught up in thinking about the most recent attack. Callie gave a soft chuckle at Jade's answer and led her into the dining room where she'd set out enough appetizer-type food to be eaten as a meal.

"I hate cooking but I like small food, so appetizers work well for me," Callie said with a smile.

"Small food is always cute," Jade said noncommittally.

"Plus you can eat a whole bunch of it and then later on when someone says, 'oh hey, did you eat?' you can say, 'just bits and bites.' You can completely avoid the guilt."

It was so obvious that Callie was trying to make Jade feel at home and comfortable that Jade couldn't help but offer her a tiny smile. She grabbed some of the pita chips and dip, sighing in pleasure when she took a bite and found out it was some kind of spinach-cheese dip.

"I know, right?" Callie said, taking a big bite. "It's like they finally found a way to make spinach taste good - put it with a bunch of cheese and make it a dip. Genius. I'd marry the person that thought of it if I could."

By the time Paris came back inside, Callie and Jade were waxing poetically about dumplings, plum sauce and dry ribs as well. Until Jade said, "I'd marry the person that invented nachos."

Callie groaned in delight. "Oh my God. Nachos. I would've made them myself but they actually take preparation and assembly. We'll have to go out after this is all over and get some. With extra jalapeños. And guacamole."

"I'm not a fan of the guac," Jade said with shrug.

Callie clasped her heart dramatically and gasped. "What?" she asked, horrified.

"It's mushy and green. That's weird."

Paris joined them at the tail end of their conversation and made a strange face at both of them as he grabbed a plate and stocked it with food. "When will you get over this strange obsession with appetizers?" he asked Callie.

"Never!" she cried dramatically, shaking her fist in the air and Jade snorted a laugh as she ate another dumpling.

She could feel the tension and anxiety of the evening starting to drain out of her as they ate around Callie's table, using their fingers to serve themselves and paper towels for napkins. Callie brought out some soda and the entire affair felt comfortable and easy. It was obvious that Callie and Paris had been friends for years. They had simple affection for and camaraderie with one another - easily maintaining light conversation. She felt sorry when dinner was over and Paris suggested they leave for his place, calling it a night.

Jade froze up a bit in surprise when Callie lurched forward at the door and pulled her into an impromptu hug. Her tiny frame was full of surprising strength as she gave Jade a solid squeeze. Jade was able to relax into it after a moment and tentatively raised her hands and patted awkwardly at Callie's back. Callie hugged Paris next, their embrace much more familiar and familial - quick and fierce.

"I'll meet you guys at the Covenstead tomorrow, okay?" Callie checked, making eye contact with both of them.

Paris nodded. "We'll be there."

On the drive home, Jade didn't know how she was going to sleep that night. She was anxious to get to the Covenstead and start checking people out - seeing if she could figure out who wanted her power. Then maybe this whole thing could be finished and she could see if she would settle into coven life.

After obsessing over it for several days, she realized she did want to stay. All the drama, demon deals and uncertainties aside, she enjoyed practicing magic. She felt like she could fit in with the coven better than she had elsewhere. Although she still chafed a bit when she thought about how Paris had lied to her at the start, not telling her about needing to break her magic if she left. However, when she sat down and thought it through, she could appreciate his point of view. He'd been hoping she would decide to stay and he wouldn't have to tell her. It made perfect sense and if she was honest, she would have done the same thing.

She really hated having to be reasonable and adult about things sometimes. It would be easier to stay mad at him, at the Coven, at the world just because she felt like it. But if she did that, she'd be no better than her parents - insecure and lashing out at whatever was closest just because they could, because they wanted to.

Back at Paris' house, she went up to her room, wondering if she'd move back to the little cottage after this was all over or if she'd find some other place to live. She had kind of liked the cottage. It was small and cozy and reminded her of...

She frowned, her eyes setting on her little shoebox, the one she took everywhere with her. It was resting on the nightstand next to the bed. With a sigh, she sat cross-legged on the mattress as she pulled the box toward her, opening it and sifting through its contents. She kept all sorts of odds and ends: a multicolored pencil, one of her report cards from grade school, a deck of cards - worn and well used, a bright pink shoestring, some rocks and finally, at the bottom, photographs.

She pulled one out and stared at it, fingering the tattered edges. She should put it in one of those special photo protectors or get it scanned and save it digitally. But there was something about holding a photo that was more tangible than looking at a picture on a screen.

The knock at the door startled her and she looked nervously around at her stuff all spread out on the bed. Innocuous enough, she supposed.

"Yeah, come in."

Paris poked his head in. "Are you all right? I made a pot of coffee and was a little surprised you weren't beating down the stairs for it."

"Yeah, just thinking."

"May I ask about what?"

She shrugged and she saw his eyes looking over her collection spread out on the bed. "Just stuff," she said noncommittally.

"What've you got there?" He indicated the photo in her hands.

"Nothing. Just a picture." She put it off to the side and started gathering all her things to put them back in her shoebox, feeling embarrassed and silly.

"Is that you?" he asked, coming closer.

Before she could stop him, he snatched the picture and examined it. She felt her heart clench, and much like when she was with the demon, she willed herself remain motionless, not to move a muscle.

"It looks like you but... Her eyes are green. Yours are grey. I didn't know you had any other family. A sister?" he asked, his tone light and easy. "That would explain why the demon couldn't pull you through the portal when it tried. You didn't say you had a sister." He flipped it over and her stomach felt sick, knowing he'd read the writing on the back.

"'Lily. Six years old.'" He looked back at her and she wondered how she must appear, preternaturally still, jaw clenched, hands reaching for the photo. "Who is she?" he asked, an eyebrow raised questioningly.

She took the photo back, harsher than she'd intended. "I don't. That's... That's just a photo. It's me. It's just... Me."

He looked at her carefully, studying her expression and she jutted her chin out defiantly, daring him to call her a liar.

"It says 'Lily' on the back," he said calmly.

She shrugged, not looking back up at him. "I changed my name. So what? I have documents if you want to see," she challenged. Her defenses were on full alert - she didn't talk about Lily, she never talked about Lily. Not to anyone, not ever.

"I'm sorry. I didn't mean to upset you."

Jade stuffed everything back in the shoebox and put it on the floor. "You didn't. I'm not." She looked back up at him, kept her face blank. "So, Covenstead tomorrow? Catch a demon-dealing witch if we're lucky?"

"Strange definition of lucky," he said, giving her the impression he was letting her change the subject. "But yes, hopefully this will all be over soon. Have you...?" he trailed off, like he was unsure and then he plowed forward. "Have you given anymore thought to staying here, at the Coven?"

"I have. Given it more thought," she said evenly. She didn't know why she was being so cagey. She was leaning toward staying. Just ten minutes earlier she'd been almost certain of it. But thinking about the past, thinking of Lily always made her twitchy and nervous. Made her feel like a little girl again, uncertain and spooked - like she couldn't trust anything or anyone. Paris waited for her to say more and when she didn't, he didn't push, just nodded solemnly.

"Very well. I'll see you tomorrow. Good night."

"Yeah. 'Night," she said offhandedly as he turned and left her room, shutting the door behind him.

Her eyes rested on the shoebox again and she couldn't even think about sleeping until she'd taken out all the items again and put them back correctly, in their proper order. She ran her fingers over the edges of the box when she was done. Even if she stayed at the Coven, she wondered if she'd ever feel ready to tell anyone about Lily.

Perhaps it was a secret she'd keep forever.

CHAPTER FIFTEEN

It was certainly true that things felt worse at night, with the darkness of the dying day pressing in on you. Jade didn't know if it was the notion that the day was over, never to be yours again, and the lack of light that made things seem worse after the sun had set, but there was something to be said for the start of a new day. Maybe it was all that mumbo-jumbo about starting over, maybe it was receptors in your eyes reacting to the light, or maybe it was just getting some sleep to reset the brain. At any rate, Jade felt like an overexcitable puppy the next day - bursting at the seams with energy and eagerness.

She wanted to catch a witch.

She kind of felt like how she imagined a wolf would feel, going out into the forest to catch some dinner. Sure, there were bigger things out there than her, but she was going to catch something and worry it with her teeth - maybe pull it apart a bit before it died.

Gruesome, but accurate. She liked to think of it as a 'winning attitude.'

It occurred to her she probably shouldn't be so excited to see if she could catch someone who kind of seemed to want her dead, but at the same time, she felt a little glee in her vindictiveness.

Maybe this is what all the self-help books preached when they professed leading a proactive life. She smirked to herself. Those books probably didn't have this scenario in mind.

Her enthusiasm was slightly dampened by the sight of herself in the mirror. The wound on her head was bruising spectacularly, blossoming yellow and purple around the edges of the bandage. She still sported welt-like marks on her neck and, of course, her cast was a black splash against her reflection.

Well, she didn't need to look like a model to catch a witch. Brains over beauty.

To date, she'd managed to avoid getting outrightly killed and had faced down a demon of the underworld. So, things could be looking up.

Jade was showered, dressed and already through one cup of coffee before Paris came downstairs. It was still really awkward to put her hair in a ponytail while one of her hands was in a cast, but she managed.

Barely. It was kind of lopsided and a bit messy, but it would do.

Paris took one look at her and raised his eyebrows. "Your power is dancing around you. Good mood?"

"I'm feeling very proactive today," she said gleefully, bouncing a bit in her seat.

Paris poured himself a cup of coffee. "How so?" he asked while he added two heaping spoonfuls of sugar to his mug.

"The promise of a new day," she said, giving him a mock salute with her own mug. He frowned at her.

"You're very odd sometimes."

She waved him off dismissively. "It's part of my charm. Can we go now?"

He chuckled good-naturedly at her and forced her to wait while he made some toast, pushing two pieces at her and indicating she should eat as well. She ate her toast like a sandwich, hurriedly crunching through it and then swigging down the rest of her coffee. She looked over at him and his three remaining pieces of toast.

"Wrap it in a paper towel, let's get going." Jade commanded, slamming her mug down emphatically and then heading for the door.

"Honestly. The most powerful witch in the Coven," he muttered behind her.

"Still don't care, get a move on." She tossed the words over her shoulder, stuffing her feet into her shoes and then pitching him the car keys.

"Dare I ask what your plans are?" Paris asked once they were in the car and on the road.

"You're going to get me the files of the people who work in the building and I'm going to go around and make like a bloodhound. Someone's doing demon magic and I'm going to find them," she said assertively.

"*We're* going to find them," he said, correcting her.

She waved her hand. "Fine. We. Whatever." She paused for a moment, having a new thought. "Hey, when we do find whoever, what happens then?"

"What do you mean?"

"Well, is there like a witch justice system or jail or what?"

She looked over at Paris and saw his jaw tightening. "There's the Council which deals with all supernatural creatures, but I would hesitate to turn anyone over to them. It's weighted heavily with Fae, as they are the largest supernatural group, and their justice can be... Strange. They value things differently than we do. Something you or I may take offense to, they would not. Similarly, something we may consider innocuous could be worth a blood bath to them. As far as coven justice or law goes, it's a little unclear. I'm afraid we have no formal penal code, at least, not a modern one. It's been a long time since we've required one."

"But you have an ancient one?" At his terse nod she continued. "What's it say?"

He grimaced. "The most common sentence is burning at the stake."

She felt her stomach clench a bit. "Yuck. Messy. I thought that's what other people did to you guys. I mean, us guys. I mean, you know, witches."

"Yes, but our persecutors ironically learned it from us. It... It cleanses the magic from a witch. Burns it out and releases it back to the universe."

The punishment seemed like it made a sick sort of sense, and although it should have been in line with the rest of her bloodthirsty thoughts that morning, it was a little overboard. Even for her.

"I'm guessing since I haven't seen any witches burning at the stake in the news you guys don't do that anymore?"

"No. Not in ages. I don't even know what other covens use for a justice system. I've been giving it some thought and at the very least, I think we'll have to break the witch that is doing this. Break their power."

She swallowed hard feeling a bit of a chill. "Like you were going to do to me."

"I told you I won't break your power." He stopped for a moment, making a move like he was going to pull the car over and have a more prolonged discussion, but he kept driving.

"Because you can't," she added quietly.

"Because I won't," he clarified. She wasn't sure why since to her mind, it amounted to the same thing.

Even though she felt like she could have a place in the Coven, felt like she could stay there, she thought that might always be a sore spot with her. Like a sliver of glass left in a wound that healed over - it didn't cause any real trouble, but it was always there, under the surface.

She pushed it down, hoping to force it deeper and ignore it. "So, witch-breaking," she said, continuing. "Think that will be enough?"

"I don't know. I guess we'll have to see. It would depend on you as well."

"Me?" she asked, her voice rising up a bit.

"Yes, you. What would you be satisfied with?"

She felt a rush of vindictive, heady power and she wanted to blurt out that maybe she'd only be satisfied with death too. Maybe she wanted to be a little bloodthirsty after all? Perhaps she wanted to give the rest of the Coven, or anyone else who was interested, a little bit of a warning: mess with me and I'll gut you like a fish.

She knew in part it was her childhood, her past talking - the small child in her that would always want retribution and revenge for everything. But she didn't know if she could live like that. It seemed like a worthy idea in the moment, but how would she feel two, three or five years down the line?

If there was one thing she knew about herself it was that her impetuousness quite often got the better of her. And she always paid dearly.

Jade fiddled with an imaginary thread on her jeans. "I think maybe you shouldn't leave it up to me," she said finally, her voice quiet.

"I would value your input."

She huffed wryly. "You really shouldn't."

Once at the Covenstead, they headed to Paris' office. It was the first time Jade had seen it. They entered through one of the doors off a hallway on the third floor into a small sitting room area that held a medium size desk. Past that, there was a door that Paris headed directly to and Jade surmised the smaller area was for his assistant. She followed Paris into his office and stopped dead in her tracks.

Okay, she was starting to get the whole 'most powerful witch in the Coven' thing. His office was cavernous. Natural light poured into the enormous space from the bay windows looming behind a large cherry-wood desk, setting the room aglow. Bookshelves, not unlike the ones at his house, lined almost every scrap of real estate along the walls. They were full of more grimoires, books on leadership, politics, on other supernatural creatures, on the history of magic, chemistry, and supernatural relations.

She felt a little dumb just reading some of the titles.

There was also a small sitting area with two large, wing-backed chairs and a tiny, intimate fireplace.

Probably where he had groundbreaking meetings with werewolves or vampires, she thought with a laugh. Jesus, no wonder he thought she was amusing for mouthing off at him. She shoved her hands into her pockets and tried to make herself a little smaller. Ugh, she felt really out of place.

Even the carpet was opulent. She didn't want to step any further into the room without removing her footwear. Her tennis shoes sunk in a little into the plush softness and she wanted to back up and try to smooth out the fibers or run a vacuum over the area to clear it up.

"Why are you just standing there?" Paris asked from behind his desk. He was already seated, the big windows framing him wonderfully. "I thought you'd be all over the bookshelves by now."

"Yeah. I'm just gonna..." She shrugged and rocked on her feet a bit. "I'm good right here."

"It's going to take me some time to pull the files," he said, looking at her like she'd lost her mind a little bit.

She glanced around the lavish room again, looking for a safe place to park her butt. Her only option was the two wingback chairs. She squared her shoulders and marched over to one, sitting down gingerly.

It was like butter. The dark, chocolate leather felt so soft she almost mistook it for some other cloth or fabric. She ran her fingers over it, marveling at its texture. She mouthed the word, 'wow' even as she tucked her feet up underneath her. At the last minute she remembered she was wearing shoes and stopped, dropping them back down on the floor. She looked over at Paris and found him smiling at her.

"Like the chair?"

She laughed at herself. "Yeah, it's pretty nice."

After a few minutes of chair appreciation time, she pushed herself out and finally made it over to the bookshelves, reading the spines of the books. She heard Paris on the phone, arranging for the files to be collated, then speaking to Callie letting her know where they were, then to someone she didn't know about a meeting with a werewolf pack that he apparently couldn't put off any longer.

Jade raised an eyebrow and glanced over at Paris as he got off the phone.

"Werewolves?"

"There's a pack very close by and we've been having some... Magic overlap issues with them."

"Werewolves have magic too?"

"Werewolves *are* magic. All supernatural creatures are magic to some extent," he explained. "Witches can use that magic at their will. The things that we've been doing recently, the amount of magic bleeding off us with the demon warding and the other spell-work you've been learning..." He trailed off. "It's leaking into their territory and they don't like it. I can't say I blame them. Normally, they probably wouldn't notice, but demon magic does have a certain... Feel to it." He rubbed his fingers together as if he were feeling the greasy taint of demon magic even then.

She toed the carpet a bit with her shoe, feeling chastised. "Sorry."

"Well, it's not really your fault. It's not anyone's fault. Something I'll have to make clear to their Alpha."

"So is it more political or magical? Your job?" she asked.

"It's both, usually in equal parts."

She made a humph sound. "Sounds crummy."

He laughed a bit. "Well, I wouldn't have used that word exactly, but it fits."

"What time's your big meeting?"

"One," he said, looking at her like he was trying to decide something. She eyed him right back.

"What?"

"I don't know what to do with you."

"Gee, thanks," Jade said dryly. "First of all, I'm not something you have to 'do' something with. Second, what's that even mean?"

He shook his head like he was trying to clear it. "I just meant that I'm uncomfortable leaving you on your own but at the same time, werewolves have a formal introduction process when meeting new people in a political setting and I don't have the time to introduce you before bringing you."

"And that would be a problem because you're kind of already on their shit list with the over-spillage of magic?" Jade asked, guessing the heart of it immediately.

"Right."

She shrugged. "So don't bring me. I can hang out with Callie in the dungeon. I'm sure Henri will be there too. Yeah 'Bob,'" she said, making air-quotes around the pseudonym she was still using for Seth, not risking his name out loud, "showed up here the other day, but he can show up anytime from what I gather. And it doesn't seem like he's actively trying to hurt me. And Doug? Well, Doug apparently favors mirrors. I can avoid those."

"So far Doug favors mirrors. We don't know what else could be coming. Portals out of the wall, out of thin air. Anything."

"Thank God you're here. I feel so much better with you around," she deadpanned.

He pursed his lips at her. "I'm just saying that we've been lucky so far."

"Lucky?" she said incredulously as she waved her cast in front of him and pointed at her face. "Have you seen me lately? I haven't been this beat up on a regular basis since I was twelve."

Jade immediately wanted to take the words, and their implication, back. Impulse control. She really had to get some for her mouth.

"I meant that it could be worse," Paris clarified.

"Again, I'm feeling so much love," she said sarcastically. "Just... Go to your little werewolf meeting and smooth some feathers. Or fur. Or whatever it is you have to do," she paused. "Although if there is some kind of freaky ritual involved, I must admit, I'm curious and I want you to tell me later." She shook herself, trying not to be distracted. "But, I will stay here, at the Covenstead with Callie and

Henri. We can stay in the cafeteria or someplace really public and visible. It'll be fine."

Paris appeared to be thinking about her proposal, tapping his fingers against his desk. "Why don't the three of you use my office? While we can't really ward any place in the Covenstead, I do feel as though there's a certain amount of power associated with this room, this space. It's been used by coven leaders for years."

"Okay. Works for me." Jade shrugged. "We can eat in here, right? You won't get freaked out if we get mustard on the carpet or something?"

"You're all adults. I'm sure you'll do fine," he said dryly.

#

Jade's unease about squatting in the formal space lasted until Henri spilled his half-filled latte cup and stained the carpet.

After that, it was like some kind of seal had been broken.

Callie, Henri and Jade lounged on the floor, leaning up against the high-backed chairs and the front of Paris' desk while they kept on in their research into demon magic. Jade liked to think of it as Demonology 101.

Although frankly, she could do without all the sexual positions, depictions and graphic sketches in many of the books. She didn't know if she was desensitized or just grossed out at that point. She didn't really care anymore and she snapped the book she was reading shut.

"I can't look at any more dirty pictures!"

Henri looked up with a smirk. "You know, when I was sixteen, I thought if I looked at enough porn, I'd eventually get to that stage." He shrugged. "Never did."

Callie made one of her snort-laughs, hiding behind the long curtain of her hair.

"I'm serious!" Jade continued. "I'm not even that much of a prude, I just want some actual knowledge to be in these books and not just whatever dirty fantasies or outrageous positions came across the writer's mind. Half of these books don't contain any real information. It's all just second hand tales or urban legends or kinky stories." She kicked at the book with a disgusted toe, nudging it further away from her. "I just want something that will help."

"Paris' mom's books are the best so far," Callie said quietly, all tones of laughter gone from her voice.

Jade nodded. "Yeah. Almost too good. It's like I don't know enough to follow along quite yet. Her stuff is like, advanced mathematics and I'm still learning how to count. There are one or two spells I think I could try, but the rest," she shrugged, "I don't know. I wouldn't even know how to attempt them without breaking something or blowing shit up. It's like I can't even figure out how she structured them."

"She was quite the witch," Callie said. "And coven leader."

"And you guys never got any hinky vibes off her?" Jade asked, looking at each of them. "Paris was shocked when I found those grimoires. He had no clue."

They both shook their head. "No," Henri replied, checking with Callie to see if she agreed and she wore a similar expression. "Nothing. She was the perfect coven leader. I mean, really, she was!" He continued at the face Jade made. "She was kind most of the time, but stern when she needed to be. She knew everyone in the Coven, knew their magic. She would remember stuff about you and ask. She was at all the public events, did all the ceremonies for the solstices and equinoxes. I didn't know her personally, but I would have never guessed."

"I knew her," Callie said. "I mean, like a child knows an adult, you know? Paris and I've been friends for years, so I was always at their house or she was picking us up from something. Or my mom and her were sitting together at some event. She was just... Paris' mom. And our coven leader."

Jade pursed her lips and stared at one of Sakkara's grimoires that she was still studying in fits and starts. It gave her a headache if she worked on it for too long and she wasn't sure if that meant something, or if it was just because of the scrawled handwriting.

Paris' desk phone ringing startled her and she jerked upright. She then poked her head out toward the small desk where his assistant should be sitting. Her plan was to accompany Paris to the start of the werewolf meeting and then come back, but it didn't look like she'd returned yet. With a shrug, Jade picked up Paris' phone.

"Uh, yeah. Paris' office," she said, sticking her tongue out at Callie who was smirking at her.

"This is Suki, Paris' assistant. I just got an email that the personnel files you requested are ready but you'll have to go to HR to pick them up. We can't transmit that kind of information over external email."

"Uh, sure. HR. Where is that?" Jade asked, grabbing a sticky note and pen.

Suki gave her directions to the HR department in the Covenstead and Jade jotted down the bare minimum.

"How's the wolf meeting going?" Jade asked, curious.

Suki made a disgusted sound. "Ugh, if I see one more preening and posturing wolf that tries to sniff me, I'm getting a silver cane and I'm going to start using it as a bat."

Jade had never met Suki, but she liked her already. "Sounds like you're having fun."

"I can't wait for this day to be over. All I can smell is wet dog." Suki added. "By the way, Paris wanted to check in and see how you're doing. All okay?"

"Yep. Just hanging out at his office, wrecking the joint." Jade stuck her tongue out at Henri this time who was still trying to move one of the chairs to cover his latte stain. He gave her the finger and she laughed.

"I'll let him know," Suki replied, sounding amused.

They said their goodbyes and Jade hung up, plucking the sticky note off the pad and fastening it to the back of her hand.

"My files are ready. I'm going to pop down to HR and get them. Who wants coffee while I'm up?"

Callie and Henri both raised their arms high and straight immediately and Jade huffed in amusement.

"Can there be pastries too?" Henri asked, batting his eyelashes at Jade.

"Moment on the lips, lifetime on the hips, Henri."

"I hate you for being right." He slumped dejectedly.

"Hate the game, not the player," Jade said smartly as she left the office like a dervish.

She read her haphazardly scrawled directions on the post-it note and figured she could either try to get to HR, on the second floor, by navigating down to it from the third, or she could head to the second floor and go from there. She wanted to get a good look at some other witches and the entire third floor appeared to be offices so she decided to start there.

She became one of those obnoxious people who walked down hallways and peered into every open door. Everyone looked up at her as she did. Some said hello and asked if she was lost, some offered to help her find what she was looking for, some appeared really annoyed and didn't say anything. She just stared at each of them thoughtfully, trying to figure out if she could sense any demon magic around them, on them, in their vicinity.

She was pretty sure she came off like a creeper. But it was collateral damage and she didn't care if they thought she was socially maladjusted or some kind of misfit. She only cared if she got a sense off them or not.

She did get a vibe from most people - a kind of generic, non-specific air. If she had to categorize it, it was vaguely cattle-ish. They were all sort of the same - she got a vague impression of magic but it was mostly superficial and bland. Nothing that really pinged her radar.

There were several folk she couldn't quite get a handle on, and she made a note of where their offices were located. She was better with numbers and spaces than names so she'd have to look up who they were later based on their location but that was okay. She could do that easily once she had the files.

Human Resources must have been the forgotten step-child of the Covenstead because their office was at the far end of one of the second floor wings, tucked into the last office down the hallway.

Although, as she stepped in, maybe it wasn't so neglected. A large window wrapped around the corner, flanked by massive drapes and liberally allowing streaming sunlight into the office space. Filing cabinets and shelves dominated the inner walls, and the soft *whirr* of computer or server fans carried into the room from an open door. It was a quiet, cluttered space with a large desk set off to the side of one of the windows, covered in papers and files.

"Hey?" she called out. "I'm here to get the personnel files?"

A bookish guy came out from behind one of the shelves, pushing up his glasses on his face as he came toward her. He had messy brownish hair which kind of matched the nondescript brown of his eyes. He was so very ordinary that she shouldn't have noticed him at all.

Except she did. Every fiber of her senses were tingling but she didn't get any magic off him at all.

Nothing.

Magically speaking, it was like he wasn't even there.

"I have them arranged in a trolley for you," the bookish guy said, indicating to the side of the desk. He came closer to her and she instinctively took a step back as he moved. He looked up at her questioningly as he went behind the desk and shuffled a few things until he found a key and handed it out to her.

"That's a lot of files," she said, taking the key and trying for casual conversation while she stared at him.

"Well, yes. We've a lot of people working in the coven. If you tell me what you're looking for, I can perhaps narrow it down."

She looked him up and down, trying to find something about him that she could pinpoint, other than his general blankness, that was making her want to spit fireballs from her hands. Casual slacks, casual shoes, casual shirt - all of it was just so bland and normal.

And then she saw it. A golden chain flashed from around his neck and hanging from it, a small obelisk - the same obelisk she spotted in the scrying mirror. Her eyes darted down to the desk where a nameplate sat. Matthew Caulder.

She thought about the shape that had been trying to form in the mirror, right before it cleared. An 'M.'

"You," she practically hissed.

After all the buildup, *this* was her nemesis it seemed. She was a little put out as a matter of fact. He was so boring, so innocuous, she could have passed him by three or four times since she'd gotten to the Coven and never even noticed until she started looking for magic.

He didn't seem surprised or concerned. In fact, he appeared sort of annoyed and unperturbed by her accusation. He sighed a bit, like he'd been expecting this.

"I really didn't want to do this here. It's going to be a mess to clean up this office."

This would be another classic example of when her impulse control failed her. She could have just left, could have just dodged back and run out into the hallway, but she was so livid that she didn't even register what she was doing until she was already up and over the desk, feet sliding on papers and files, tackling him like a linebacker.

She knocked him over and they slammed into the unyielding floor. She immediately kneed him in the groin and punched him with her cast.

"You son of a bitch!" she shouted even has he managed to get a foot up between them and push it against her chest, kicking her off. She hit the desk sideways, wincing with the blow, feeling the sharp edges digging into her hip and shoulder as she collided with the solid wood.

He shouted some curse and she felt it brush by her, cloying and sickly sweet - demon magic - and hear the door slam shut behind her, heard the *snick* of the lock engaging and the demon hex locking the door.

Matthew was already murmuring something under his breath and she had this quick flash in her mind of 'oh shit,' and she *knew*, she knew she had to keep him from finishing that spell or hex - whatever it was, it wouldn't end well for her. She pushed off from the desk, using her good arm and made another lunge for him, scrabbling at his feet. He kicked out, easily avoiding her grabbing hands and finished his spell, spitting out the last words.

She heard an unnatural sound. A horrible, keening sound from off to the side, behind one of the curtains and she was afraid to look, afraid to turn her head and see what it was. It was like glass grinding or metal twisting - shrill and harsh. She locked eyes with Matthew and he smiled.

"I may not have a lot of power, but I can call someone, *something* that does. And he'll get me your power. Power meant for a coven born witch and not some," his face twisted a bit in disgust as he said, "some mundane who can't even wield it properly."

"Fuck you," she said as she conjured a fireball and tossed it at him, feeling a little bit gleeful as it set his shirt on fire. He started screaming, rolling on the ground to put himself out.

She had a moment to enjoy her petty victory before two strong arms seized her from behind, lifted her towards the ceiling and tossed her hard against a line of bookshelves. She landed with a sick crunch and felt the impact travel up every single one of her bones. She shook her head, looked up and didn't know how to process what she saw.

From behind the curtain, she could see part of a mirror and it was missing a section, a shape in the form of a man, a shape that was lumbering toward her, fluid and sinewy - sliver and slick - like he'd crawled out of the mirror and taken part of it with him. It moved with a foreign, abstract grace that made her brain stutter to watch.

As it slid toward her, flowing through the air, she started shuffling backward on her feet, trying to think of something, a spell, a hex anything she'd read in the grimoires. She remembered the one she'd used on Seth and she worked the incantation and spat it out, pushing it at the quick-silver shape.

It rolled off him, like water off an oily surface, sliding to the ground and pooling at his feet.

"Definitely 'A' for effort."

She yelped at the voice in her ear and scrabbled away, turning to find Seth staring at her, crouched low, watching her with gleeful eyes.

"I didn't call for you," Jade said quickly.

"No, but I'm pretty hopeful you will," he said, tipping his head toward the door. "Door locked by demon magic, so unless someone in your coven can work the hex, you're on your own." Seth then looked at the looming silver shape. "Lesser demon coming after you, partially trapped on the other side but still, pretty strong." He finally looked over at Matthew. "And the demon is bent to his will. I reckon, since you just gave him third degree burns on his chest and arms, if he did harbor any misgivings or second thoughts - you just burned them out of him."

The silver shape was on her, reaching out with massive paws for hands. Jade flipped over onto her stomach and tried to slither way from it, around the corner of the bookshelf. Everything hurt. In the movies, people got tossed around all the time and still got up to fight but in reality, even with her adrenaline, it fucking hurt and she didn't know if she could trust her legs to hold her.

It grabbed her by the ankle and started pulling her toward the mirror. Her shirt rucked up and the floor burned her skin, scraping along it painfully. She kicked, she wiggled, she struggled but couldn't break her foot free. She looked around desperately for something to use as a weapon. There was nothing. Jade managed to grab a shelf on her way by and felt an awful pop in some of her joints as the demon kept his relentless tow, dragging her towards the mirror.

"Once he gets you on the other side, he'll try to extract your magic," Seth said conversationally, hunkering down next to her. "I'm doubtful it will even work. Old witch legend at best. Take the heart of a witch, take their power. Unfortunately, it does mean he's going to carve it out while you're still alive."

Jade kicked again, trying to yank herself back and away from the silver demon. It was faceless, expressionless - like fighting an automaton. Her arms, hands and fingers were exploding in agony from the strain she was exerting to keep herself anchored to the bookshelf.

"Still not willing to deal?" Seth asked, his bottomless eyes hopeful.

"No," she said, jaw clenched.

Jesus, if she could just hang on long enough for Paris to get here. Surely someone had heard all the ruckus, or Callie and Henri would figure she should be back and would call him. She wasn't above needing a rescue, she could admit that much and keep her individuality.

The silver demon pulled and she shrieked. Holy God, her fingers were starting to slip as they cramped and popped. She just couldn't gain enough leverage.

"Are you sure?" Seth asked, crouching even closer, putting his face in front of her.

She didn't get the chance to curse at him before her hands gave out and she slid hard across the floor, being dragged mercilessly by the demon. Jade yelped, clawing at the ground, becoming more frantic in her movements, kicking, thrashing, twisting. She managed to break free for a moment and scramble to her feet only to feel arms wrap around her waist and pick her up off her feet and carry her backward toward the mirror. She was screaming, frantic, loud, wordless screams but she still couldn't say the words Seth needed to hear. Even in all the chaos, she had this sense that if she agreed, if she said yes to him, it would somehow end up worse than this. Seth's smile and his eyes were so much more horrifying than the faceless demon because Seth looked human but wasn't.

The silver, faceless demon may overpower her but Seth... Seth could outsmart her and she had no idea what she would be getting into.

Her hands pinwheeled out, trying to grab onto something, anything. She heard an awful, sick, sucking sound behind her and then her hands collided with something and she realized it was the frame of the mirror. The demon had already stepped in and was trying to pull her in with him. She felt the mirror at her back, felt its resistance and remembered what Paris said about having an anchor on this side, something that was keeping her here. She thought it might be her secret, the one she would carry for life, Lily, but she couldn't be certain.

Lily was dead.

She grabbed at the edges with clawed hands, her fingers feeling stuck permanently in place. She kicked out with her legs and managed to find the outside of the mirror with them and wrapped her ankles around the frame.

She felt pressure around her chest, under her ribs, demon-strong arms pulling at her, trying to yank her backward.

"Possum, come now," Seth said, standing in front of her. "Valiant effort, but one word and I can help you out here. Just say it. 'Deal.' That's it. So easy. Everyone deals. I'll keep you from crossing over, and I'll even take care of him for you." Seth jerked his head toward Matthew and Jade's eyes flickered over.

He was still on the floor - his shirt a charred mess, sticking to his burned flesh where her fire-spell had caught him. He was clutching the obelisk in his hands and...

He was still spell-casting.

There was another solid heave and she felt something cold and sharp pierce under her ribcage, stealing her breath. Pain radiated out from her body and she looked down and saw blood blossoming out from her shirt.

"Or if he can't get you all the way over, I suppose he can just take your heart like this," Seth said easily with a shrug, staring at the red liquid pooling from where a silver prong had pierced her. "I still don't think it will work. Either you'll be dead or you'll be powerless. I'm betting on dead." He leaned in closer, his lips almost touching hers, so close that she had to go a bit cross-eyed to keep looking at him. She gasped in pain as a second spike started punching its way through her skin.

"Say the word, possum. Seal our deal."

Jade turned her head and focused instead on Matthew. The squirrely HR stooge was clutching that obelisk like his life depended on it.

Matthew who, according to Seth, was controlling the demon.

She'd been fighting the wrong thing. Stop Matthew and she'd stop the demon. She'd been focused on the demon because it was horrific, it was big, it was powerful.

But it was still just a tool. And Matthew was wielding it.

Jade tried to conjure her fire but couldn't square her focus. Another spike of pain shot through her and she shrieked. She tried to think of something else, of anything else she knew of her magic which didn't require her full attention, because, holy God, her attention was on the unbelievable suffering directed at the middle of her chest. But she couldn't think, she couldn't focus, she just wanted Matthew to stop.

Just stop what he was doing, just be incapacitated by something, anything that made him stop.

Pain made her vision double and blur for a moment but then she focused on the gold of the chain, around Matthew's neck. The obelisk swinging a bit as he clutched the chain, back and forth, back and forth. She felt like she had in the lab when Paris was testing her power, getting sleepy and dazed, watching it move back and forth, back and forth.

Then it stopped and Matthew grabbed at it with his fingers and Jade pushed at him as hard as she could, pushed with all her power, thinking of what she wanted him to do, pushed so hard she felt something give a little in her brain and it hurt, like a blow to the head.

"Oh, possum," Seth breathed. "You are fun."

Matthew plunged the obelisk into his eye, blood spurting out spectacularly as he pressed it in deep and started screaming. He reared back, clawing at his face, shrieking.

Jade dropped like a sack of bricks and she unceremoniously fell to the ground with a *thud*, pain radiating throughout her entire skeleton. She turned slightly and looked at the mirror behind her.

It was solid glass, her reflection staring back her. She had blood running down from both her nostrils and a little bit from one of her ears. The bandage on her forehead was leaking vitae as well, trailing down her face. She was bruised, battered, her hair a mess, her cast broken a bit at the edges. She kicked out as hard as she could against the mirror and it star-cracked once before falling to the floor and breaking into pieces.

Matthew was still shrieking behind her but she was functional enough to shoot a barb in his direction.

"Oh, shut up you big baby. It's your own fault," she said as she slumped into a little pile of misery on the ground. She could hear pounding on the door to the room - loud, thunderous against the heavy oak of the door. And she thought she heard Callie yelling her name, maybe Henri too.

Seth leaned over her, eyes bright and fond.

I can't do anymore, she thought. *I got no more left today.* Her brain felt heavy, thick - like she couldn't get her thoughts to process correctly. Her vision started swimming at the edges, making Seth look strange and foreign.

Or maybe it was just him. He seemed larger, leaner, more like an animal. She thought she could feel a tail curling around by her feet, swishing just out of her range of vision.

Of course that could just be brain-damage talking, she thought darkly. She felt like she might vomit. Her breath hitched a bit on a sigh. Jade wanted to pass out. Being unconscious would be pretty nice right about now and then hopefully she would wake up on some pain-killers and all would be right with the world again. But she couldn't allow herself to slip under with Seth still there, slinking around her like a snake.

No. Stay awake.

Seth clapped a tiny little golf clap and gave her a mock bow. "Very nice." He brushed back some of the strands of hair that had come lose and she batted at his hand. He laughed. "I think we'll be good friends."

She heard something in the general direction of the door give a loud groan and Seth looked up, past her toward the door. "That'll be your friend," he said, sneering a bit, "and his demon magic finally breaking that lock. Too bad he missed all the fun," he signed dreamily and looked down at Jade and then over at Matthew who was moaning now, clutching his eye. Blood dripped red and bright from his fingers. "You do wonderful work."

He shimmered and disappeared before she could tell him to go fuck himself.

She was a little disappointed about that, actually.

The door burst open with a crack and she waited until she could make eye contact with Paris, be sure it was him and see him coming toward her before she let the soporific pull tugging at her drag her down into oblivion.

CHAPTER SIXTEEN

Jade's first thought upon being dragged back up to consciousness was that she might be dead. She quickly discarded the idea when she heard a faint beeping sound. She doubted they had machines in the afterlife and cracked open one eye to peer from the small slit. She was back in the medical lab, lying on one of the incline beds. Even though the light was dim, she squinted against it as she opened both eyes. Her vision was hazy, the edges of everything she saw blurred, making things seem like they disappeared into nothingness at the fringes of their existence. Jade heard soft clicking noises and she rotated her head slightly. Paris sat in the hideous overstuffed chair, hunched over a laptop. He had a lamp directed at papers on the arm rest. As she watched, he bent over the papers, running his finger along lightly, and then made some notes with his laptop, then bent over the papers again. He paused for a moment to rotate his neck in a circle. His vertebrae made loud, cracking noises as they slid over one another. He checked his watch and went back to work. She watched him for five minutes before he tilted his head slightly, as if listening. He looked up slowly, his gaze meeting hers.

"She wakes."

His voice was low and quiet, barely above a whisper. She opened her mouth to say 'hi' but the word got stuck in the dryness of her throat. She started to cough, but that made it worse and her eyes teared as she tried to clear the tickle that irritated her vocal chords. Paris stood and poured her a glass of water from a small nightstand. He placed the straw to her mouth and as soon as the cool liquid touched her parched lips and tongue, she thought she had never tasted anything so refreshing in her life. She finished the entire glass in three big gulps. By the time he refilled it and handed it back to her, she had managed to calm her coughing. Jade cleared her throat once more and took another sip.

"Hi," she finally got out.

He handed her a tissue and she swiped at her eyes with it, clearing away the tears that her coughing spell had unearthed. He pulled his chair closer to the bed and sat down again.

"How do you feel?" he asked solemnly.

She coughed again, a dry, hacking sound with no real heft behind it. She swallowed hard around her now sore throat. "Stiff." Jade finally answered as she tried to move her limbs and found her joints slightly swollen and unwieldy. She started through her usual body check but gave up as soon as she realized her fingertips were sore.

If her fingertips were sore, for crying out loud, the rest of her must just be shit. Most of the pain seemed centered around her ribcage and she poked a little bit there, wincing and hearing the crinkle of bandages.

However, she was feeling the pleasant haze of some good drugs. She felt like a warm terry cloth towel, fuzzy and soft.

She remembered then. Things poking into her. Piercing. She shuddered and the heart monitor started beeping faster, betraying her. With a groan, she pulled the clip off her finger, noticing Paris wave away Dr. Gellar who came to check as soon as the machine didn't register a pulse. He flicked off the machine quickly, leaving them in silence.

"You were batted around quite a bit from what we could tell. Nothing broken, other than the wrist from before. Amazingly," he added.

"I have tough bones."

"Lucky for you," Paris said.

"Yeah. I feel really lucky," she snorted.

"Other than the stiffness, how are you doing?"

She paused. "Not bad. Tired. I've a headache." She rolled her neck and then gingerly touched her temple. "Feels fuzzy up here. My magic feels weird. Dull. Like an overused pencil."

"I've been meaning to talk to you about that," he said grimly, pulling the chair closer and sitting back down.

"If you tell me I'm dying after all that I just went through, I will punch you in the head. With my cast."

"No, you're not dying," he replied with a slight smile and then sobered. "Your magic is different than everyone else's. Or, rather, *you* are different than the rest of us."

She wanted to make some kind of joke, make light of situation but all she could think was, *again. You're different than everyone else again.* She didn't want to be different. She wanted to fit in somewhere. Finally.

"You know you're very powerful," he continued, waiting for her to nod a bit, "but you weren't born in a coven. You weren't born a witch and apparently that's a big factor in how your power works. I meant to talk to you about this sooner but-"

She saw him clenching his fists on his lap and felt an uncharacteristic rush of sympathy for him. She could only blame the drugs. "We had a lot going on." She offered him a way out.

He nodded gratefully. "As it turns out, your brain is not entirely made for magic and using it, using a lot of it is... Hard. On your brain. On you. I'm sure Dr. Gellar can give you the specifics if you'd like but it's more of a magic conversation than a medical one. You have to be careful how much magic you use. Especially at one time."

She thought about how violently she pushed at Matthew, how much she wanted him to stop what he was doing. She wanted it with her whole body, her entire being and she'd made him gouge his own eye out. She remembered the sharp pain in her own head afterward, knowing she'd just broken something in her brain.

"Is it permanent? When I overuse magic? Did I give myself brain damage?" Jade asked, horrified.

"No. Not that we can tell."

Jade laughed inappropriately. Not that they could tell. Fantastic. She was probably lucky she wasn't a drooling idiot.

"It's all about learning your limits and staying within those limits," he counseled solemnly. "I can help you with that. The coven can help you with that. If you agree."

Oh, right, she still had to make an official decision.

She had to clear her throat a bit and she opened her mouth twice to speak before she could get it out. "I'd... I'd like that. I think. Um. To stay," she stammered.

Paris smiled at her and it was the first big smile she'd ever seen from him. Teeth, crinkled eyes and apple cheeks. He looked just like that picture she'd seen of him as a boy, with his mother - happy and open.

"I'm glad, Jade. I'm very glad."

"You probably won't be as glad when you get the bill for renovating the HR office," she said dryly.

She took another mouthful of water, swished it around in her mouth, unceremoniously spat it back in the cup and handed it to him. He took it without comment and set it back down on the small table.

"Speaking of," he said, resting his elbows on his knees, "can you tell me what happened?"

She snorted. "Matthew didn't confess all, sobbing and broken, like one of those cop shows?"

Paris looked pensive. "He's been an incoherent mess," he finally said, his tone frank. "We tried talking to him, I tried talking to him but he keeps talking about his deal, and how he owes now and can't pay and wants to know if we can protect him. That and he lost one eye and is... Distraught about it," Paris continued diplomatically. "He's not exactly a dependable witness."

"Can you protect him?" she asked, fiddling with the edge of her new, bright pink fiberglass cast.

Part of her wanted to tell Paris that Matthew could rot for all she cared. When she thought about what he'd been trying to do to her - have some creature, some demon take her heart out, in the hopes that it would give him her magic, it was difficult to drum up sympathy for the guy.

Even for making him gouge one of his own eyes out.

"I don't know," Paris said honestly. "I know we have the demon wards, but from what I can understand of his raving, he's got a deal. I don't know what that means." Paris paused, seemingly waiting for Jade to make eye contact with him again. "At the very least, I'll be breaking his magic."

"You can do that? I mean, he's not very strong?" she asked, remembering what Paris had told her about breaking her own magic.

Paris nodded grimly. "Yes. I can break Matthew's magic. It's probably why he wanted yours. He's never been very powerful. I'm not even sure how he managed to wage a deal with a demon, frankly, or what his leverage was. It's very odd."

She nodded a bit, uncertain what else she could say without starting to yell, *throw the book at him! I don't care how hard!*

"So, will you tell me what happened?"

Jade tried to give him the 'short version' of what happened, starting with her arriving and seeing the obelisk necklace Matthew wore. Of course, it all deteriorated after that. Paris went stiff and tense when she mentioned Seth arriving and she had to endure a barrage of questions from him regarding exactly what

Seth had said and that, yes, Jade was absolutely certain she didn't get into a demon deal - not by words nor by implication nor by non-verbal assent.

It was a little insulting, but since he seemed genuinely concerned for her safety, she tried not to bristle and answered his questions honestly and repeatedly. She explained that it had taken her some time - time in which she got spectacularly beaten up - but that she'd finally figured out it was Matthew she needed to stop, not the demon. She faltered a bit when she explained how she pushed Matthew with her mind, pushed him into mutilating himself. She couldn't quite explain how she did it, and even though it saved her life and she wasn't sorry for it, it was still a gruesome memory, burned into her retinas and grey matter.

She finished by telling him about Seth, at the very end and his very clear and continuing interest in her. Jade looked him straight in the eye, knowing she must look like death warmed over but needing him to know how serious she was and how non-negotiable her plans were.

"I know you've said that you don't know people that deal in demon magic. Well, now you do. I'm going to learn. I'm going to be good at it. And you can't stop me." Jade's voice didn't waver or falter. She kept her gaze steady and calm even as Paris clenched his jaw a bit.

He nodded. "I understand. I'll... I'll help you any way I can."

She let out the breath she didn't know she'd been holding. "I want to study your mother's grimoires. Study her, if possible."

Again, he seemed tense, conflicted. But he nodded again. "I agree. Her books seem to be the best source we have on the subject. And although I'm stunned to learn she dealt in demon magic, I still trust no one's magic more than hers." He hesitated and then added, "I know her intentions must have been good."

"Okay," she said lowly, feeling more settled. She rubbed her eyes a bit and then ran her fingers through her hair and grimaced.

Yuck. She was glad she didn't know what she looked like.

"So, it looks like I'm moving to the Coven," she said, trying to infuse her tone with brightness. "Wanna come over and help me demon-ward my house?"

#

It had been three days since 'the incident,' as most of the Coven was calling it. Jade liked to call it 'that time I kicked ass and took names' but apparently that was a little long and hard to say.

So 'the incident' it was.

Paris let her know that Matthew had been evaluated by several doctors and psychiatrists who concluded he was mentally ill. Whether he'd been before his demon deal or as a consequence of it, no one could say for certain. They had a lot of big fancy words for his diagnosis and Paris let her read the official statement. In the end, it merely amounted to 'bat-shit crazy.'

They determined the best thing would be a psychiatric facility for supernatural beings where he could receive counseling and care by professionals who dealt with preternatural people on a regular basis. He was being transferred at the end of the week.

As soon as Paris broke his magic.

Breaking a witch's magic was a solemn, serious affair and normally for only four people to witness - the accused, the witch breaking the magic, a third party to evaluate the procedure at the end and a medical doctor.

Paris asked if she wanted to observe.

She said yes.

They were in a small room in the dungeon of the Covenstead, separate and apart from the library. It was cold and clammy and there was the faint smell of copper and burnt ashes in the air. There were no windows, no furniture and no light fixtures. The only light came from three torches pressed into sconces on the wall. Paris explained they'd discovered it was best to not have any technology surrounding them as sometimes it interacted unpredictably with the magic involved.

There was some kind of incense burning and it made the air thick and hard to breathe. She'd been taking little, shallow breaths but felt like she wasn't getting enough oxygen and had to give up and breathe in deeply. The smell clung to her soft palate and she just had this feeling like all the mouthwash in the world wasn't going to clear it out for days.

She shivered a bit and wished she'd brought an extra sweater. She was still stiff and sore all over from the fight and if she caught too much of a chill down here, her bones would ache for the rest of the day, no matter how many hot showers or pain-killers she took. Jade kind of wanted to stand closer to Paris, to get a little residual heat, but he was putting off some serious 'don't come near me' vibes. His posture was ramrod straight and his movements were stilted and slightly awkward. His entire being screamed how much he didn't want to do this, but also contained an echo of duty, responsibility and obligation.

She kept her distance.

There was an itchy spot underneath her cast and she was contemplating finding a ruler and jamming it down there when she heard the approaching feet. A heavy wooden door swung open soundlessly, its hinges well-oiled and immaculate. Matthew was led in by a man Paris had told her was named Josef. He worked in the Counter-Magic Department and Paris said he was a fair and trustworthy witch. He was older, perhaps in his fifties, with greying hair and a long, pointed nose. He kind of reminded her of a really fit Geppetto from Pinocchio.

Matthew was wearing a collar around his neck and one on each wrist - silver and adorned with runes and markings. Paris told her they were binding collars and they were keeping Matthew from using any magic until Paris could break it. Jade thought they looked beautiful - too pretty to be put to such a grim task. She studied them, wishing she could get a better look at their surface, but the flickering fire-light of the torches didn't give her much to work with.

Jade told herself it was because she was interested in the markings and not because she was avoiding looking at Matthew's face.

She couldn't restrain herself any longer and her eyes flickered up, into Matthew's one remaining eye – that eye was staring directly at her. She felt her heart stutter a beat at the empty, blank gaze but she managed to stay still and not move.

He blinked at her a few times, like he was trying to remember her or place her and then he smiled.

It creeped her out and this time she couldn't stop herself from flexing her shoulder blades in an effort to make the space between them stop tingling.

Dr. Gellar came in behind Matthew, a small medical bag in her hands. She nodded at both Paris and Jade and then took up a spot in one of the corners of the room, away from the center.

Josef led Matthew to the center of the cell where some kind of warded circle had been etched into the stone. It looked like it had been drawn over with chalk and Jade wondered if Paris had done it himself or if they had someone at the Coven who specialized in things like that. Matthew stood in the center of the circle and spun around - making a full rotation until he was again staring at Jade.

She held his gaze and willed herself not to move.

Paris held a heavy, thick book in his hands and it kind of reminded Jade of being in church - the whole six times she'd been.

When Paris started to talk, his voice was quiet, almost soft, but the small space had no furnishings to absorb any of the sound and it seemed to resonate for much longer than it should. He iterated the charges Matthew was facing which had slightly formal words like 'persecution of a fellow and kindred witch,' and 'consorting with darker elements for the malediction of a brethren coven member.'

She supposed no matter what you called it, it still amounted to 'bat-shit crazy.'

Matthew kept his one eye focused on Jade the entire time and she refused to look away. Out of the corner of her eye, she could see Paris flipping the pages of the book until he found what he was looking for and then he started to read, his words foreign and strange, sounding like all consonants and no vowels.

Matthew started to twitch and flinch slightly as the circle beneath him glowed. Paris continued to read and Matthew started to make a whining sound, way in the back of his throat. It made the hair on the back of Jade's neck stand up straight and she wanted to cover her hears. Then, Matthew started to scream, his voice drowning out Paris' low, even tone. In the circle, Matthew curled up on himself, falling to his knees, shouting senselessly and Jade thought she could see his magic inside him, folding in on itself, crumpling, like a tin-can being crushed underfoot.

It was awful.

Matthew's voice was shrieking, high-pitched and shrill and he clawed at the collar around his neck, his fingernails gouging into the skin and drawing blood. Dr. Gellar made a move to go forward to him but Josef held up a hand and stopped her with a look.

Paris didn't falter, didn't pause, but when Jade was finally able to look away from Matthew and look at Paris, she saw a sheen of sweat breaking out across his brow and his lips. She saw him starting to shake and tremble with supreme effort.

Jade didn't want to imagine what it would have been like for her to have her magic broken, if they had even been able to find someone to do it, but she couldn't stop from picturing herself in the center of a glowing circle, screaming her lungs out.

There was a terrible ripping sound, like wet fabric filled with liquid tearing open and Matthew yelped loudly, wildly and then... Then he stopped.

He started whimpering quietly, lying down on the floor in the fetal position and Josef motioned that Dr. Gellar could go to him now. She was on him in a moment, checking his vitals and murmuring softly to him, smoothing his hair back.

Jade turned and looked at Paris. He was pale and sweating, the fire-light dancing across his face and casting strange and bizarre shadows. He panted a little, like he'd just jogged around the block quickly. He closed his book and looked at her. His eyes were glowing slightly, bright blue and other-worldly.

She didn't know what to say, if she should say anything at all. Thanks? Good job? That was one of the most horrible things I've seen and I've seen some crazy shit?

Jade managed a curt nod that he returned brusquely before he turned and left the ritual room.

Josef and Dr. Gellar led Matthew out, his head hanging low although he managed to shuffle his own feet and move under his own steam. Heedless of the chill now, Jade leaned back against the cold, clammy stone and took a few shaky breaths.

So this was coven life.

#

Jade felt like she'd been waiting for a shoe to drop all week.

She still had to go back to her apartment and pack her things, break her lease and quit her job. To be honest, she had visions in her head of walking in and saying loudly, 'screw this. I quit!'

Instead she typed up a rather bland resignation letter, apologizing for the lack of notice but offering to be available via email and phone if anything came up for which she was needed.

Responsibility sucked.

Callie and Henri threw her an actual housewarming party and she got to meet their boyfriends. Callie brought all appetizers. Henri contributed a chocolate cheesecake and told her that as long as they ate standing up with the fridge door open, calories didn't count.

She might love them just a little.

Paris helped her demon-ward her little cottage. The portal in the pantry was no more but every time she reached in for a can of soup, she got a little chill down her spine.

She planned to remove the food and turn it into a storage closet. Though it didn't really help, she told herself it was because she was worried there was bad woo-woo left behind which could spoil the food. Her decision had nothing to do with her stark fear of her first visitor through the portal.

Hannah shipped some books on demons and demon magic to Paris for Jade to start studying. Jade was apparently going to meet the all-knowing, ever-wise Hannah shortly and get her tarot cards read. She didn't know if she should be nervous or not.

She spent most of her time in the library, a few tables away from Callie, working on her laptop. She didn't like to read the demon magic books alone - they kind of freaked her out. She liked the idea of someone being close by and she and Callie would often go for lunch or coffee during the day. Josef had come by and asked her if she'd like to work with him in Counter-Magic and she'd tentatively agreed. Starting next week, she'd be taking lessons from him as well as from Paris.

She must have been getting the hang of the demon magic because she felt the air shift and she looked right to the spot where Seth appeared, grinning.

"Clever, possum. Look at you! You make me proud." He clutched at his heart with a dramatic smile.

This was the only downfall of not working in her home - no warding. But she couldn't stay locked up forever. She'd had enough of that as a child.

"I thought you might show up," she said crossly.

"I must admit, I was horribly disappointed when you didn't deal with me. But I can't hold a grudge." He shrugged. "I'm sure there'll be other opportunities."

"Why don't you hold your breath until I say yes?"

He waved a hand. "Wouldn't kill me anyway. Besides, I'm sure once you find out all the things I can do, that we can do together, I'm not even going to have to ask you. You'll be the one asking."

"I doubt it," she said, not taking her eyes off him.

He looked at the books she was studying, making some faces. "God, these are old. So outdated. So misinformed. If you want, I can tell you where to find some better books." He looked coyly at her through his lashes.

"No."

Seth tapped his finger on the cover of one of the books. "You play so hard to get, possum. But I think I know something that will pique your interest."

"Not listening," she said, turning back to her book. He leaned over her, draping his arm over her shoulder and she glared at his hand resting casually on her arm. His lips were close to her ear, his breath hot and sticky-sweet.

"What if I told you all about Lily?"

She felt her heart rabbit-beat and she tried hard not to react.

"That's the thing, possum. You think she's your secret. But I'll tell you something. I've got a bigger one about you both."

She took a deep breath, trying not to think about the sickly sugar smell, about the way his words made her skin itch. "You're a liar."

"Yes," he said unequivocally. "But not about this."

"I don't believe you."

"Yes you do."

Jade turned her face to him. He was millimeters away, his eyes dark, deep and wrong. There was no reflecting surface in them, just darkness.

"Prove it," she challenged.

He made a *tsk-tsk* sound. "You'll never buy the cow if I give away the milk for free." He tapped her on the nose. "I'll let you stew on that for a while. Don't worry, I'll be back." He straightened and took a step away from her. "Or you can always call me. Anytime."

He shimmered and vanished, leaving behind his scent, clinging to her clothes, to her skin. She stared at the space where he'd just been, thinking.

Callie poked her head around the corner, blonde hair swinging. "Hey, who you talking to?" she asked, eyes wide and innocent.

"No one. Myself," Jade muttered, finally looking away from where Seth had been and up at Callie.

Callie gave her a fond look. "You know what they say about talking to yourself?"

"That it's fine as long as you don't answer back?"

Callie laughed. "That too. But I was gonna say that it usually means it's time for a coffee break. Henri just texted me. He wants to go to Crema. It's happy hour in twenty minutes and that means half-price coffee. You in?"

"Yeah," she said closing her book and her laptop. She looked up at Callie's smiling face. "I'm in."

She tried to push Seth's words from her head as she followed Callie out of the library, listening to her bright voice telling her about the upcoming Coven Ball, but she was only half listening. Her brain was stuck on what Seth said, about what he'd implied. About how far she'd be willing to go to find out.

What if I told you all about Lily?

"Jade!" Callie said, standing outside the Covenstead, staring at where Jade was stopped still, staring into space. Callie shook her head at her. "What's got you so pre-occupied?"

Jade shook her head and faked a smile, one of her best. "Text Henri if we beat him there, he's paying."

She tried to concentrate on Callie's sharp laughter, warm and bright and not the chill that settled in her chest.

You think she's your secret. But I'll tell you something. I've got a bigger one about you both.

The cold feeling settled deep in her stomach. Jade wondered how long she could hold out against a statement with that much promise.

#

AUTHOR BIO

Margarita loves the art, creativity and romanticism of storytelling. Sometimes, however, the act of putting pen to paper proves challenging. She works to develop genuine, relatable characters which grow in the hearts of her readers. From that foundation, the stories flourish into a warm friend.

She enjoys pursuits which blur the lines between the analytical and creative sides of her brain. This includes her day job in electronic data management, where she uses her creativity to solve logical problems, and also her lessons learning to play the cello, where she finds beauty in the structure of music and the instrument. She believes there is a place for both logic and imagination to work together. When they do, the results are magical.

The 'label' she identifies most with is 'storyteller.' According to Wikipedia, storytelling is the conveying of events in words, and images, often by improvisation or embellishment. It seems to fit pretty well with how she feels about her work.

Get Books 2 and 3 of Covencraft, Counter-Hex and Double-Sided Witch, online at Amazon

Get the free short story (Book 2.5 of Covencraft), Carnival Moon, online at Amazon, Smashwords, Apple and Kobo

At www.margaritagakis.com, you can sign up for her newsletter to get updates on her current work and upcoming releases.